THE DOCTOR
DIGS A GRAVE

THE DOCTOR
DIGS A GRAVE

Robin Hathaway

ST. MARTIN'S PRESS
NEW YORK

A THOMAS DUNNE BOOK.
An imprint of St. Martin's Press.

THE DOCTOR DIGS A GRAVE. Copyright © 1998 by Robin Hathaway. All rights reserved. Printed in the United States of America. No part of this book may be used or reproduced in any manner whatsoever without written permission except in the case of brief quotations embodied in critical articles or reviews. For information, address St. Martin's Press, 175 Fifth Avenue, New York, N.Y. 10010.

Design by Nancy Resnick

Library of Congress Cataloging-in-Publication Data

Hathaway, Robin.
    The doctor digs a grave / Robin Hathaway. —
1st ed.
        p. cm.
    ISBN 0-312-18568-5
    I. Title.
    PS3558.A7475D6   1998
    813'.54—dc21   98-5375
                                                          CIP

First Edition: May 1998

10 9 8 7 6 5 4 3 2 1

To my husband, also a cardiologist,
who remembers things past

ACKNOWLEDGMENTS

As much as I would like to, it would be impossible for me to thank all the people who have helped me with this book.

I must be content with expressing my heartfelt thanks to my husband, Robert Alan Keisman, M.D., cardiologist, for his exhaustive contribution to the medical content of this book. My deepest gratitude to Dr. Herbert C. Kraft, professor of anthropology and director of the Archeological Research Center and Museum at Seton Hall University, for his careful reading of my manuscript and his willingness to share with me his vast knowledge of the Lenni-Lenape Indians. And to Fred Kafes, medical librarian at Our Lady of Lourdes Medical Center, Camden, New Jersey, my thanks for providing essential medical material.

To all the rest—family and friends, mystery writers and mystery readers, editors and agents—please know that I am profoundly grateful for all your help, and I wish I could thank each of you individually.

The Indian Burying-Ground

In spite of all the learned have said,
 I still my old opinion keep;
The posture that we give the dead
 Points out the soul's eternal sleep.

Not so the ancients of these lands;—
 The Indian, when from life released,
Again is seated with his friends,
 And shares again the joyous feast.

His imaged birds, and painted bowl,
 And venison, for a journey dressed,
Bespeak the nature of the soul,
 Activity, that wants no rest.

His bow for action ready bent,
 And arrows with a head of stone,
Can only mean that life is spent.
 And not the old ideas gone.

Thou, stranger, that shalt come this way,
 No fraud upon the dead commit,—
Observe the swelling turf, and say,
 They do not lie, but here they sit . . .

PHILIP FRENEAU

THE DOCTOR
DIGS A GRAVE

CHAPTER 1

SATURDAY, OCTOBER 29, 4:45 P.M.

The driver edged the van carefully through the alley (there was no more than a two-inch leeway on either side) and entered a gloomy space about the size of a suburban backyard. Although still daylight, the enclosure was dim because it was surrounded by the rear ends of tall buildings—a bank, an apartment house, a parking garage, and a hotel.

Making a neat U-turn, the driver backed the van across the entrance to the alley, blocking a view of the enclosure from anyone passing by on the street. He jumped to the ground, moved around to the back of the van, and opened the twin doors. He drew a spade from inside and, choosing a spot a few yards from the van, began to dig. Now and then he stopped to wipe the sweat from his forehead with his sleeve. It was warm for October, and the dirt was packed down hard. It took almost an hour to dig a hole two feet by four feet and about five feet deep.

Satisfied, he tossed the spade into the back of the van and wiped his hands on his jeans. The rectangle of sky framed above the four buildings was still light. Too light to finish the job. The smell of hamburger reached him from a nearby McDonald's.

1

He was hungry. Hopping into the rear of the van, he lifted a corner of an oil-stained tarpaulin. The tarpaulin covered a mound slightly smaller than the hole he had just dug. A quick glance underneath, and he let it fall.

Slamming the back doors, the driver made his way around to the front. The sound of the motor starting up reverberated in the small space. He backed the van carefully over the hole he had just dug and parked. He walked once around the van, checking to make sure the doors were locked, before turning down the alley on foot. It wouldn't hurt to leave for a few minutes, long enough for him to grab a bite. By the time he got back, it would be dark and he could finish the job.

CHAPTER 2

SATURDAY, 5:00 P.M.

D r. Andrew Fenimore stepped out the back door of the hospital for a breath of fresh air. Even with the level of pollution in Philadelphia, the air outside was fresher than the air in the doctors' lounge. It was balmy for October. Indian summer. He shed his suit coat and headed for the doctors' parking lot. As he neared his car, he spotted the boy. Either a tall twelve or a short sixteen, wearing a dark baseball cap—visor in back—he was jogging between the cars, head down. When he crossed an aisle between two rows of cars, Fenimore saw that he was carrying a sack. Not carelessly, swinging it at every bumper and fender as you might expect, but cautiously, protectively, as if it contained the crown jewels. (The loot from a nearby jewelry store, more likely. Why, Fenimore? Because his skin is dark? He's probably taking some groceries home to his mother.) The boy halted beside a lone sycamore at the edge of the parking lot. When the land had been cleared for the lot, the tree had been spared and the ring of earth around it had escaped the macadam. Bending, the boy began to scratch in the dirt with some tool that Fenimore couldn't see. The parking lot attendant rapped sharply on the inside of his glass booth. With a sullen look, the boy darted into the street.

Fenimore opened the rear door of his car and tossed his suit coat into the backseat. He snapped the door shut and sauntered out of the lot. With no particular destination in mind, he headed east on Walnut Street toward the river. He had an hour to spare before the Cardiology Department meeting at six. An odd time for a meeting. But the chairman had just returned from a sojourn on the Riviera where he had been chalking up continuing education points (of one sort or another) at the Nice-Hilton. Fenimore couldn't care less. His calendar was rarely full, but he imagined that some of the more socially active doctors (not to mention their wives) were unhappy about it.

The street was empty except for an occasional panhandler or a stray tourist heading back to the hotel after a look at the Liberty Bell or the Betsy Ross House. A standard Saturday in the city.

As he waited for the light to change at Seventh Street, he caught sight of the boy again. Poised at the entrance to the park, he glanced around and Fenimore got a good look at him. His face, the color of strong tea, framed eyes of a much deeper brown. Hispanic, probably. His expression was belligerent and anxious at the same time. Fenimore concentrated on a row of tattered posters announcing the arrival of a famous rock star—six months ago.

From the corner of his eye, Fenimore watched the boy turn into Washington Square. He was no longer jogging; his feet dragged. Homeless people lounged on the benches on either side. Fenimore paused to look at the Eternal Flame, a memorial erected to the unknown rebel soldiers who were buried there after the American Revolution. When he looked up, the boy was gone. To his surprise, he was annoyed. The boy had piqued his curiosity more than he realized. What the devil *was* in that sack, anyway? As Fenimore moseyed along the bench-lined path, the boy's head popped up from behind an azalea bush a few yards away. It disappeared and reappeared several times. Each time it appeared, a shower of dirt flew across the path. From a different direction, a tall man in a neat gray uniform strode purposefully toward the bush. Fenimore sat down on the nearest bench to watch.

The park guard collared the boy, seized his digging tool—a rusty toy shovel—and reached for the sack. The boy lunged for the sack.

Fenimore intervened. "What's the trouble, Officer?"

The guard turned on Fenimore. "Look at that!" He nodded at a hole about the size of a soup bowl next to the azalea bush. "These vandals cause thousands of dollars worth of damage a year." He gave the boy a shake. "He oughta be locked up." The boy cringed. "But we aren't allowed to do that nowadays."

"Officer, you must have more important criminals to take care of. Why don't you leave this one to me?"

The boy and the officer both eyed Fenimore with suspicion. Fenimore saw himself through their eyes: a small, conservatively dressed man hanging around the park picking up teenage boys. Hastily, he drew out his wallet and handed the officer his card, hoping to establish credibility with the boy as well as the guard.

"A doctor, huh. I don't see what you can do for him, unless you're a shrink." He gave the boy a disgusted look but let go of his T-shirt. "All right. But fill in that hole." He tossed the shovel at him. "And don't let me catch you around here again." He left them to attend to more urgent business—harassing a homeless man on a bench nearby.

The boy kicked the dirt back into the hole and grabbed his sack, preparing for a quick exit.

"Hold on." Fenimore stopped him. "What have you got in there?"

The boy swung the sack behind him.

"Don't worry, I'm not going to take it. I'd like to help you."

Something—either Fenimore's words or his tone—got through to the boy. "My cat," he cried. "A car got him this morning. I want to bury him. But you can't bury anything in this fucking town. Everything's cement or brick or tar, and the parks are full of fuzz." He turned away.

Fenimore waited until the sniffing stopped. "I know a place," he said.

The boy wiped his nose down the length of his sleeve and looked at him.

"Come on." Fenimore headed out of the park. The boy followed—a car's length behind.

On Saturday there were few shoppers on Walnut Street and no commuters to get in their way. The boy walked behind Fenimore, Indian file. Fenimore turned only once to make sure he was still there. Between Broad and Thirteenth, he stopped at the entrance to a narrow alley flanked by two buildings, a cart track long ago. On the wall of the facing building, the words "Watts Street" were carved deeply into the stone, a reminder of more permanent times. He turned in. The boy followed. The alley ended in a small open space—a swath of hard-packed dirt walled in on three sides by tall buildings. The only occupants of the area were a couple of pigeons and a gray van. The pigeons took off with a rush of wings and Fenimore noted the license tag on the van: SAL123. He wouldn't be apt to forget that. His cat's name was Sal and her litters never exceeded three.

"This was an old burial ground set aside over three hundred years ago by William Penn for Indian . . . er . . . Native Americans," Fenimore explained, "and the deed still prevents anyone from building here or paving over the ground. People shouldn't be allowed to park here. The Lenape Indians have unmarked graves, but there should be a historic marker or sign." He made a mental note to bring this to the attention of the Historical Society soon. But for his present purpose, it was better to have the place unmarked, anonymous. A historic secret. "Only a few people know about this place," Fenimore told the boy. "Just the Lenapes and a few history buffs like me."

The boy looked down. The ground was smooth and black and hard. But not macadam. Real dirt, packed down by feet and tires. He tested the surface with the toy shovel. It grated. He looked up.

"We'll need something better than that." Fenimore glanced at his watch: 5:45. Nearly time for that damn meeting. "Tell you what. Meet me back here at eight. I'll bring my spade."

The boy's eyes shifted, still suspicious.

"On second thought, come to my office." Fenimore pressed his card into his hand.

The boy glanced at it.

"One-five-five-five Spruce."

He nodded and started off.

"Hey." Fenimore stopped him. "I don't know your name."

The boy hesitated. "Horatio." Then he quickly added, "My mom calls me Ray. My friends call me Rat."

Horatio. Fenimore savored it. He didn't know what he'd expected, but not the name of one of his boyhood heroes—Horatio Nelson, the great admiral of the British fleet. "How did you come by a tag like that?"

He shrugged. "I'm the sixth kid. My mom ran out of saints. She picked that one off the TV and stuck me with it. Some old movie she was watching. She likes the sad ones."

That Hamilton Woman, Fenimore thought. Vivien Leigh played Lady Hamilton and Laurence Olivier was Nelson. It was sad, all right. "Mind if I call you by your full name?"

He looked as if he minded.

"He's kind of a hero of mine," Fenimore explained. "He beat

the French with a sleight of hand. Split his own fleet in two. Won the battle but lost his life. Lost an arm and an eye before that."

The boy danced from one foot to the other, eyeing the exit.

"See you at eight." Fenimore watched him retreat down the alley, holding the sack carefully at his side.

CHAPTER 3

On the way back to his van, the driver picked at some french fries in a cardboard container. Sucking up the last one, he let the red and yellow box drop to the ground. He started the van and moved it forward a few yards. He got out to check the hole. It was still there. Unlocking the back doors, the driver climbed inside. He reemerged with the slight body of a woman slung over his shoulders in the traditional fireman's grip. Before climbing down, his eyes darted around the enclosure. The space was empty and, except for the shush of traffic at the other end of the alley, it was quiet.

Bending down, he eased the body slowly into the hole. Despite his care, the head, arms, and legs flopped like a doll's. With one hand, he jerked the body upright into a sitting position. Then, with both hands, he shoved it backward until it rested against the back of the hole. The torso remained vertical, but the head persisted in lolling to one side. With a curse, he reached for the spade and began tossing chunks of earth into the body's lap. He paused, spade in midair. Letting the spade fall, he climbed back into the van. When he reappeared, he held a small canvas

9

bag in one hand. Shoving it roughly down beside the body, he continued to fill up the hole.

A rustle. He spun around.

A pigeon waddled toward him out of the dark. He feinted hitting it with the spade and went back to his work. When he had finished, the rectangle of earth looked like a flower bed waiting for tulip and daffodil bulbs.

As the driver nosed the van out of the alley into the street, he noticed that all the passing cars had their headlights turned on. The job had taken longer than he thought. He might have to jack up the price.

CHAPTER 4

P*rasas!*" Fenimore edged his way out of the room in which the meeting of the Cardiology Department was just breaking up. *Prasa* was the Czech word for "pig." Fenimore's mother was Czech, and she had taught him about "The Three Little Prasas" early in life. The Czech word had more oomph than the English one, he thought, as he surveyed the broad back of the chief hospital administrator. That monument to the medical establishment had just treated the doctors to a lecture on how moving their offices into the hospital complex would increase their "dollars up front." And his three little MBA assistants had nodded in unison.

Fenimore hurried down the hospital corridor hoping to avoid any further encounters with staff administrators who might want to discuss "cash flow" or "market share." Vultures! Jackals! Before Fenimore could call up any more unsavory members of the animal kingdom, someone hailed him from across the hall.

"Off on a house call, Fenimore?" Another cardiologist, clad in an expensively tailored suit and Gucci shoes, eyed Fenimore's rumpled jacket and creaseless trousers with barely disguised disdain.

"Right, Thompson. Gotta eat."

"It must be nice to be able to know your patients," Thompson said, keeping pace with him. "Mine are in and out."

Yes, and you're never *in* to hear their complaints, Fenimore wanted to say, but restrained himself.

Failing to get a rise out of him, Thompson left with a wave.

Off to the squash courts, no doubt. Fenimore remembered when the Medicare law was first passed, in 1965. He had been just a kid, about ten years old. A friend of his father's had come for dinner that night, an older doctor who had recently retired, and they had discussed the new law. Growing increasingly agitated during the discussion, the older doctor had finally said, "I'm glad I'm out of it, Fenimore. Mark my words, twenty years from now you won't know this profession." Then, leaning across the table, he had pointed his dessert spoon at Fenimore's father. "It will become a business, like any other."

That was thirty years ago, and how often those words had come back to him. The old doctor was long dead. His father had also died. And here he was trying to make a living in this "business."

Spotting another colleague he wanted to avoid, Fenimore ducked into the mail room. As usual his box was overflowing with notices for more meetings. He tossed the whole lot in the wastebasket. He attended only the ones he had to attend in order to stay on the staff. He had to have one hospital affiliation, a place to admit his few patients when they needed hospitalization. Few, because he practiced solo and all his colleagues practiced in groups. It was hard for one doctor to develop a practice today, when the competition was so highly organized and the group doctors all referred their patients to each other.

He detoured down a back stairway, avoiding the elevator and any further unpleasant encounters.

He'd stick it out awhile longer. But he had to admit that his patient load was dwindling. The older patients he had inherited from his father were dying out, and their children tended to join HMOs. You could hardly blame them. They heard the ads on the radio and television and they signed up. He had made a pact with his cat, Sal: He would practice solo until he could no longer afford cat food. Then, and only then, would he sell out. Being an independent sort herself, she didn't object.

As he made his way toward the men's room, he thanked God for his other little business, his sideline. If it weren't for his private investigating, he wasn't sure he could keep his sanity—or his solvency. He didn't need a big brick building, a lot of shiny equipment, or a team to keep his clients happy. There were few forms to fill out, no client review boards, no government inquiries. It was a one-on-one relationship. And the only people he had to answer to were his clients—and himself.

While washing his hands, he inadvertently glanced in the mirror, something he usually tried to avoid. God, what a face. What did Jennifer see in him? He had none of the attributes women usually go for. He wasn't tall or dark, and he certainly wasn't handsome. In one of their more intimate moments, she had murmured something about his "deep brown eyes." He had immediately thought of a cow. Another time she had spoken about his hands. "You should have been a surgeon," she said, tracing his fingers with one of her own.

"Have you ever seen a surgeon's hands?" he asked.

She looked at him.

"They're almost always short, thick, and muscular."

"Hmm." She had looked back at his hand. "Then I wouldn't want them to touch me."

"If you needed an operation, you would."

She laughed. "Then I'd be asleep and wouldn't care."

"Fenimore!"

He turned. The tall young man at the next sink was looking quizzically at him. "I spoke to you three times."

"Sorry, Larry."

"What do you think about that case in 340? Mr. Liska. The boys want to do an angioplasty of course, but he's eighty-six. Don't you think we could handle him medically?"

Larry Freeman was Fenimore's favorite resident, one of the few who actually put the patient's welfare before the almighty dollar. "I agree. His coronaries aren't that bad, and his heart is working well." Fenimore rubbed some soap vigorously into his hands.

"It won't be easy." Larry frowned.

"No, but they haven't scheduled the procedure yet, and if we stick together . . ."

Larry grinned. "You're on."

Fenimore tossed the crumpled towel in the basket and followed him out. As he pushed through the back door of the hospital, he was already planning his strategy for treating Liska with a conservative, noninvasive approach. Running into Larry was a breath of fresh air. There are a few of us left, he thought. And Larry was young. That was a good sign. As he strode toward the doctors' parking lot, he began to whistle.

CHAPTER 5

Same Evening, 8:00 P.M.

Horatio had no trouble finding Fenimore's old town house, the one that served as both his office and home. A yellowed sign rested in the front window. ANDREW B. FENIMORE, M.D., it read, and underneath, BY APPOINTMENT ONLY. A relic from when Fenimore's father had practiced there. There had been no reason to change it—the name was the same. Mounting the three marble steps in a bound, the boy leaned on the bell. The doctor had been waiting.

Together they set off—Fenimore with the spade, Horatio with the sack. Side by side this time. As they walked, Fenimore couldn't resist giving the boy a history lesson.

"Long ago, all this," his hand swept over the city street, "was nothing but forest, populated by a few Indians."

Horatio tried to imagine a dark and silent forest in place of the neon glare and traffic din.

"They lived and hunted happily here before the European settlers came. Then everything changed. The settlers had strange ways. Instead of sharing the land, they fenced it off into small parcels and protected it with guns." He glanced at the boy to see if he was listening.

Horatio, eyes front, gave no clue. But he seemed more relaxed, less wary. Maybe he had decided that an old codger (anyone over thirty was old to a teenager) who gave long-winded lectures on American history must be harmless.

"They cut down the trees and built houses, stores, and churches," Fenimore went on, "and turned the forest footpaths into roads for carts and wagons. A few settlers treated the Native Americans fairly. Paid with goods for the land they took, instead of just stealing it. The most famous, of course, was William Penn."

"That dude on top of City Hall?"

Fenimore nodded. "He was an honest man and made a treaty with the Indians that stipulated—"

"Huh?"

"He saw to it that certain Indian burial grounds remained sacred and no one was allowed to build on them, like this one we're headed for now." They paused at Broad Street for the light. "Somehow, through all the growth and change in this huge city, that little plot has remained intact." They crossed and came to the alley. Fenimore started to turn in, but Horatio hung back.

"What's wrong?"

"Are there . . . Indians buried there now?"

"Yes, but they're nothing but dust."

"But their ghosts . . . ?"

"Don't worry." The doctor smiled and shook the spade. "I'll take care of them."

The site seemed smaller at night. Damn. He'd forgotten his flashlight. He glanced up to remind himself there was sky overhead. A few pinpricks of stars convinced him they weren't sealed in a tomb. When he first touched the ground with the shovel, it made a rasping sound. They both jumped.

It was no easy job to dig where the earth had been trampled

16

for a couple of generations. Without any real hope, Fenimore felt around blindly with his shovel for a softer spot. Unexpectedly, he found one. As his eyes grew accustomed to the dark, he realized that the softer area was where the van had been parked that afternoon. The van was gone now, and the space where it had been was dug up. Strange. He felt the boy watching him and began to dig. Within a few minutes he had made a nice cavity, just about the right size for a cat. One more shovelful. As he dug, his shovel bounced a little, as if hitting something resilient. He reached down, probing, and snatched his hand back. He had felt something remarkably like a clavicle.

The boy moved closer. "Is it ready?"

"Not quite." Fenimore pulled the shovel out, moved a few feet to the left, still keeping to the soft patch, and began to dig again.

"Hey! What was wrong with that one?"

"I hit a rock," Fenimore lied, digging feverishly. When he finally had a new hole the same size as the old one, he reached for the sack.

"Let me." Horatio gently lowered the sack into the hole.

"Here." Fenimore handed him the spade.

Carefully, the boy shoveled the loose dirt over it. When the hole was filled, Fenimore said, "Do you want to say anything?"

Horatio shook his head.

"What was his name?"

"Danny."

Horatio's mother, obviously, had not had a hand in that one. "Good name. My best friend's name is Dan." He refrained from mentioning that his friend was a cop. Fenimore was finding it hard to concentrate on the funeral ceremony. His mind kept leaping back to that first hole. He had a strong desire to recite "The Jelico Cat" by Eliot, but thought better of it. Instead, he fell back on the old litany, "Ashes to ashes, dust to dust. Amen."

The boy crossed himself.

17

Fenimore steered him through the alley, back to the street. "I've got a cat," he said. "Her name's Sal. She's due for a litter in a month. Stop by and I'll save one for you."

Horatio nodded and took off. Relieved of the encumbrance of the sack, he loped easily down the street.

Fenimore waited until the boy was out of sight before he headed for the nearest phone booth.

"Dan?"

"Yeah, Doc."

"Can you get over to Walnut and Watts, right away?"

"What?"

"Yes. Watts. That alley behind Fidelity Bank."

"Watts up?"

"Funny. This is serious."

"But the Phillies are beating the Braves. *That's* serious."

Fenimore could picture Rafferty's big frame hunched over his desk, peering intently at the little black-and-white TV set, the only one the department allowed.

"Sorry, Dan. And bring a powerful flashlight." He hung up on his friend's groan.

Fenimore went back to the burial ground to wait. The street sounds were muted and far away. A man came out the rear door of the hotel, dumped some trash in a can with a clatter, and went back inside. It was even quieter after he had gone. Fenimore wished he had his pipe. The red glow of a pipe, or even a cigarette, was a comfort in the dark. As he raised his eyes, the band of lighted windows on an upper floor of the bank turned black. He jingled his keys in his pocket, a faintly cheering sound. He was itching to investigate that first hole again. But he had no flashlight and only a crude spade. Besides, police procedure was very strict about that. Where was his spade, anyway? He glanced around. He was sure he'd left it leaning against the bank wall when he'd ushered Horatio out. It wasn't there now. That call to

18

Rafferty had taken only a few minutes. Could someone have nipped in and swiped it while he was gone? He turned to scan the rest of the enclosure and caught the full force of the spade on his left temple.

"Fenimore . . . Fenimore . . ."

Someone shaking his shoulder. A bright light in his eyes. A searing pain in his head. He shut his eyes.

"Wake up. It's me, Dan."

Moan.

"What happened?"

"Take that damned light away."

It went away. He tried to raise himself to a sitting position. Another moan.

"Easy. Someone's given you a whack on the head."

"Thanks for the diagnosis." Fenimore gingerly felt his left temple. His fingers came away wet.

"Don't touch it. What the hell were you doing here, anyway?" Rafferty glanced around. "Planning a Halloween party?" Suddenly an idea struck him. "How the hell did you manage to call me *before* you got mugged?"

"Neat trick, eh?" Fenimore attempted a grin, but it turned into a wince. He felt in his back pocket. His wallet was still there, crammed with the bills he'd withdrawn that morning from the ATM machine. He showed it to Rafferty.

Rafferty was crouching in front of Fenimore, who was slouched down against the bank wall. "Start at the beginning," he said.

Between jabs of pain, Fenimore slowly recounted the story of the boy, his cat, and the grave. When he had finished, Rafferty stood up and went over to the patch of ground that Fenimore pointed out to him. He knelt, and, as Fenimore had done before him, prodded in the soft dirt. And, like Fenimore, he snatched back his hand.

19

CHAPTER 6

SAME EVENING, 9:30 P.M.

Did you say this was an Indian burial ground?" Rafferty was slouched against the bank wall next to Fenimore, waiting for his homicide squad to arrive. He had put the order through on his radio a few minutes earlier.

"That's right," Fenimore said.

The policeman had offered to call a squad car to take Fenimore to the hospital, but Fenimore had refused. After suffering this much, he was damned if he was going to miss all the fun.

"I feel their spirits watching me right now," Rafferty said.

"Whose?"

"The Indians'." He stirred anxiously, glancing around. "I wish I had a pint."

"How did somebody who's afraid of ghosts get to be a top cop in Philadelphia?"

"Ghosts aren't Philadelphia's problem."

"Shall I sing?" Fenimore was beginning to feel better.

"Please don't."

That was all the encouragement he needed. He began to croon, "When Irish Eyes Are Smiling."

"Can it. Why did you have to go and dig up a corpse two days before Halloween? Tomorrow's Mischief Night. We have to work extra shifts, and the department's overworked as it is."

"That's why you had time to watch the Phillies?"

"Can it."

"You're getting repetitive."

"Can—" Rafferty got to his feet and began pacing the perimeter of the small space, careful to avoid the hole and its occupant. The limited exercise seemed to give him no relief. He disappeared down the alley to look for his reinforcements.

As soon as he left, Fenimore's head began to throb again. After what seemed a long time, he heard heavy footsteps in the alley, and Rafferty reappeared with his personal army in tow: two police officers, a detective, the medical examiner, and a photographer. From then on business was brisk. Fenimore, feeling uncharacteristically useless, remained against the bank wall.

"Hey, Fenimore, look at this!"

Fenimore leaped to his feet and nearly fainted. The pain surged through his head, almost blinding him. A combination of curiosity and sheer willpower carried him the few steps to look into what had now become a large hole.

There was nothing unusual about the woman's appearance. Eyes closed, tawny skin, black hair. She was simply dressed in a T-shirt, jeans, and sandals. And there were no visible marks on her face, arms, hands, or feet. It was obvious she had been buried recently, within the past two or three hours. There was no evidence of decomposition or decay, and the medical examiner had assured them that rigor mortis was just beginning to set in. It was her posture that was unusual. Instead of lying flat, in the accepted burial position, her body was flexed, knees tucked under her chin, arms crossed over her chest.

Fenimore whistled. "And look how she's facing."

Rafferty stared at him.

Fenimore returned his stare. "It's traditional, among the Lenni-Lenape Indians, to bury their dead in a flexed position, turned toward the east.

CHAPTER 7

SUNDAY AFTERNOON, OCTOBER 30

Fenimore lay on the sofa, pressing an ice pack to the side of his head. The TV was on, but he wasn't watching it. He never watched it, unless he was too sick to read or in too much pain to sleep and needed an excuse to do absolutely nothing without appearing to be brooding.

Sal lay curled at his side, her head turned pointedly away from the screen. She shared his opinion of TV. Every now and then an image on the screen would catch Fenimore's attention—an obnoxious news anchor, an idiotic commercial, or a pretty girl, oops, attractive female person. The first might extract an oath; the second, a snort; the third, a grin. That was the extent of his reaction to the media. Today he felt too terrible to react at all.

Fenimore lay perfectly still in order not to jar his head while he stroked Sal. Most of the time he kept his mind a perfect blank, but every now and then the events of the previous night intruded. Questions rose up. Who hit him? Why? He would stop stroking Sal to ponder these questions until she registered her annoyance with an abrupt *"Meow!"* Then he would resume stroking.

Was the person who had assaulted him the same person who had buried the body? Or an accomplice? How did this person know he had discovered the body? He had been so careful not to let on to the boy. Had the person been lurking nearby when he and Horatio had been engaged in their funeral rites—an uncomfortable thought—and bashed Fenimore on the off chance that he had discovered the body?

"*Meow!*"

Stroke, stroke, stroke.

Had the person meant to do more than injure him and been interrupted? Sal reacted to his too-vigorous stroking by leaping off the sofa.

The phone. He reached for it.

"Andrew?"

Jennifer.

"Dan just called to say you needed cheering up. Is something wrong?"

Blast him. "Not a thing. Can't imagine what . . . he ran into me at the wrong time . . . right after a department meeting. You know how they always funk me up. What are you doing today?"

"Oh, Dad has me inventorying some books that came in Friday from an estate on the Main Line."

"Can they read out there?"

"Snob. Actually, these books belonged to a judge, and they're quite dog-eared."

"Not the usual mint condition, chosen because the binding matched the drapes?"

"No, seriously, he even has an impressive collection of mysteries. Mostly trial stuff, but there are a couple of early Chandlers."

"Hey, could you save me those? I'd like to take a look at them."

"I have a better idea. I'll bring them over."

"Uh, I'm sort of in the middle of something. Billing time . . . end of the month."

"I thought Mrs. Doyle took care of all that."

"Usually, but she was on vacation this month. Things pile up."

"I see." She sounded hurt. "I'll let you go then."

"Maybe you could invite me for dinner some night, and your dad could fill me in on the Lenni-Lenape Indians."

"Why?"

"They're a subject of interest to me right now."

"We have a shelf of books about them."

"Great. I'll be over soon."

"Shall I serve venison and wild rice garnished with—"

"Poison ivy?"

"That depends."

"On what?"

"Lots of things." On this enigmatic note, she hung up.

Fenimore examined his motives. Why had he put Jennifer off? Had he really not wanted her to come? Or did he fear being comforted? Did he secretly yearn to be fed bouillon and read to and generally have his hand held? In short, was he getting soft? If that was the case, he was in the wrong business. Instead of an income supplement, his little sideline might quickly turn into a health hazard. Not that brawn was a weapon he often relied on in his investigations. He didn't have any. His method was to match wits with his adversaries. But even matching wits required a certain amount of independence and self-reliance. That's why he had put Jennifer off.

CHAPTER 8

MONDAY, OCTOBER 31

It was Monday morning. Halloween morning to be exact. The city had made it through another Mischief Night relatively unscathed. So had Fenimore. He had recovered from his head wound enough to sit in his office and read a coroner's report.

Mrs. Doyle, his nurse-secretary for more than fifteen years, and his father's before him, was at her typewriter. (Fenimore had offered to buy her a word processor, but she had emphatically refused. None of those bits and bites and chips for her, thank you. She'd stick to her faithful old Smith Corona.) The fiery hair of her youth had mellowed to a dusty rose (redheads never turn gray), and her curves had acquired some padding. To the patients she resembled a comfortable old sofa that welcomed them into its depths, offering comfort and solace. But underneath all that mellowness and padding lay a keen mind and a sharp tongue, which, like a taut spring, could break through the upholstery at a moment's notice.

The spring had sprung that morning when she walked into the office and saw Fenimore's face: black and blue from eyebrow to chin on one side and a nasty scab over the left ear. "What hit you?" she demanded belligerently. Her concern for the doctor always took the form of anger.

Fenimore, in response to her concern, always acted like a truculent boy who didn't want to explain things to his mother. "Nothing much. Just a small shovel."

"A large bulldozer, more likely." She punctuated her observation with a loud snort. "Have you seen a doctor?" A rhetorical question; she already knew the answer.

Fenimore didn't disappoint her. "I *am* a doctor," he said and returned to his report.

She drew a sharp breath. Every now and then the doctor fell into a pose so like his late father's that it gave her a turn. They were similar in appearance—slight and wiry with a tendency toward balding. And they both suffered from weak eyesight. Father and son each had the habit of leaning on his right arm while reading and making a visor of his right hand to shield his eyes against the lamp's glare. Today one was swollen shut.

Fenimore scanned the first page of the report:

Name: Unknown
Address: Unknown
Phone number: Unknown
Social Security #: Unknown
Sex: Female
Age: Between 23 and 25
Hair: Dark brown
Eyes: Dark brown
Weight: 118 lbs.
Race: Native American
Marks of identification: Scar on chest; evidence of
    heart operation in childhood to correct tetralogy
    of Fallot

27

"Tetralogy of Fallot?"

Mrs. Doyle looked up from her typing. "Doctor?"

He was reading again.

> Stomach contents: Residue of recent meal. Shreds of
> beef, mushrooms, onions, peppers, lettuce, toma-
> toes, bread
> Cause of death: Heart failure

The phone rang at his elbow.

"Ready to man the battlements for Liska?" It was Larry Freeman, his resident.

Fenimore outlined the plan he had conceived to rescue Mr.
Liska from one of the more aggressive cardiology teams at the
hospital. He gave the young doctor detailed instructions. When
he hung up, he was satisfied that another blow had been struck
for the welfare of the patient. He had barely replaced the receiver
when the phone rang again.

"Help."

Rafferty. "The pathologist just left. She was here for over an
hour jawing about blue babies. I didn't understand a word. Can
you get over here and translate?"

"I'll be right over." Fenimore fumbled in the side drawer of his
desk. He found what he wanted and stuffed it in his pocket. "I'm
going out, Doyle. If there's an emergency, get me at Rafferty's
office." He disappeared down the long narrow hall.

"Doyle"? He called her that only when they were about to
embark on a case. That, combined with the state of his face, assured her that he was up to something. Mrs. Doyle returned to
pounding her typewriter. If there had been a law against typewriter abuse, she would have been serving time long ago. But she
wanted to finish her office work in order to be free to help with
this new case—and more important, to get her hands on the
monster who had banged up the doctor's face.

When Fenimore came in, Rafferty examined him critically. "Typical doctor, won't see a doctor."

"Don't you start. I've just escaped Doyle. And what's the idea of squealing to Jennifer?"

"I just thought you needed a little TLC."

"Well, next time you feel like playing cupid, don't."

"Whew. What side of the bed did you get up on?"

"I slept on the couch. So you want to know about blue babies?" Fenimore swiftly changed the subject.

"Yeah. And keep it simple. That pathologist talked a lot of gobbledygook." He rubbed his temples. "What's that?" He was quick to notice the bulge in Fenimore's jacket pocket.

Fenimore took out an object about the size of a softball and set it on Rafferty's desk. It was a small plastic model of a heart. "Take it apart."

Rafferty, after a startled look, began to dismantle it, laying the pieces in a neat row in front of him. When he had it all apart, he looked up like a good child expecting a pat on the head.

"Now for the hard part," Fenimore said. "Put it back together."

After a few false starts, Rafferty succeeded.

"Good. Now you're ready." Fenimore launched into a definition of tetralogy of Fallot.

"Tetralogy of Fallot is a heart condition found in some newborns that causes cyanosis—the so-called blue babies. The cyanosis is caused by some of the blood not getting enough oxygen in the lungs. Blood without enough oxygen is blue." Fenimore pointed to the veins in his left hand. "After the blood gets oxygen in the lungs, it becomes red. In tetralogy of Fallot there are four, or tetra"—he held up four fingers—"factors that prevent blood from getting to the lungs and receiving oxygen. Oh, and Fallot is the French fellow who discovered it all. Now there's a surgical operation that can correct this condition, and with the help of medicines, the kid can live a relatively normal life."

"How come you didn't just say, 'This condition keeps blood from getting to the lungs to pick up oxygen'?"

Fenimore sighed. "And have you think I spent all those years in medical school drinking and carousing?" That was how Fenimore had met Rafferty. One balmy spring evening he and some other medical students had been involved in a harmless, drunken prank (hurling water balloons at unsuspecting passengers seated next to open windows in trolley cars). Rafferty, barely more than a rookie himself, had threatened him and the others with arrest on charges of assault and battery. The lean, dark policeman (he could have been a stand-in for a young Gregory Peck) had even had the temerity to accuse Fenimore of being the instigator. But the silver-tongued medical student had managed to convince him that no harm had been done. Not only did Rafferty let them go, he agreed to meet Fenimore later, when he was off duty, for a few beers at The Raven, a shabby dive with pretensions to having once served the famous author, Edgar Allan Poe. It had been their favorite haunt ever since.

"Now let's get down to the important business." Rafferty tipped back in his chair, clasping his hands behind his head. He still looked like a movie star, albeit an aging one. His black hair had some gray in it, and there was the slightest hint of a bulge at his waist—even though, Fenimore knew, he worked out regularly—but his eyes were the same deep blue, and his gaze was, if anything, sharper and more penetrating. "Could the condition revealed in the coroner's report cause sudden death many years after the operation?"

Fenimore pondered. "It's a definite possibility. You see," he pointed to the septal wall in the model, "this area where the surgical repair took place is also where the electrical conductor of the heart is located. When this conductor is disturbed by surgery, it may not conduct beats properly. And more important, years after the surgery it might cause ventricular arrhythmias that could result in ventricular fibrillation and syncope—"

"Whoa!" Rafferty held up his hand. "You're beginning to sound like that pathologist. Back up and give me those last three again."

"Sorry." He took Rafferty's pencil and wrote down the three technical words. " 'Arrhythmia' is any disturbance in the rhythm of the heartbeat: 'Fibrillation' is when the heart muscle stops contracting and merely quivers, making ineffectual wormlike motions, and the blood doesn't get pumped around: And 'syncope' is fainting due to lack of blood getting to the brain."

"And all these developments are bad?"

"Very." He nodded.

Rafferty was thoughtful. "If someone knew this woman's medical history, could any of these disturbances be artificially induced, by, say, the introduction of a drug?"

Fenimore looked up. "You think her death was unnatural?"

"Her burial sure was."

"Not for a Native American."

"Come on, Doc. How many Native Americans bury their friends and relatives in vacant lots?"

"That 'vacant lot' happens to be a sacred Lenape burial ground. But you have a point. It's been neglected and it's unprotected. A Lenape would not be likely to use it, unless . . ."

"Unless?"

"Unless they wanted the body to be found."

Rafferty pondered this, drumming his fingers on the desk. Then he said, "Another thing. If this was a traditional Lenape burial, why didn't the family lay her out in something more appropriate—some kind of ceremonial dress? She was wearing jeans, a T-shirt, and sandals."

"True. But not all Lenapes own ceremonial garments. The

younger ones may have lost or discarded them, the way we might give our grandmother's wedding dress to a thrift shop or rummage sale."

"Yours, maybe. If I did that, my grandma would come down and haunt me 'til I bought it back." Rafferty had been pacing the office; now he turned on Fenimore. "And if this was a simple family burial, how do you account for someone bashing you on the head? Is that a quaint Lenape family custom too?"

"Totally unrelated. Some mugger—"

"Who left a wallet behind with two hundred bucks."

"He might have been interrupted."

"By what?"

"You."

"And disappeared into thin air?"

"No, into the back of the hotel. I saw a man come out of there to dump some trash. It wasn't locked."

They sat in silence, glaring at each other. Finally Fenimore said, "Turn up anything in Missing Persons?"

"Thought you'd never ask." Rafferty shot a computer printout across his desk.

Fenimore scanned the list:

MISSING PERSON	REPORTED BY	DATE	TIME
Adams, Mary	George Adams, husband	07-31	4:30 PM
Corinsky, Joseph	Anna Corinsky, wife	08-09	6:20 AM
Facciolli, Nicholas	Angelo Brullo, friend	09-02	2:15 PM
Fairfax, Sally	Michael J. Fairfax, father	10-30	3:05 PM
Field, Joanne	Ted Hardwick, fiancé	10-30	11:15 PM

He paused. There was a small penciled cross next to Field. "Let's see this description," he pointed.

Rafferty had it ready. He passed it over.

JOANNE FIELD: Age: 24. Height: 5´4˝. Weight: 118 lbs. Hair: Dark brown. Eyes: Dark brown. Race: Native American. Marks of identification: Scar transecting lower left quadrant of chest.

Fenimore raised his eyes to Rafferty's. "What are you waiting for?"

"A small canvas bag was found buried with her," he said. "There were no obvious forms of identification in it, but the contents are being examined now and I'm waiting for the report."

Fenimore pulled the list of missing persons toward him again and studied it. "I know a *Ned* Hardwick," he said slowly.

Rafferty perked up. "Could this be his son?"

"Could be. Have you notified him yet?"

"Not yet. Would you like the pleasure?" He placed his feet on his desk.

"How much time do I have?"

"We have to notify the next of kin within twenty-four hours of identification."

"Fiancés aren't 'next of kin' ".

"You must've been a whiz at genetics."

Ignoring him, Fenimore asked, "Does she have any blood relatives?"

"When the fiancé reported her missing, he mentioned she had a brother."

"Where is he?"

"South Jersey, near Riverton."

"That figures. The Lenapes settled around there."

"There you go. At last you can put that history hobby of yours to some practical use." Rafferty enjoyed poking fun at Fenimore's academic pursuits.

"Look, do you think you could bend the rules a bit?" Fenimore asked. "I have a light schedule today, and I think I may know these Hardwicks. Maybe I can dig something up."

"Haven't you dug enough up?"

Fenimore waited patiently, like a child who has asked for a special treat.

"Okay," Rafferty brought his feet back to the floor with a thud. "You can have 'til nine o'clock."

Fenimore was heading for the door when Rafferty hailed him. "You left your heart behind."

He turned and grinned. "Why, Raff, I didn't know you cared." He pocketed the plastic model and exited before the policeman could throw something at him.

CHAPTER 9

STILL MONDAY MORNING

In the dim corridor outside Rafferty's office, Fenimore waited for the elevator and thought about the Hardwicks. Ned was already an established surgeon when Fenimore was a mere intern. As soon as Ned had begun practice, he had married Polly Matthews. Because Polly came from a prominent and wealthy Philadelphia family and her father was chief of surgery, everyone thought Ned had made "a good match." This had nettled the young surgeon at the time, because he prided himself on his own origins. His family was of old Boston stock; his ancestors had arrived on the *Mayflower* in 1620. But the Hardwicks had lived in Philadelphia for only two generations, relegating him to a slightly lower rung than Polly's on the social ladder, even though her ancestors had not arrived in Philadelphia on the *Welcome* with William Penn until 1682.

Giving up on the elevator, Fenimore took the fire stairs.

While a young doctor, Fenimore had seen the Hardwicks fairly often. Polly was famous for her dinner parties. (People in Polly's circles never asked you over for dinner—they invited you to dinner parties.) She often invited a few younger staff members to liven up the parties, and Fenimore, known even then for his witty repartee, was frequently included.

Fenimore had early grown tired of the Hardwicks' form of entertaining. By the time he was thirty, he preferred to spend his spare evenings at home with Sal and a good mystery. (That was before he met Jennifer, of course.) Now, Hardwick was a prominent surgeon. There wasn't a prestigious board in Philadelphia that didn't bear his name, and the only time Fenimore ever saw the famous surgeon was when he bumped into him at some medical meeting. Funny, he couldn't remember his son, or any of his children, for that matter. Of course that was more than twenty years ago. The children would have been very young at the time and not permitted to eat with the grown-ups. They probably lived their small lives upstairs under the watchful eye of an expensive nanny.

Fenimore pushed open the fire door and stepped into the foyer of the Police Administration Building. He captured a pay phone and dialed his office. After learning that there were no messages, he gave Mrs. Doyle her instructions. First, call Dr. Hardwick's home and ask for Ted. If Ted answers, or is called to the phone, pretend to be doing a television survey and ask what program he's watching. If the person who answers has never heard of Ted, say, "Sorry, wrong number," and hang up. Second, call Dr. Hardwick's office. If he's in, ask how long he'll be there. If he's out, ask where he can be reached.

While Fenimore waited for Doyle to call back, he jealously guarded his pay phone and surveyed the scene before him. Armed men in blue uniforms led scruffy, handcuffed youths in and out of a network of mysterious rooms. None of the offenders looked particularly upset. On the contrary, they had the air of being in a familiar place, following a well-known routine and being bored with the whole procedure.

The telephone jangled in his ear. He grabbed the receiver to learn that Ted Hardwick had answered Ned Hardwick's home

phone; he did not watch morning television. Dr. Hardwick was not in his office. He was on his way downtown to chair a meeting at the Philadelphia Society of Physicians and Surgeons at 1:00.

Fenimore glanced at his watch. 12:30. "Thanks, Doyle." Dodging an assortment of police officers and alleged criminals, he reached the sidewalk and hailed a cab, a luxury he indulged only in cases of emergency. He gave the cabby the uptown address, "Eighteenth and Spruce."

The home of the Philadelphia Society of Physicians and Surgeons, or PSPS (pronounced "pisspiss" by some heretical nonmembers), was an imposing combination of brick, marble, and wrought iron, located in the once fashionable part of town near Rittenhouse Square. The doctors who had founded the society in 1789 had held monthly meetings there to parade their titles and degrees while partaking of tea, sherry, and elegant pastries. The present members carried on this time-honored tradition.

But the society wasn't entirely social. It had some excellent academic resources: a museum with such tantalizing exhibits as the largest tumor excised in the United States before 1900; a library containing a firsthand account by Benjamin Rush of the yellow fever epidemic; and a small but exceptional herb garden providing specimens of plants and herbs used for healing before the advent of pharmaceuticals. Finding these resources useful on occasion, Fenimore paid his annual dues and skipped the social gatherings.

The wrought-iron gate stood open. He followed the brick path that wound through the herb garden. Strolling slowly among the beds, he could keep an eye on the gate without appearing to be overtly watching for someone. Now and then he stooped to read a label attached to a plant. "Marigold (ointment for ulcers)." "Horehound (tonic for colds and coughs)." "Rosemary (liniment)." "Garlic (antiseptic)." "Foxglove (heart fail-

ure)." He snapped a leaf from the last and found a seat on a nearby bench.

A batch of early trick-or-treaters, wearing costumes and masks, scurried past the iron gate, giggling. A cat, a skeleton, and two witches. Funny about masks. He had been scared to death of them when he was small. When the trick-or-treaters had come to the door, he had dived under the dining room table. But he had soon outgrown that and donned the most hideous monster masks, all green and mottled and oozing with blood, and loved scaring the other children.

"Fenimore. What a coincidence!" Ned Hardwick loomed over him. He was a large man, immaculately groomed, his silver hair glinting in the sun. "Substantial" was the word that came to Fenimore whenever he saw him. "Sorry, old man," the surgeon apologized. "Catching a catnap, were you? Can't blame you. Don't get much sleep, I guess. Hear you still make house calls?" Suddenly he noticed Fenimore's face. "What happened? Run into a door? Ha ha."

"Slipped on some stairs," Fenimore said casually, knowing that Hardwick's concern was only curiosity. He was still puzzling over Ned's greeting. What coincidence?

"Polly was just bugging me this morning to call you about a little problem we're having. Not medical, mind you." He leaned forward, lowering his voice, and Fenimore caught a strong whiff of expensive aftershave. "Has to do with that little sideline of yours."

None of Fenimore's colleagues approved of his "little sideline," as they described his occasional forays into private sleuthing. But their reservations miraculously disappeared whenever something came up in their own lives that required his services. He waited patiently to hear the nature of Ned's little problem.

"This is the thing. My son's fiancée has disappeared. She's only been missing a little over twenty-four hours, but Polly's

upset. You see, the wedding's in three weeks and there's all the arrangements. My own theory is she's just panicked and run off to think things over. Women are as jittery about marriage as men these days, you know. Afraid of losing their independence, jeopardizing their careers . . . They've been living together, of course, for over a year. 'Significant others' and all that. But actually tying the knot is a different thing, you know. Er . . ." Suddenly remembering Fenimore's bachelor status, he said, "I guess you don't know. But let me tell you—"

Apparently, Ted had neglected to tell his father about notifying the police. "When," Fenimore broke in, "did your son last see his fiancée?"

Hardwick wrinkled his massive brow. "That's the funny part. We were all together at our home Saturday afternoon. Polly had arranged a party in her honor. She had invited a few family members and some old friends we wanted her to meet."

To pass judgment before allowing her into the sacred family circle, no doubt, thought Fenimore.

"It was a nice affair. Polly always goes all out, you know, even though it was just a picnic."

Fenimore did know. He had sat through a number of the Hardwicks' parties, usually drinking too much and counting the minutes until he could escape. Maybe Ted's fiancée had had similar feelings.

"Everyone liked the girl . . . uh . . . young woman. She's a dear child. Dark beauty. Ind . . . er, Native American background. I always kid her, tell her her ancestors go farther back than mine, although mine came over on the *Mayflower*. Her anglicized name is Joanne Field, but her Indian name is Win´gay´musk, which means 'Sweet Grass.' "

Fenimore's face, from long experience as a physician and private investigator, gave nothing away.

"Can't get over running into you like this. Never see you at the monthly meetings," Ned chided.

Fenimore mumbled something.

"Well, what d'ya think of our little problem?"

Why the "little"? To make it seem smaller? "I can't say, Ned. For a start, I'll check out Missing Persons and give you a call tonight."

Ned wrinkled his brow again, mentally flipping the pages of his crowded social calendar. "Think we have the orchestra tonight. But we're dining in. You can probably catch me at home between six and seven."

Accustomed to the odd priorities of people in Hardwick's circles—the orchestra took precedence over a missing prospective daughter-in-law—Fenimore nodded and they parted. Hardwick's broad, imposing back headed up the marble steps of the society while Fenimore's slighter frame slipped through the wrought-iron gate and turned down Walnut.

CHAPTER 10

MONDAY AFTERNOON

Mrs. Doyle looked up from her typewriter and glanced at the clock. Fenimore had been gone for more than two hours, and all that had transpired were three routine phone calls and one teenage patient off the street with no appointment. The patient was a disreputable-looking youngster who could very well wait. She had told him the doctor wasn't a pediatrician, and he had given her a very hard look. Much too hard for such a young person, she thought. It had quite rattled her. She told him to take a seat, the doctor would be in shortly.

That was twenty minutes ago and he was still there, staring straight ahead, not touching the magazines. Maybe he couldn't read. From his appearance, that was possible. Faded jeans and a ragged T-shirt. Mrs. Doyle softened toward him. Illiteracy was a terrible thing. She volunteered at her local library to teach reading, and it was pitiful to see people older than herself who had lived their whole lives without reading a word. No lurid newspaper accounts. No sizzling romances. How did they stand it?

"Well, Horatio!" The doctor's greeting resounded in the waiting room. "If you've come for your kitten, I'm afraid you're too early. My cat doesn't produce on demand." He picked up Sal, who had been rubbing against the boy's leg.

"Uh, no. I came about somethin' else." He stared at Fenimore's bruised face but made no comment.

"Well, come on back then." Fenimore led the way to his outer office, his nurse's exclusive domain. "Have you met Mrs. Doyle?"

The boy nodded sullenly.

Mrs. Doyle pressed her lips together and continued typing.

"I see." He waved him into his inner office, leaving the door ajar. "Well, what can I do for you? You look healthy enough." Sal, who had been dangling over his arm all this time, leaped to the floor as Fenimore seated himself at his desk.

There was an awkward pause. Then the boy blurted, "Do you have some work for me? I could come after school."

Fenimore felt Doyle's displeasure emanating from the outer office. He ignored her. "Have a seat." He waved him into a chair that had started life in a Sunday school, moved on to a second-hand furniture store, and was ending its days in Fenimore's office. "D'ya know your alphabet?"

"Sure." He looked offended.

"Good. Then you can file. Can ya read?"

"I'm fourteen, for Chrissake!" (Mrs. Doyle regretted her wasted sympathy.)

"Good. Then you can sort the mail. Can you type?"

He shook his head and muttered, "Do I look like a fucking secretary?"

"Good." Fenimore glanced warily through the door at his nurse. "We wouldn't want to put Mrs. Doyle out of business."

Mrs. Doyle, like the queen, was not amused.

"Well, Doyle, what d'ya think?" he called to her. "Can we find something for this young fella to do?"

She was still "Doyle," at least. Her mood mellowed. Maybe this boy could lighten her load and she would have more time

42

to work on important things—like this new case. She could attend to his language later. "Oh, well," she shrugged.

"Fine. When can you start?" Fenimore asked.

"Tomorrowrightafterschool." It came out as one word.

"Five dollars an hour. If you do well, we may up it to six."

A flicker of a grin.

"And, Horatio?"

Mrs. Doyle blinked at the name.

"If Mrs. Doyle doesn't have work for you one day, would you be willing to do odd jobs? Clean the cellar or the backyard?"

His nod was quick.

"Okay. It's a deal. See you tomorrow. You can let yourself out."

Fenimore came back to the outer office and settled into his favorite battered armchair. To avoid his nurse's eye, he fussed with his pipe.

"Since when do we need help around here? I've always thought I managed this office perfectly well. Your father never had any complaints."

"Of course you do, Doyle. I wanted to give the kid a break."

"Is he honest?"

"I haven't the faintest idea. I met him only yesterday. But he passed Sal's inspection." He cast a fond look at his cat, who had settled herself on the windowsill. "Did you see how she wrapped herself around him?"

Unimpressed by Sal's preferences, she said, "Well, the first time I notice anything missing . . ."

"That goes without saying." Fenimore finally had his pipe going and eased back in his chair. "Let me tell you how I ran into him," he began, and out came the story of the burial of the cat, the discovery of the body, and his recent encounter with Ned Hardwick. He passed lightly over his own injury.

Mrs. Doyle listened attentively. When he had finished, she was silent.

"No comment?"

"I'm speechless."

"A nice little Halloween story, eh?"

The phone.

Fenimore grabbed it ahead of his nurse. As he listened to the caller, a look of incredulity spread over his face. "That's bizarre." He hung up.

"What's bizarre?"

"That was Rafferty. A small canvas bag was found buried near the woman's body. Would you care to guess what was inside?"

"A pair of smelly jogging shoes?"

"A Walkman, a wooden weaver's shuttle, and a jar of peanut butter." He recited a verse he had learned in school:

> "The Indian, when from life released,
> Again is seated with his friends,
> And shares again the joyous feast . . ."

"Of peanut butter?" she made a face.

"Tastes differ, Doyle." He leaned forward. "Native Americans believe that life goes on after death."

"So do we." Mrs. Doyle was a good Catholic; Fenimore, a bad Anglican. He went to church only twice a year—Christmas Eve and Easter Sunday.

"But not in the same way. We believe we leave our earthly desires and satisfactions behind—eating, drinking, lovemaking. The Native Americans don't. They believe they carry them along, all intact. They are still able to eat, drink, make love—or war—after death. That's why some of their most treasured possessions are often buried with them."

"Should we envy or pity them?"

He took a long drag on his pipe and stared morosely at the brick wall outside his window. When he spoke, his tone was sober. "Pity the young man who may have lost his Indian maiden."

44

The rest of the afternoon passed routinely for Fenimore. He ate a bologna sandwich on rye and saw three patients—a stomachache, a sore throat, and a head cold. Most cardiologists would consider it beneath them to treat such minor ailments. Not Fenimore. He liked his patients and enjoyed making them well, no matter what ailed them. Besides, they helped put bread on the table (and cat food in Sal's bowl).

As Mrs. Doyle was preparing to leave, she couldn't resist offering him one of her home remedies. "Tea leaves soaked in warm vinegar and applied as a compress."

Fenimore grimaced.

"There's nothing like it, Doctor, for reducing the swelling."

When she was safely out the door, Fenimore placed another call to Rafferty. "Was there a tape in that Walkman?"

"Yeah."

"Anything on it?"

"What did you expect, a complete description of her death and burial for police and reporters?"

"Zip?"

"Blank. Her friends and relatives gave her a blank tape, probably to dictate her impressions of the hereafter—record those choirs of angels, the creak of St. Peter's gate."

"I imagine that's pretty well oiled," Fenimore said.

Rafferty laughed.

"By the way, Joanne Field had another name," Fenimore said. "Sweet Grass."

"Sounds like a pseudonym for marijuana."

"It's a translation of her Algonquin name. Win´gay´musk." Fenimore quickly filled him in on the Hardwick story.

Before Rafferty let the doctor go, he reminded him of his deadline. He must bring Ted Hardwick into the morgue to make a positive identification by nine o'clock that night.

When Fenimore hung up, he was alone. Mrs. Doyle and Horatio were long gone. Even Sal had disappeared on some mission

45

of her own. Except for the hum of the little refrigerator, which held his patients' blood and urine samples (and a couple of cans of soda), the office was still. Sitting immobile at his desk, Fenimore postponed the inevitable moment when he would have to cause pain. He could not put it off much longer. Rafferty had issued his ultimatum. Tomorrow morning, *The Inquirer* would have a full account of the discovery of the body, the radio would be bleating the news every fifteen minutes, and the TV would have a team of photographers panning the ancient burial ground. He glanced at his watch. 5:30.

He reached for the phone.

"Ned? This is Andrew. I'm trying to reach Ted. Yes, something has turned up. I'm sorry. I can't discuss it over the phone. I must speak to Ted first." Fenimore moved the receiver an inch from his ear. People as prominent as Ned Hardwick were not accustomed to being refused anything. "Could you tell me where I can find your son?"

According to his father, Ted was teaching a class at the university and would be finishing up around 6:30. No, he didn't know which class or what classroom building. That would be up to Fenimore to ferret out. Fenimore called the registrar's office.

Armed with the necessary information, Fenimore arrived outside a lecture hall labeled ART HISTORY 101 just as the doors burst open and a crowd of noisy freshmen piled out. He waited while Ted answered the question of a last, lingering student. When the teacher was finally alone, Fenimore entered the hall, closing the door carefully behind him.

46

CHAPTER 11

MONDAY EVENING

No son could resemble his father less, in figure and personality, than Ted Hardwick. (He was actually Edward Hardwick, III, but his grandfather was Ed, his father was Ned, and to avoid confusion, he was called Ted.) Where the father was rock solid, the son was reed slim. Where the father was egocentric, the son was self-effacing. Where the father was hard and uncompromising, the son was gentle and unassuming.

Ted had decided not to become a doctor early on, he explained to Fenimore. Or, rather, his total lack of aptitude and enthusiasm for scientific subjects had automatically eliminated him from the field, he said with a self-deprecating smile. It was a deep disappointment to his surgeon father. Instead, Ted had chosen to teach art history. At present he was employed as an instructor here at the university.

Fenimore let him talk on, cowardly postponing his news.

"This is where I met Sweet Grass," Ted said. "She's an instructor in American Indian studies, specializing in arts and crafts, weaving and pottery. She's a talented weaver as well," he added with some pride.

47

Fenimore flinched at Ted's use of the present tense.

"You have news?" Ted was suddenly wary.

Fenimore looked past the young man, so anxious and vulnerable, through the window at the statue of Benjamin Franklin, casting its long shadow across the grassy quadrangle. If only he could draw strength from that solid, bronze back. "We've found a body that fits Sweet Grass's description."

"Roaring Wings!" blurted Ted.

Fenimore drew back. From his first impression of Ted, he had expected a different reaction—a collapse or breakdown. Instead, his mild expression had turned ugly, and he had spoken with tremendous force.

"What do you mean?" Fenimore asked.

"Roaring Wings. He's Sweet Grass's brother. He hated me. He was against our marriage from the start. I might taint his sister's pure Lenape blood." He shook his head slowly. "And this is how . . ." He staggered, leaning against the lectern.

Fenimore led him, like a child, to a seat in the front row of the empty lecture hall.

When Ted had recovered sufficiently, Fenimore drove him to the morgue. After identifying his fiancée's body, Ted acquiesced to letting Fenimore take him home.

"You can leave your car in the university lot overnight," Fenimore told him.

Ted nodded. He was silent while Fenimore dealt with the heavy city traffic. But once on the expressway, he said tersely, "You won't let him get away with it."

"Who?"

"Roaring Wings, of course."

"We have no proof."

"You're a detective, you can get proof."

"Sometimes, but—"

"You can start now. I'll tell you everything I know."

Traffic had thinned. The dark road spread out before them.

48

"Well," Fenimore began gingerly, "for a start, you could tell me everything you remember about your fiancée before she disappeared. Her activities, her conversations, her thoughts."

"I didn't see much of her these last few weeks. You see, we were both still working and trying to get ready for the wed . . ." He faltered.

"Are you sure you want to do this?" Fenimore pressed his arm.

"Yes." He shifted in his seat. "Where was I?"

"Getting ready for the wedding."

"Well, she went shopping a lot. Or rather, she was supposed to go shopping. My mother had given her a list of things to buy for the ceremony and the wedding trip."

A vivid image of Ted's mother, Polly Hardwick, popped into Fenimore's mind. Tall, big boned, imposing. She could have been her husband's twin, and her son bore little resemblance to either of them. Fenimore remembered one dinner party he had attended at their house. A guest had rashly disagreed with Ned Hardwick on some current political issue. Polly had fixed him with an imperious stare and said, "We seldom tolerate such opinions in my home." Startled, the guest had flushed, stuttered to a halt, and (to Fenimore's disgust) remained silent for the rest of the meal.

"On Friday," Ted went on, "Sweet Grass went to see Roaring Wings. He lives on a reservation in south Jersey. He's not like his sister. He refuses to be assimilated into contemporary society. His main interest is preserving his native heritage and his Lenape blood. He refused to come to the wedding. She went down there to try, one last time, to persuade him to come. He's her only living relative, and as children they were very close."

"Have you talked to him since?"

"No. He doesn't have a phone. One of his many quirks. When I realized she was missing, I sent a message to him. Eventually he got back to me saying he hadn't heard from Sweet Grass since her visit. She had left him the next morning when she realized that he wasn't going to change his mind. She had to get back for the party anyway."

"Party?"

"Yes. Mother gave a party for us Saturday afternoon. Actually, it was only a picnic. She wanted to introduce Sweet Grass to some relatives and old friends of the family. Sweet Grass seemed to be feeling a little low afterward. Mother's friends can be a bit overwhelming at times."

I'll say, thought Fenimore.

"And what with her brother refusing to come to the wedding, I think she was depressed. I wanted to drive her home, but she had her car, and since she was going to visit a friend in the hospital, she said I'd only be in the way."

Fenimore got off the expressway at the Gladwyn exit and burrowed into the heart of the Main Line. "What friend?"

"Doris," Ted said, "the one she's rooming with temporarily. She was operated on last week, and Saturday was the first day she was allowed visitors."

"Did you talk to Sweet Grass after that?"

"No." There was a catch in his throat. "I called her at the apartment later that night, but she didn't answer. I left a message, but she never called back."

"And the next day?"

"I still got the answering machine, so I went right down there. There were a couple of women standing around in the hall. They told me Sweet Grass had scheduled a weaving class that morning, but she hadn't shown up."

"What did you do then?"

"Well, first I contacted Roaring Wings. Quite a production because of that phone thing. When I finally learned that he hadn't seen her, I called Doris. She said Sweet Grass had come to the hospital but hadn't stayed long. She had complained of a headache and dizziness. That's when I got really concerned and wanted to call the police. But my parents wouldn't have it. It would be too embarrassing if we involved the police and it turned out Sweet Grass was just suffering from a case of prenuptial jitters. They suggested that we wait awhile and see if she turned up."

"And you agreed?" Fenimore struggled to hide his surprise.

"Yes. But I wasn't happy about it. And I told them so. That's when Mother thought of you and bugged Dad to give you a call. Dad dragged his feet all Sunday. I couldn't stand it. Without telling them, I called Missing Persons. Then, this morning, Dad ran into you at the herb garden. Quite a coincidence!"

"Quite." Fenimore wondered if Ned would ever have contacted him if he hadn't staged their "accidental" meeting. "There are some things I need to know. Do you have something to write on?"

Ted pulled a small notebook and a pen from his pocket.

Fenimore flicked on the overhead light. "I need Roaring Wings's address or some place where I can reach him."

"You can leave a message at the Lenape Cultural Center in Riverton. They have a phone, and he'll get it eventually." Ted jotted the number down for him.

"And the name of her friend?"

"Doris Bentley."

"And the hospital?"

"Franklin Hospital." He wrote both these things down. "But I don't know her room number."

"Was Sweet Grass on any medication for her heart problem?"

He nodded. "She takes . . ." He paused and said deliberately, "She *took* a pill once a day. I'd pick them up for her sometimes at the pharmacy."

"Do you happen to remember the name?"

"Digoxin."

"Write that down."

He did.

"Had she gotten a refill recently?"

"Yes, as a matter of fact. I picked one up last week. I think she said it would last for three months."

Fenimore paused at an intersection and asked which way to turn. His visits to the Main Line were infrequent, and it was easy to lose your way on the narrow twisting roads. Once back on track, he asked, "Do you know the name of her physician?"

"Robinson. She's at Jefferson. Her office is in the hospital."

Fenimore knew Dr. Robinson. A competent cardiologist. Not overly aggressive. Board certified, like himself. Less experienced, of course.

They drove in silence for a while. Suddenly, Ted began to talk quietly, almost to himself. "It was so unlike her, not to call. She always called before she went to sleep at night. We would tell each other about our day and . . ." Abruptly remembering that he was not alone, he said, "You see, we shared an apartment until a few weeks ago when the lease ran out. Since then we lived apart. I lived at home and Sweet Grass stayed with Doris. Mother's idea. 'It would be more practical,' she said. 'More proper,' was what she really meant." He paused, probably regretting those weeks with Sweet Grass that he had lost. "After the wedding we were going to move into a small town house in Society Hill. We've been working on it off and on all year. Getting it into shape. The floors were the toughest. All that sanding. All that dust. Sweet Grass isn't much of a housekeeper. She . . ." he trailed off.

It was after nine o'clock when they passed through the gate, brooded over by two stone lions, into the Hardwick property. It took a long time to circumnavigate the driveway to the house. The house itself was a mix of French château, medieval castle, and English country estate. Only a combination of inherited wealth (Polly's) and a surgeon's income (Ned's) could possibly sustain such a spread. There was no car in the circular drive in front of the house and only a few lights on downstairs. The

Hardwicks, it seemed, had not returned from the orchestra. Fenimore felt uneasy about leaving Ted alone. He had been silent for some time. As they crunched to a halt, Fenimore said, "How about if I come in for a while."

"No. I'm all right." He tore the sheet from his notebook, handed it to Fenimore, and got out quickly. "Thanks for the ride." The courtesy was automatic.

Fenimore waited while Ted disconnected the burglar alarm and unlocked the front door. A large black Labrador rushed out to greet him. He knelt and hugged the dog, pressing his face into its fur. Fenimore waited another half minute before sliding into gear and starting back down the curving drive.

CHAPTER 12

LATER MONDAY EVENING

As Fenimore groped his way through the dark suburban roads, the image of the young man burying his face in his dog kept coming between him and the windshield. When that image disappeared it was replaced by another—of a young woman lying in the city morgue.

A screech of tires and brakes. To his left, in the glare of headlights, an angry man was shaking his fist and shouting something that sounded remarkably like "Damned drunk!"

From the breadth of the driver's shoulders and the set of his jaw, Fenimore decided not to defend his sobriety. He pressed the accelerator and did not let go until he was deep on a wooded road requiring his high beams. The incident had jolted him out of his numbing depression. He craved action. Technically his services were no longer needed. He had located the young woman he had been asked to find. But he wasn't satisfied. Intuitively he sensed that there was more to this than a simple missing person's case followed by a natural death and burial. Why had Ted blurted "Roaring Wings" as soon as he had learned of his fiancée's death? And there was something else Ted had said about his brother-in-law-to-be: "He feels very strongly about preserving his native heritage and his Lenape blood." He must talk to Roaring Wings before the police did, before they put him on his guard. He glanced at his watch. Almost ten. Too late to tackle New Jersey back roads. These suburban roads were a piece of cake compared to the unmarked roads of south Jersey at night. Besides, it would be nearly midnight before he arrived. Hardly an appropriate time to inform someone of a death in the family. One thing was in his favor, however. Roaring Wings had no phone. And he was sure the police would not bestir themselves to notify the man of his sister's death until the next morning.

But sleep was out of the question. He would only toss and turn. There must be something, someone. Doris Bentley, Sweet Grass's roommate. She was a patient in the hospital. Often patients recuperating from surgery had trouble sleeping. Perhaps she would welcome a nocturnal visitor. But he must not tell her about Sweet Grass, as such a shock might delay her recovery. He would have to pretend they were still searching for her and he needed Doris's help.

While working out this plan, Fenimore had been driving automatically. When he took stock of his surroundings, he was surprised to find that he was approaching the entrance to the expressway. The efficiency of his automatic pilot always amazed him. He was only ten minutes from center city and Franklin Hospital. He pulled onto the ramp and waited for an opening between the stream of cars.

At night, the cavernous lobbies of big-city hospitals depressed Fenimore. They reminded him of deserted railway terminals. But instead of waiting for trains, the few people dotting the landscape were waiting for news, often of life and death. And there were no cheerful attendants in blue and gold uniforms, eager to answer their questions. The only attendants were interns who appeared sporadically, in garish green tunics often stained with red—to let you know they had been dealing with serious matters. They wore their stains with an air, a sort of "red badge of courage." They were young, of course. The older doctors no longer indulged in such histrionics, and they never showed up in the lobby.

Fenimore rarely came in the front entrance of a hospital. At his own hospital, he always came in the back, directly from the parking lot.

On his way to the information desk, he skirted a large sofa that had become home base for a woman and her three children. The youngest was curled up asleep against her thigh, but the older two were restless, darting around the room, engaged in some game. The woman made a halfhearted attempt to restrain them in Spanish, but its effect was short-lived and they were soon up and at it again.

The lone receptionist was deep in a paperback.

"I'd like the room number of Doris Bentley, please."

The woman looked up and yawned. "Visiting hours are over."

"I'm a physician." He showed her his card, not bothering to tell her that he wasn't on the staff.

"Oh, sorry, Doctor," she flipped through the card file. "Room two-one-four."

"Thanks."

Fenimore got off the elevator and made his way down the corridor. He passed the nurses' station where a party seemed to be in full swing: Nurses, orderlies, and assorted staff engaged in hilarity while the lights on the call board behind them flashed with the SOS's of patients. If it had been his own hospital, he would have read them the riot act.

In this grim mood, he scanned the room numbers: 210, 212, 214. He tapped lightly on the half-open door. If she was asleep, of course, he wouldn't disturb her.

"Come in."

In the soft gray light of a small TV set suspended from a bar above the bed, he made out the young woman. Like Sweet Grass, she was sitting in a flexed position, knees bent. But this woman was alive—and facing west.

"My name is Dr. Fenimore. . . ."

Obligingly, she turned off the TV with the remote control and pulled a string that turned on the light above her bed. The room, illuminated as if by a camera flash, revealed someone in the early stages of convalescence after major surgery. Her pale face was set in a manner Fenimore recognized instantly—someone who has recently suffered severe pain and is still anxiously awaiting its return. She smiled tentatively, as if expecting yet another test or examination.

"I'm sorry to bother you at this hour—"

"No bother," she stopped him. "A visitor is always welcome in the hospital. It relieves the monotony."

"Then you must be feeling better."

She smiled. "A little."

"I'm a friend of Ted Hardwick. He—and his father—have asked me to help look for your roommate."

"They haven't found her?"

"Not yet." Fenimore hated lying, but he told himself that in this case the end justified the means. "I wonder if I could talk to you for a minute."

"Of course." She indicated a chair by the bed.

"When did you last see Sweet Grass?"

"Saturday. She dropped by and brought me those." She pointed to a pretty basket of violets on the windowsill. "I haven't heard from her since."

"Does that strike you as odd?"

"Not really. She's awfully busy with the wedding and everything."

"When she was here, did she mention anything about going away, to think things over or . . . ?"

"No. Nothing like that. She talked a little about the Hardwicks' picnic. That's where she was before she came here. And she complained about how hectic things were getting ready for the wedding. She and Ted wanted a simple wedding, but his parents insisted on the works."

Fenimore nodded. "Parents tend to do that."

"Sweet Grass had just joined a Friends Meeting and wanted a Quaker wedding," Doris told him. "They marry themselves, you know. It's a very simple ceremony. No minister. They sit in silence until the spirit moves their friends or relatives to speak about them."

"Yes, I know."

Fenimore was a great authority on weddings, of course. A bachelor for forty years, he had never even been engaged. Although Jennifer Nicholson was his frequent companion, he hesitated to make a permanent commitment because of the difference in their ages (she was fifteen years his junior). He could envision Jennifer in her prime, while he was doddering around some nursing home. It wouldn't be fair to her, he thought. The fact that Jennifer might disagree didn't occur to him.

"I'm a Presbyterian, myself," Doris said, "but I went to a Quaker school . . . but I'm rambling. That's what happens when you're stuck in the hospital without anyone to talk to."

Fenimore laughed. "Yes, hospital staff would rather stick needles into you, or take pictures of you, or roll you around on trolleys, than converse."

She started to laugh but stopped abruptly, pressing her hand over her abdomen. "Not quite ready for that." She smiled wanly. "Would you like some candy?" She gestured to a box of chocolates on her bedside table.

Why did people insist on giving bonbons to people recovering from abdominal operations? "No, thanks."

"I don't like them either. Pickles and salami are more my line. When I'm well, that is," she hastened to add.

Fenimore went to the end of the bed and glanced at her chart. Expecting to find notes on an appendectomy, or at worst a gall-bladder operation, he was dismayed to read "hysterectomy." When he looked up, the young woman was watching him. He came back to his chair. "Did you know that your roommate's brother had refused to come to the wedding?"

She nodded, relieved that he was not going to discuss her personal health problem. "She was very upset about it."

"Did you know him?"

"I met him once. He's . . ."—she plucked at the blanket, searching for the right word—"intimidating."

"In what way?"

She frowned. "He's very quiet."

"Shy?"

"Oh, no. Still."

"Still?"

"Yes. You know how most of us fidget—rub our chin, play with our hair?" She began to fiddle with her own gold braid as if to illustrate. "Well, he doesn't do that. He just sits, hands in his lap, and stares. His eyes are full of intelligence, and he fixes you with this gaze." She shook her head. "It's very disconcerting."

"Thanks for the warning. I'm going to see him tomorrow."

"Oh? Do you think he has something to do with her disappearance?"

"Well, we have to explore every angle."

She looked at him hard. "Are you some kind of detective?"

"Uh, unofficially. I like to solve puzzles. It's not too different from diagnosing people's ailments. You take a history, do some tests, use some judgment based on experience, and make a diagnosis."

"And the cure?"

He shifted uncomfortably. "That's not so easy." He changed the subject. "Ted told me Sweet Grass wasn't feeling well when she came to see you."

"Yes. That's true. She complained of a headache, and she felt dizzy and a little nauseated. She thought it was a migraine coming on. She's subject to them. She blamed it on all the tension over the wedding. She left here early because of it."

"Did she say where she was going?"

"Straight home to bed."

"Were you aware that your roommate was on medication?"

"Oh, yes. She took a pill once a day."

"Do you happen to know the name of it?"

She thought a minute, then said tentatively, "I think it was digoxin."

Fenimore examined the young woman's face—as a doctor, not a detective. It was pale and drawn. It was time to bring the interview to a close. "You've been a tremendous help." He rose. "Now try to get some sleep before they wake you up to give you your sleeping pill."

She started to laugh but remembered in time and settled for a grin. "Let me know as soon as you find out anything."

"I will."

As he walked past the nurses' station, where the party was still in full swing, he considered the unfairness of things. Two young women; one denied the right to give life, the other denied the right to live.

"Doctor!" The cry came from room 208. It sounded like a bona fide cry of distress. He poked his head in the door.

"Doctor, I've been pressing my buzzer for over an hour, but no one comes. I had a hip replacement today and I need something for my pain." The speaker was a frail, elderly woman with a determined set to her jaw. Engulfed in pillows and sheets, she looked as if she were buried in a snowdrift.

"I'll see what I can do." On his way out, he turned. "How did you know I was a doctor?"

She seemed astonished. "You look like one."

"But I'm not on this staff."

60

She sniffed. "You'll do."

Fenimore retraced his steps to the nurses' station. No one noticed him. All eyes were trained on a young woman in a white uniform who was relating what seemed to be a particularly entertaining anecdote.

"Who's in charge here?" He forced his tone to be pleasant.

The woman stopped in midsentence and her audience looked annoyed.

"There's an elderly woman in room two-oh-eight requesting a sedative. She says she's been ringing for over an hour."

The young woman glanced at the board lined with lights. The one next to 208 was dark.

"It's not flashing now, because I said I'd take care of it."

"And who are you?" the woman demanded.

Reminded that he wasn't on the staff of this hospital, Fenimore smiled weakly and said, "A friend. Would you please take care of her."

To his surprise, the woman returned his smile and set off down the hall at a rapid clip.

As Fenimore headed for the elevator, he pondered the old adage, "Honey catches more flies than vinegar."

CHAPTER 13

TUESDAY, NOVEMBER 1, 6:00 A.M.

Fenimore slept fitfully for three hours, fell into a deep sleep for a fourth, from which he was jolted awake by the alarm clock at 6:00 A.M. Feeling anything but refreshed, he shoved Sal off the end of the bed with both feet (to which she responded with an outraged squawk) and padded into the bathroom. He made a point of never looking at his face above the chin while shaving. He couldn't count the number of times he'd wished for the physiognomy of Cary Grant. (Fenimore did have a small cleft in his chin, but that's where the resemblance ended.) Vanity about his physical attractions was not one of Fenimore's deadly sins. (As for his mental attributes, that was another matter.) He stole a quick glance at his face this morning. He was glad to see that the black and blue was fading to green and yellow. Soon he'd be back to normal.

It took him fifteen minutes to dress—five to shower, five to shave, three to tie his tie, and two for the rest. (Only five to dress for an emergency call in the middle of the night, minus the shower and shave.) Five minutes for breakfast—a doughnut and "swill"—powdered coffee dissolved in hot tap water, a recipe he had picked up as an intern—which he consumed standing at the kitchen counter while catching up on the morning news via a midget radio. Besides his own face, the only thing he couldn't stand the sight of early in the morning were TV anchorpeople, primped and polished, serving up the news between generous dollops of kittenish banter. He preferred his news served brisk and undiluted, like his shower: Cloudy skies. Temp. 58 degrees. Winds 20 mph. Tie-up on the expressway due to jackknifed tractor trailer. Dow Jones average down 15 points. Phillies took one from the Mets, 4 to 2. His only objection to the format was that it presented the most important fact last. He flicked the radio off before the listing of overnight fires, shoot-outs, and stabbings.

He threw together a tuna sandwich, which he shoved into a small cooler along with a can of Coke and some cookies. Last of all, he fed Sal and changed her litter box. Not sure when he would be back, he scrawled a quick note to Mrs. Doyle, in a hand only her practiced eye could decipher, asking her to reschedule his morning appointments (more colds and sore throats) and, in case of an emergency, to call Dr. Reilly.

When he let himself out the front door, it was only six-thirty. True to the weather report, the sky was the color of putty and the temperature mild enough to leave his coat unbuttoned. Instinctively, he looked left and right, checking for enterprising early-bird muggers. Darts of pain still pierced him when he moved his head too quickly, a reminder of his last mugging. He headed for his car parked only a block away—by city standards, very convenient. Pausing at the corner, he dropped some coins in the newspaper dispenser and took out a morning *Inquirer*. A glance at the Metro section revealed full coverage of discovery of the body but no mention of any identification. Fortunately, that had occurred too late to make the morning edition. Now he could only hope that Roaring Wings's disdain for telecommunication extended to radio and television. He tucked the paper under his arm to peruse at his leisure, which probably wouldn't be until late that night.

He had crossed the Ben Franklin Bridge and was well into New Jersey before he let his mind drift toward Roaring Wings. Superhighways stimulated his thought processes. Leaving the mechanics of driving to his motor reflexes, his mind could roam freely, unimpeded. But he had to be careful not to let it roam too freely. He had been known to miss his exit.

He began by reviewing his knowledge of the Lenni-Lenapes, which didn't take long. He knew that *Lenni* meant "original" and *Lenape* meant "men" or "people." They were also known locally as the Delawares, after the river on whose banks they'd settled. Their ancestors were supposed to have migrated to America from Asia across the Bering Strait Land Bridge some fifteen thousand years ago. But the Lenapes had only been recognized as a distinct people for about a thousand years, when they settled in what was now New Jersey. The history of the Lenapes was hard to come by because it was mostly oral history and many of the older people who were familiar with it had died. Very little had been written down. What was known had been learned primarily from artifacts and the diaries and letters of early settlers, the Swedes, the Dutch, and the English. One of the most reliable of these were the letters of William Penn. He was one of the few who took the trouble to learn Algonquian, the Lenape language. He was very impressed by it, Fenimore remembered. He described it as "lofty, but narrow . . . Like shorthand in writing, one word serveth in the place of three." Fenimore had thought how nice it would be if our own language was as economical and the professional babblers of this world— specifically on radio and television—had their words reduced by two thirds.

As for the Lenapes' recent history, he had read in a newspaper account not long ago that a local tribe with ancestors from the Turtle clan had acquired a tract of land near Riverton, New

Jersey. The land had once belonged to the Lenapes, before the white man came. They had hunted and fished and farmed there. The reporter had asked a member of the tribe about their future plans. The tribesman had first thanked the Great Spirit for the land and then said something like, "Without land, it is hard to be an Indian. With land, we can bring the circle back. We can bring the hoop together."

A red Jaguar cut in front of him and the driver gave him the finger. A glance at his speedometer revealed the reason. Immersed in thought, Fenimore had been cruising at 45 miles per hour. Bringing the needle up to 65, he also brought his thoughts up from prehistoric times to the present. What was he going to say to Roaring Wings?

If Sweet Grass had died of natural causes and Roaring Wings had found her and buried her, technically his only crime was neglecting to report a death to the authorities. Ethically, he should have informed her fiancé, but he wasn't required to by law. And the burial ground in which Sweet Grass had been found was still recognized as a legal place of interment for Native Americans. If this were the case, Roaring Wings had every right to be furious with Fenimore for tampering with his sister's grave.

However, if Sweet Grass had not died of natural causes and whoever murdered her had buried her in the traditional Lenape burial ground to throw suspicion on her brother, Roaring Wings had every right to be outraged.

On the other hand, if Roaring Wings had murdered Sweet Grass (preferring to see her dead than married to a white man), as Ted seemed to think, and had buried her himself in the sacred ground . . . A horn bleated behind him. Glancing in his rearview mirror, Fenimore saw a giant oil truck bearing down on him. He pressed the accelerator and sighed. No matter what, the prospective interview promised to be difficult.

As he turned onto the exit ramp, another vehicle followed him. A pickup truck. It had almost missed the exit and squealed like an injured animal when it made the turn. The driver was wearing dark glasses and had his windshield visor down even though it was overcast. The truck remained in his rearview mirror for at least two miles before it turned into a side road and disappeared. Relax, Fenimore. Nobody's after you. That mugging was sheer coincidence. From then on, he concentrated on the road and maintaining a good speed. The most important thing was to reach Roaring Wings before the police.

Riverton's most distinctive landmark was the dome of the courthouse. Painted gold, on a bright day it gleamed and sparkled in the sun. Nothing else gleamed and sparkled in the town. In days gone by, the main street had sparkled with freshly painted Victorian houses adorned with gleaming white gingerbread. The houses were still there, but now they were shabby and their gingerbread was badly in need of paint and repair. The courthouse clock read 7:30. A few people were on their way to work, either walking or congregating at bus stops. Fenimore pulled up to one of the stops and rolled down his window. "Can anyone direct me to Camp Lenape?"

His request was met with blank stares.

"Thanks anyway." He drove on, down the hill and over the small bridge that spanned the Ashley River (formerly known as the Wisamek, or Catfish River, before the British renamed it). On the other side, he pulled into an old-time gas station, boasting two pumps and one oil-stained attendant. A Phillies cap was pulled down over the man's greasy locks. (Since New Jersey had no baseball team of its own, Jerseyites often rooted for the Phillies.)

"Help ya?"

"I'm looking for Camp Lenape."

He paused to chew something. Gum or tobacco. "You mean the injun campsite?"

Clearly, political correctness had bypassed Riverton. "That's right."

Another pause, filled with more chewing, as he looked down the street. "Take this road outta town." He spat roundly. "About two miles outside, on the right, you'll see a sign. Says 'Camp Lenape.' Ya can't miss it. There's an iron gate they keep locked. Don't know why. They ain't got nothin' worth stealin'. Only the land. And you can't steal that."

How little he knew. "How do I get in?"

"Just blow your horn. They'll open up for ya."

Fenimore thanked him and took off.

The exit from Riverton was even more depressing than the entrance, dotted with abandoned trailer camps, gas stations, and railroad tracks. The tracks, laid in the 1890s when south Jersey was a booming industrial center, were rusty and choked with weeds from disuse. He was glad to get back on the open road lined with nothing but sandy banks and scrub pines. He had gone a little over two miles when he spotted the iron gate and the sign. The sign was a surprise. It was made of polished wood with the words CAMP LENAPE inscribed in gold paint by an obviously professional hand. The wrought-iron gate had probably once belonged to the estate of a glass baron. Glass manufacturing was a big industry in that area a hundred years ago, because of the abundance of sand. But that was before World War II, when plastic took over.

The gate was well maintained, painted a satin black with no rust visible. Fenimore hesitated to blow his horn. Rude at any time, it seemed especially so at such an early hour and in such peaceful surroundings. He scanned the gate for a buzzer or bell. Halfway up one side of the gate, he spotted a small box with a wire curling from it up the drive. He turned off his motor and got out to examine it. It resembled the voice boxes on the town houses in Philadelphia's yuppier neighborhoods. There was a button at the bottom. He glanced at his watch: 8:05. If he wanted to maintain his edge on the police, he'd better hustle. He pressed the button. It made no sound, but a second later a man's voice inquired, "Who is it?"

"Dr. Fenimore. I'd like to speak to Roaring Wings."

A barely perceptible pause. "Speaking. What is your business?"

Fenimore cleared his throat. "A private, family matter."

"You may enter." As these words were uttered, the gates began slowly to open.

Fenimore hopped back in his car and drove into Camp Lenape.

CHAPTER 14

The driveway was no more than a dirt road through a field, and the only building in sight was a large barn outlined against the sky.

The sky was the most distinctive thing about south Jersey. The land was flat, and the sky seemed to go on forever. It was as close to the landscape of the West as you could find in the East. Fenimore, although an inveterate city dweller, sometimes daydreamed about buying a few acres here, building a one-room shack with a wood stove, a pump, and a privy, where he could come to smoke his pipe and contemplate field and sky without interruption, and Sal could chase mice to her heart's content. (No muggers here.) It was a luxury not to be taken lightly. Future generations might not have the opportunity to survey such limitless space—except from a spaceship.

He followed the unpaved road, wincing at every rut and bump. The shocks in his old Chevy had given out long ago and he had never bothered to replace them. The government grant that had provided the Lenapes with the land, the new sign, the intercom, and the paint for the gates must have run out before the drive could be paved. As he drew near the barn, a man came around the corner and stood waiting for him. Of average height and build, he was dressed in jeans, a plaid shirt, and a fringed leather jacket laced partway up the front with leather thongs. His hair, parted in the middle, hung to his shoulders in two neat braids. His face was impassive. As Fenimore pulled up beside him, he gave no sign of welcome. Silently, the man watched him get out of the car. Fenimore glanced at the man's feet, expecting to find moccasins; instead he found an expensive brand of sneakers. "Roaring Wings?" He extended his hand.

The man shook hands briefly and nodded. If he noticed the odd color of Fenimore's face, he gave no sign.

Fenimore found himself suddenly, and uncharacteristically, tongue-tied. He had driven all the way down here thinking about Sweet Grass's death without giving a thought to how he was going to break the news to her brother. Subconsciously, he must have decided that Roaring Wings already knew. But suppose he pretended not to know? Fenimore must pretend too. But there was always the possibility that he really didn't know.

"I'm afraid I have bad news." From long experience as a doctor, Fenimore knew there was no way to sugar-coat death, "Your sister, Sweet Grass, is dead."

The man continued looking at Fenimore. He had heard the words, but there was a delay before their sense registered, like the pause after lightning, before the thunder.

"How?"

"Heart failure."

"Ah." He placed his hand over his breast. "Her old trouble."

"No." Fenimore bit his tongue. The medical knowledge had slipped out automatically. From a detective's point of view, it would have been better for Roaring Wings to believe that his sister had died from a complication from her "old trouble," tetralogy of Fallot.

He felt the full force of the man's gaze. Doris Bentley had not exaggerated its potency. "Is there some place we could talk?"

For the answer, Roaring Wings turned and walked around the barn.

As Fenimore followed he couldn't help noticing the graceful way the man moved. He flowed across the rough ground, making Fenimore feel, with his normal gait, like a clumsy oaf. Somewhere he had read about the Indians' gait. They placed one foot directly in front of the other, toe to heel, instead of side by side with a gap between, as most people did. Long ago this enabled them to walk the narrow paths of the forest and stalk animals— or enemies—swiftly and noiselessly. A side effect of this gait, after the original purpose had become obsolete, was a dignified posture that automatically commanded respect. If this gait were taught to children in kindergarten, Fenimore thought, it would eliminate a lot of middle-age back problems.

Roaring Wings led him to a small cinder-block building that had been concealed by the barn. A ribbon of smoke rose from a metal chimney that protruded from the corrugated roof. There was no sign of the mansion to which the elegant iron entrance gates had once belonged. It must have been razed, or destroyed by fire, and the barn was all that was left of the estate. Stepping aside, Roaring Wings held open the makeshift plywood door.

The prefab exterior gave no hint of the warmth and beauty inside. Textured white walls were hung with blankets woven in warm earth tones of brown, red, and sand. Terra-cotta pots of various sizes and shapes exploded with flowers and fern. Dominating the center of the room was a cone-shaped fireplace with a long pipe soaring to the ceiling. Bright pillows were scattered before the flagstone hearth, inviting you to relax and sprawl. Roaring Wings gestured to one of them and disappeared behind a screen on the other side of the room.

Fenimore lowered himself onto an orange cushion and was glad the young man could not see his awkward descent. His stiffness was not due to age, of course, but to lack of exercise. Once settled more or less comfortably, he surveyed the room in detail. In one corner was a mattress on a raised wooden platform, its cover echoing the warm hues of the wall hangings. Another corner was occupied by a large desk smothered in papers. A word processor rested on it. A filing cabinet completed his office-in-the-home. Applying for government grants required almost as much paperwork as applying for Medicare reimbursements. Gradually Fenimore became aware of a pleasing scent emanating from behind the screen. There must be a stove back there, maybe even a refrigerator.

"I'm making tea," the man called out.

"That's not necessary."

"You prefer coffee?"

"No, no. Tea is fine." He'd prefer nothing, so he could get on with the business at hand. He glanced at his watch: 8:25. Apparently there was more to making tea than just dunking a tea bag in hot water. Finally Roaring Wings emerged from behind the screen bearing two earthenware mugs steaming with that special fragrance. Fenimore envied the ease with which the Lenape lowered himself onto a turquoise cushion while balancing the two mugs full of hot liquid. He handed one to him. Fenimore had a strong desire to take out his pipe. But somehow, seated cross-legged opposite a Native American, he felt awkward about it. He took a sip of tea. "Hmm. What is this?"

"A blend of herbs."

They drank in silence, Fenimore growing more and more ill at ease, edgy. He was not used to silence. If he hadn't been sitting on the floor and afraid of making a fool of himself as he struggled to his feet, he would have risen and paced the room, looking at things and inquiring about them to relieve the tension. But he remained where he was, waiting for his host to speak. He was surprised that Roaring Wings didn't ask more about his sister's death. Or was there some taboo in his culture about discussing the dead? He seemed to remember that it was forbidden for the Lenapes to speak the name of their dead. The residue of crushed herbs was visible in the bottom of Fenimore's cup, before Roaring Wings finally spoke.

"Tell me what happened."

Reacting like a child who has been told to be quiet and is finally allowed to speak, Fenimore poured out the whole tale of burying Horatio's cat and the discovery of Sweet Grass and the eventual identification of her body by Ted. When he had finished, Roaring Wings rose easily and, turning his back, busied himself with the fire. To hide his grieving? His face had remained impassive during the telling of the story, and Fenimore had begun to wonder if he had any emotions. He checked the time. A half hour had passed. Soon the creaky wheels of organized crime detection would begin to turn. Rafferty or one of his assistants would show up on the doorstep. Fenimore must be gone before then. Rafferty would not be amused by his meddling. The only time Rafferty condoned Fenimore's meddling was when it was instigated by him. If there was anything more to be learned from Roaring Wings, he must learn it now. "Did you know of this burial ground?"

He turned from the fire. "My uncle took me there once, when I was a child."

"Does it surprise you? That she was buried there?"

He sat down again and took a sip of tea. The deliberateness of his movements was maddening. "Nothing about my sister surprised me."

Fenimore kept silent, noting that Roaring Wings neglected to mention her name.

"You see, we chose separate ways long ago. She chose to mix with the *wasechus*. I did not."

Fenimore recognized the word *wasechus*. He had come across

73

it in his studies of the Lenape. It was a derogatory term for "white man." But he was learning the rewards of silence. He held his tongue.

"Don't misunderstand me. I don't blame her. When she was small, she had this sickness. She had trouble breathing. When we played tag and other running games, she had to squat down to catch her breath. The other children made fun of her. They called her Sitting Frog. And she was a funny color. Her skin was sometimes blue. The children made fun of that too." He looked at Fenimore. "Children are cruel."

Fenimore allowed himself a nod, without disturbing the flow.

"When she went to school, on the first day the nurse diagnosed the blue tinge of her skin as cyanosis. She insisted that my mother take Sweet Grass to a specialist. After that, everything changed. My sister went to a big hospital in the city. She had an operation. She was gone for several weeks. And when she came back, she was completely cured. She was no longer blue, and soon she was running like the rest of us. No one called her Sitting Frog anymore." He paused.

"Naturally, she was very grateful to the *wasechus*," he went on, "and afterward, she seemed to feel at home with them. She got along very well at school. The teachers loved her. And she made good grades. I also made good grades. But they did not like me as much, and I never felt at home with them." Again he paused, obviously thinking back.

"As the years went by, she grew closer to the white people, and I did not. She went away to school and became a teacher. As a result, we grew farther apart. In recent years we saw each other only now and then. And when she told me she was going to marry a . . ." For the first time, he seemed to realize that Fenimore was one of them.

Fenimore said quickly, "And what were you doing all those years, while your sister was becoming a teacher?"

74

"I am an engineer, a builder." His eyes swept the room. "I built this house." His voice held a note of pride.

"Quite an accomplishment. It's charming and very comfortable." (Albeit chairless, Fenimore thought.) "But during all those years when you were getting an education, surely you mixed with the *wasechus*?"

"Mixed, yes," he nodded, "but never blended." He glanced at the herbs in the bottom of his mug. "That I do only with my own people."

"Would you have considered burying someone in that burial ground?"

He shook his head vigorously. "Never. Very foolish. Too public. Things happen. Disturbances. Look what did happen. You and that boy. The dead do not like to be disturbed. My sister should not have been disturbed."

Fenimore felt like a child who has been justly reprimanded.

"However, I can remedy that." Roaring Wings rose and turned back to the fire. "Now we have this land."

"We?"

"The Lenapes. The Turtle band. The Great Spirit has returned this land to us in the form of a grant from the government. I am the director, in charge of development. We will turn it into a historic park, a memorial to our ancestors." He outlined his plan for the park in some detail for Fenimore. "I can bring my sister here and bury her," he concluded. "And I guarantee she will not be disturbed." He looked at him. "Where is she now?"

To Fenimore's consternation, Roaring Wings seemed ready to come back with him to Philadelphia then and there, to collect his sister's body. "Her body has not been released." The Lenape's gaze was intimidating. "Uh, the police are uncomfortable with the circumstances of your sister's death."

"The police?" He frowned. "What have they to do with this? This is a blood feud, between the *wasechus* and the Lenape. Obviously a *wasechu* buried my sister—and botched it." The word leaped out at Fenimore, from the Lenape's carefully formal sentences. "Probably that fiancé of hers . . ." His lip curled. No lack of emotion now.

"Wait a minute. You have no proof of that. Her fiancé was the one who reported her missing."

The Indian's eyes burned with years of controlled resentment, and Fenimore recalled a Lenape legend he had once read: When the Lenape met his first white man, the Lenape had a deer hanging up. The white man took all the fat parts, leaving only the neck and the feet for the Lenape. The literal translation of *wasechu,* he remembered now, was "fat taker."

"We'll see." Roaring Wings looked down, as if to hide the depth of his feelings from Fenimore. "Meanwhile," he continued, "I want my sister. I am her next of kin. It is my right to bury her."

"I'll see what I can do." Fenimore got clumsily to his feet, but Roaring Wings took no notice. His mind was filled with funeral plans—and vengeance.

On the way home, Fenimore was so absorbed in his thoughts of Roaring Wings that he took no notice of the pickup truck maintaining a discreet distance of three car lengths behind him.

CHAPTER 15

TUESDAY, AROUND NOON

The minute Fenimore stepped into his office, he sensed that something was amiss. The atmosphere was charged. Mrs. Doyle sat stiffly at her typewriter. Horatio was hunched over a file drawer, filing for all he was worth. Sal was cowering under the radiator, only an inch of tail visible.

"Good morning," Fenimore chirruped, although it was after noon. The return trip from Camp Lenape had taken longer than he had expected.

They each bestowed on him a glacial stare, Sal's the most frigid. She had emerged from under the radiator and was arranging herself artistically on top of it.

"You're early, aren't you?" he remarked to Horatio.

"Teachers' meeting. Got a half day off," he muttered.

"And you came right here?"

He nodded.

For some reason, this pleased Fenimore inordinately.

Apparently, his feelings were not shared by Mrs. Doyle.

"Any messages?" he asked his nurse.

Wordlessly, she handed him a pile of slips. Usually she commented on the more urgent ones. Not today. The first one read: "Jennifer. 10:15." No hint of trouble there. The rest were routine calls for office appointments or prescription refills.

"Any drop-ins?"

Mrs. Doyle shook her head. Horatio banged shut his file drawer.

"What *is* the matter?" asked Fenimore.

"One of your slippers is missing." "She thinks I stole it!" His employees spoke simultaneously.

Fenimore glanced at the floor by his chair that was usually occupied by a pair of disreputable slippers. Today there was only one.

Only a stranger to Fenimore's establishment would wonder at the stress Mrs. Doyle laid on this seemingly minor incident. The doctor valued his slippers more than all the gold in Fort Knox.

"What would I want with a fucking old slipper?" Horatio spat out the words.

"I didn't mean to imply that he took it," Mrs. Doyle justified herself. "I only thought he might have misplaced it." She continued pounding the life out of the typewriter.

Sal, disgusted with the low tone things had taken, landed with a graceful leap and took off for parts unknown.

"Now see here, you two." Fenimore adopted his most soothing manner. "I'm sure there's some reasonable explanation."

They ignored him, pretending to be absorbed in their work.

"A man comes home after a hard morning's work and what does he find? Dissension, dissolution, and discord."

"Piffle," said his nurse.

"Bullshit," said the boy.

"Let's begin at the beginning." Fenimore used his most conciliatory tone, the one he reserved for the interrogation of suspects in his most difficult cases. "When did you first notice the slipper was missing, Mrs. Doyle?"

"About half an hour ago."

He turned to Horatio. "Did you leave the office at any time after you arrived?"

He shook his head.

Back to Mrs. Doyle. "What was the first chore you gave him to do?"

"Clean up the waiting room."

Fenimore glanced in the waiting room. It was cleaner than he'd ever seen it. The rug had been vacuumed, the sofa pillows plumped, the magazines stacked into neat piles.

"I went into the kitchen for a few minutes to make a cup of tea," Doyle murmured defensively.

"That's when I stole it!" Horatio's eyebrows shot to the ceiling.

"Where would he have put it?" Fenimore exclaimed. "He would have had to be Houdini."

Horatio sent Fenimore a look, transmitting the complex message that if he had wanted to steal the slipper and conceal it in that brief time, he could have managed it, but what would he want with a fucking old slipper?

"I'm sure it will turn up," Fenimore said hastily. "Now let's forget all about it." He struggled into his white lab coat and went to the sink to wash his hands, symbolically washing them of the whole unsavory episode. "Who's my first patient?"

Mrs. Doyle consulted his appointment book. "Mrs. Johnson at one o'clock. You said to reschedule all the morning patients." Her voice was peevish with disapproval. Not of his rescheduling, but of his taking off for New Jersey without telling her why.

"Great, then I have time for a sandwich." He took the well-traveled tuna sandwich from the cooler and, ignoring its soggy condition, settled into his old armchair to eat it. From habit, he was about to shed his shoes and replace them with his comfortable old slippers, but he caught himself in time. He had no desire to reopen wounds. He wriggled his toes painfully in their

79

confined space (he sorely missed those slippers) and flipped open the can of Coke that had been his companion since early morning. A deep swallow of the tepid liquid caused him to grimace. But the thought of traipsing to the kitchen for a glass and tussling with an ice tray for a single cube was even less appealing. He drained the can.

The other occupants of the room followed suit. Mrs. Doyle removed her hermetically sealed lunch box from her desk drawer and methodically laid its contents on a paper napkin that she had previously spread on her desk. Salad in a plastic container, a thermos of soup, three crackers, and an apple. She believed in a well-balanced diet.

"Think I'll grab a frank." Horatio slammed shut the file drawer he had been working on and glided down the hall. His destination, the corner vendor, Fenimore surmised.

Sal made a dignified entrance, head and tail held high, padded over to her dish in the corner, and filled the uneasy silence with noisy munchings on something revolting called Kitty Chow.

It was a relief when the telephone rang.

"Fenimore?" Rafferty.

"Speaking," Fenimore responded nervously.

"I just received a call from a detective employed at the Riverton Police Department. I'd asked him to make a routine visit for me to Camp Lenape."

"To what purpose?" When nervous, Fenimore's speech became more formal.

"TO COMPLETE A WILD-GOOSE CHASE I'D SENT HIM ON!" he shouted.

"Oh?"

"It seems that a certain Lenni-Lenape, by the name of John Field, also known as Roaring Wings, had already been informed of his sister's, Joanne Field, aka Sweet Grass, death when my man arrived."

"Uh, well, I thought he should be notified as soon as possible, and since he didn't have a phone . . ."

"You took it on yourself to hightail it down there at the crack of dawn and blab the whole thing. Right?"

"Put coarsely."

"We policemen are known for our coarseness." He took a deep breath. "Now, if it wouldn't inconvenience you too much, perhaps you would be kind enough to honor me with your presence and share the essence of your little tête-à-tête?" When really angry, Rafferty could outdo Fenimore in formality.

"Er, I'm expecting a patient."

Fenimore's ear reverberated with the sound of the receiver being replaced.

Hastily exchanging his lab coat for his suit coat, Fenimore was halfway down the hall when he paused to call over his shoulder, "I won't be long, Doyle. Ask Mrs. Johnson to wait."

"Yes, Doctor." She looked after him curiously.

After Rafferty had finished raking Fenimore over the coals for being an "insufferable, interfering, amateur meddler" and had gleaned every bit of information that the doctor had acquired during his interview with Roaring Wings, he settled down to a rational, nearly-but-not quite-friendly discussion of the case.

"What was your overall impression of Roaring Wings?" The policeman's gaze was no less forceful than the Native American's.

Fenimore thought a moment. "Proud, introverted, bordering on the fanatical where his tribal origins were concerned."

"Umm." Rafferty ran his hand through his thick black hair. "I had a visitor this morning. A representative from Higgins, Marple, and Woski. It seems that Sweet Grass had taken out a life insurance policy worth a hundred thousand."

"Beneficiary?"

Rafferty drummed his fingers on the desk. "Her brother."

Fenimore considered. "That makes sense. There was no point leaving it to her fiancé. His coffers were already overflowing."

"Did Roaring Wings impress you as the greedy type?"

"Not in the usual sense of acquiring material things for himself. But he is a crusader. He has a cause. He told me about his plan to re-create a Lenape village in south Jersey. The project calls for the construction of authentic dwellings, a 'big house' or large barn for traditional ceremonies and a museum to house artifacts—weapons, pottery, ornaments—that have been found in the area. The land has already been acquired from the government. But this legacy would certainly help him with this project and to realize his dream."

"Interesting."

Fenimore, suffering from guilt pangs over Mrs. Johnson, said, "I'd better be getting back."

Rafferty made no objection, but as Fenimore rose to go he remarked, "Next time you get any bright ideas about the early bird catching the worm, forget it."

Fenimore made a speedy departure.

Once outside, he remembered that he hadn't returned Jennifer's call. He hastened to the nearest phone booth. He didn't like to make personal calls from the office with two pairs of ears flapping. Three, if you counted Sal, who understood every word he said.

"So you aren't dead." Jennifer made no attempt to disguise her relief.

"Nope."

"You're on a new case?"

"Yep."

"Can you talk about it?"

"Nope."

"How about dinner tonight, here. I have a mad desire to feed monosyllabic medical men. Besides, Dad has a new acquisition he's dying to show you."

"On the Lenapes?"

"I don't think so. But I'll show you our shelf on them. And for an aperitif you can take a look at the Chandlers."

Mr. Nicholson's *new* acquisitions were usually several hundred years old, and Jennifer's dinners were always a culinary treat. Plus the shelf on the Lenni-Lenapes and some early Chandlers added up to just what the doctor ordered, especially after a day spent with ill-tempered employees and an irate law enforcement officer. "I'll be there," Fenimore said.

Unfortunately, such a prescription was not in store for him.

CHAPTER 16

TUESDAY EVENING

Back at the office, Fenimore found not only an impatient Mrs. Johnson but also a message from Polly Hardwick marked "Urgent."

She answered on the first ring. "Andrew? Thank heavens. Could you come for dinner tonight? Something awkward's come up and we're feeling rather low." The request itself hardly qualified as urgent, but her voice held a desperate note that he could not ignore.

"Of course. What time?"

"Sevenish."

For the second time in ten minutes, he uttered the words, "I'll be there." Being in two places at once defied even Fenimore's extraordinary abilities. Reluctantly he dialed Jennifer's number. She was disappointed, but somewhat mollified when he promised to come the following evening.

In contrast to his former visit, tonight the Hardwick mansion was brightly illuminated and the semicircular drive was filled with three cars—a red Jaguar, a white Audi, and a blue Mercedes. How patriotic, Fenimore thought, as he pulled up behind them in his battered, mud-brown Chevy, destroying the whole effect. (Mud-brown wasn't his favorite color, but it had been in stock and cheaper than the azure blue.)

Polly must have been watching for him, because she opened the door before he touched the bell.

"Come in." She grabbed his arm and drew him into a small room off the center hall. Cluttered with books and papers, it appeared to serve as an office or study. "I wanted to talk to you before we joined the others." Her face was drawn and her voice held an unusual quaver.

He waited for her to regain control.

"Ted thinks Sweet Grass committed suicide. And," she paused, "he thinks we're all to blame."

"Nonsense."

"He's convinced of it, and he's making us all miserable."

"I'll talk to him."

"Would you, Andrew? I don't think I can go through another day like this."

"What happened?"

"He accused each of us, individually, of insulting Sweet Grass. And he blamed me for"—her voice trembled and her eyes were too bright—"for pushing her over the edge."

"Where did he get this idea? There's no evidence of suicide. The cause of death hasn't even been established." He failed to mention that the last time he had talked to Ted, the young man had accused Roaring Wings of killing Sweet Grass. "He's just upset."

"He found her diary."

"Oh?"

"He refuses to read it to us, but he says she recorded things we said and did that hurt her deeply."

"I see."

"Andrew, don't look at me like that. I feel so dreadful. I'll admit I didn't think she was right for Ted in the beginning. You know how mothers are about their sons. No one's good enough for them." (Actually, he didn't know. His own mother had had no delusions about her sons and would have been pleasantly surprised if anyone had wanted to marry them.) "But I didn't mean any harm," she finished.

"Social slights are not a common cause for suicide," Fenimore said. "It may have relieved Sweet Grass to write about them in her diary. Many diarists do that. Even the famous Pepys. But to kill herself over them?" He shook his head. "I seriously doubt it."

"Could you convince Ted of that?"

"I can try."

"I knew I could count on you." She squeezed his arm. Her normal color had returned, and her voice had regained some of its old assurance. "We better join the others. They'll be wondering what happened to us."

Polly ushered Fenimore into a pale green and ivory living room, highlighted here and there by small objects of silver and brass. Although the entire family was assembled, Fenimore did not feel he was interrupting anything. No conversation or interaction of any kind seemed to be taking place. Ned Hardwick was fixing himself a drink in the bay window where the bar supplies were arranged. Ted, holding an untouched drink, was staring moodily into the cold fireplace. A sturdy, compact woman sat on the sofa, ostentatiously reading a book. A younger, frailer woman with a cloud of white-blond hair was hovering over the fish tank, making "kiss-kiss" noises to some tropical fish. A third woman, in a long lavender print dress, her dark hair pulled back in a bun, reclined in a Victorian chair. Her bemused expression remained unchanged while Fenimore was being introduced.

"You all remember Dr. Fenimore. Bernice?" Polly spoke sharply, and the compact woman on the sofa closed her book. *Flora of Japan* was the title.

"Good to see an unfamiliar face," she said and energetically shook his hand.

"And Lydia?"

The woman with the bemused expression lifted her right arm at the elbow and languidly wiggled her fingers at him.

"Kitty! I wish you'd leave those fish alone."

Kitty turned, startled by her mother's waspish tone.

"Sorry, dear, but I wanted you to greet Dr. Fenimore."

She made a little dip, a remnant of the curtsy she had been taught at dancing school, and turned back to the fish.

A look of pain crossed her mother's face. "That's the lot. Except for Ted, of course." She smiled tentatively at her son. He gave Fenimore a quick nod. Polly went over to the coffee table and plucked a cigarette from an exquisite porcelain box.

"Mother!" came from two directions at once. Ted was absorbed in his thoughts and Kitty in her fish, but Bernice and Lydia both cast their mother stern looks.

She stopped, the cigarette halfway to her mouth. "Oh, very well," she said and dropped it back in the box, flipping the lid shut.

I don't know why you keep the filthy things around," said Bernice.

"They must be horribly stale." Lydia made a face.

"I keep them for my guests. Andrew, will you have one?" she offered in a mocking tone.

"No, thanks. I prefer this." He took his pipe from his jacket pocket.

"How naughty," Lydia said.

"And a doctor, too," Bernice added.

"I also drink," he said placidly.

"What'll you have?" Ned, taking the hint, spoke from the bay window.

"Scotch, please, with a little water." He took a seat on the sofa next to Bernice.

87

Polly wandered restlessly around the room. Ned left the bay window to play host. "Well, Fenimore, what d'ya think of my little harem?" He handed him his drink.

"I'm overwhelmed." He took a deep swallow, insulation against the difficult evening ahead.

"My 'Mayflowers' I call them." He bestowed a doting glance on each of his daughters in turn.

"And what do you call Ted, Father?" Lydia inquired with a mischievous glint.

"My only son and heir," he said quickly.

Ted remained entranced by the empty fireplace.

"Mother's money goes to us girls," Lydia informed Fenimore, "to make up for Daddy's medieval ideas."

"Really, Lydia, must we divulge all our family secrets?"

"Oh, I'm sure they're safe with Dr. Fenimore, Mother. He's taken the Hippocratic oath."

"I don't know if that applies to money matters," her mother said.

"Put your fears to rest, Polly," Fenimore hastened to reassure her. "I rarely discuss money matters. They bore me."

"How quaint," said Lydia. "That isn't true of most of your colleagues, I understand."

"True," her father broke in, "some doctors have more interest in the financial rewards of medicine than others. But I assure you, Fenimore is the exception. Didn't I see you drive up in that same old Chevy you had as a resident, Fenimore?"

Fenimore laughed. "That would be a miracle, Ned. I shelved that car fifteen years ago." Fenimore was known for driving ancient cars and hanging onto them until they fell apart. "But this one's the same color and a similar model." Before the Hardwicks could delve any deeper into *his* finances, Fenimore directed their attention to the musket hanging over the mantel. "Is that a family heirloom?" he asked.

He couldn't have chosen a better topic. His host beamed and

immediately launched into the story of the weapon's origins. It seems it belonged to an ancestor who had fought at Fort William Henry in the French and Indian War. Ned gently removed the musket from its place of honor and handed it to Fenimore to examine. It was a handsome specimen, immaculate and well oiled, ready for instant use. He trusted it wasn't loaded. Carefully, Fenimore returned it to its owner.

"My ancestor fought with honor against the French," Ned said, replacing the gun on its rack.

"Did your ancestor die in that battle?" Fenimore asked politely.

Ned nodded. "First Lieutenant Willard S. Hardwick, of the King's Regiment. He was one of fifty soldiers massacred by the Indians who were fighting with Montcalm. You may remember the incident?"

Fenimore nodded. The British had already surrendered when some Mohawks on the French side had set on the unarmed soldiers and killed them.

"A dreadful thing, actually. Some of the Indians who had joined the French cause got out of hand and tomahawked . . ."

Ted looked away from the fireplace for the first time and stared at his father. "I didn't know you were such an expert on Indian folklore, Dad."

"Not folklore, Son. History."

A deep flush spread from Ted's neck to his face.

Polly, stepping into the breach, turned the conversation swiftly. "I'm planning an unusual exhibit for the Flower Show this year, Andrew."

Everyone who's anyone in Philadelphia gardens. Polly was exceptionally talented in this field. She was president of a prominent garden club. Her own garden was a showplace. "It isn't until March," she said, "but the preparations began last summer." She took a seat near the fireplace and seemed more relaxed as she discussed her favorite subject. "The theme this year is 'Gardens:

Past and Future.' At first, we toyed with the idea of a Martian rock garden, but the possibilities seemed a trifle limited."

Fenimore silently agreed.

"So we decided to stick to the past and do a garden from ancient Rome."

"But, Mother, Rome has entirely different flora from North America," Bernice objected. "It's a drier, much warmer zone. How do you plan to protect the plants?"

"Now, darling, a Ph.D. in botany doesn't give you the right to dictate my choice of plants for the Flower Show. There are such things as greenhouses. Some of the specimens—the hibiscus, oleander, and olive trees—have already been shipped from California and are doing quite well."

"Yes, but once you get them into that great, drafty mausoleum downtown, I wouldn't give you two cents for them."

"The club is taking every precaution. We're creating a kind of atrium and installing electric heaters behind a network of mosaic walls."

"As you can see, Doctor, expense is no object," Ted spoke sharply. "And when the club has exhausted its funds, the members will be more than happy to dig into their own coffers to take up the slack, right, Mother? That's why, to become a member, you have to be pretty well-heeled."

"Darling, you know how I hate those vulgar expressions." Polly rose. "I'll be right back. I want to show Andrew our plans." She was back in a minute, bearing a large roll of paper under one arm. Unfolded, it was the size of a world map, and when she spread it out on the coffee table, two thirds of it drifted to the floor.

The next half hour was spent admiring the blueprint for a Roman garden, circa 100 B.C.

Bernice leaned over to take a look. "Good heavens, Mother, olive and orange trees? And who's going to construct all this?"

She indicated the maze of walls and pathways with a sweep of her hand.

"Some of the husbands have volunteered, and . . . a few of the sons." She looked at Ted, who ignored her.

"Oh, Mother, you must have a pool!" Kitty joined them. "There's room for one right there." She pointed a small finger with a much chewed fingernail. "And I could pick out the fish. Oh, please let me, Mother."

"We'll see." Her mother cast her a puzzled glance, as if unsure who she was or where she came from.

Lydia was the only one who declined to offer an opinion on the plan. She remained draped in the Victorian chair, observing. Fenimore was unsure whether she felt above it all, or was simply bored by a scene she had witnessed many times: her mother showing off her expertise before another audience.

A uniformed woman appeared in the doorway. "Dinner is served."

One by one they filed into the dining room. Fenimore found himself seated on Polly's left, Lydia's right, and directly across from Bernice. As he shook out his linen napkin, he wondered who would be the first to mention Sweet Grass, the only reason he had come. Would it be up to him? He hoped not. The grapefruit course passed in silence. But when the soup arrived, Lydia turned to him and asked, "Are you related to the author?"

It had been a long time since anyone had connected him with James Fenimore Cooper, the prolific author of books about a more youthful America. Had the nation's recent interest in preserving the wilderness and helping Native Americans sparked a renewed interest in his works? "Yes and no," he said.

"How yes?" She arched a perfect jet brow.

"I'd rather begin with the no. My father claimed absolutely

no connection with the great author. He said all his ancestors were rascals and rogues."

She smiled. "And the yes?"

"One day my mother became annoyed with this routine and decided to look into the matter. She was from Prague and could trace her origins back over five hundred years, and she always wanted to do the same for my father."

"Prague?" His dinner partner's eyes shone. "Kafka country!"

"Er . . ." Fenimore cleared his throat. "I don't think Mother was a big Kafka fan."

Lydia looked crushed.

"Anyway," Fenimore went on, "Mother hightailed it to the Historical Society and did a little research. And a few weeks later, at breakfast, she presented my father with a neatly typed genealogy that proved, beyond a shadow of a doubt, that he was a distant cousin of James Fenimore Cooper."

"How fascinating. What did he say?"

"Nothing. He wouldn't speak to her for a week."

When Lydia laughed, she showed two rows of perfect pearly teeth.

"Why such an interest in Cooper? I didn't think anyone read him anymore. Don't the schools these days feel that literature begins and ends with Hemingway?"

"Not my school."

"Which was?"

"Briggs."

Fenimore sighed. Of course. The exclusive day school for young ladies, founded before the Civil War, that had not revised its curriculum since. "So you've actually read Cooper?"

"All of him."

It was Fenimore's turn to raise an eyebrow. Even *he* hadn't read all of him. "Are you a teacher?"

She shook her head.

"What do you do? Besides read Cooper, I mean?"

She smiled mischievously. "Shop, garden, sleep, eat." She helped herself to a perfectly browned veal cutlet from a serving dish the maid offered her.

Fenimore felt as if he were in *Alice in Wonderland*. In her own way, this woman was as daring as the kids in the sixties who had refused to go to Vietnam. He would have been less shocked to find himself seated next to a dinosaur. "Forgive me, but how do you justify your existence?"

"You mean, why didn't I become a doctor, lawyer, merchant, chief?"

He nodded.

"Life is theater, doctor. There are the leads, the supporting roles, the minor parts, and the walk-ons. All are necessary to carry off the play." This rebuttal sounded stale and rehearsed. She must have used it many times in self-defense.

"You forgot the director."

She wrinkled her nose. "Not for me."

"Or stage manager?"

She brightened. "Now there's a thought. I might fit in backstage."

"And of course there's the audience." He remembered the detached way she had observed her mother's performance during the cocktail hour.

Before she could answer, Ned Hardwick interrupted, addressing the party. "You all know why Dr. Fenimore is here tonight. We were just beginning to recover from the shock of a death in the family, when another unpleasant discovery was made." He paused and looked at his son. "Ted has found Sweet Grass's diary and discovered that she recorded certain feelings she had about all of us. As a result, Ted has jumped to the conclusion that his fiancée committed suicide—and somehow we are to blame. I think this is unlikely, but I've invited Dr. Fenimore here to serve as a neutral party, someone outside the family to give his opinion on this painful matter. If he's willing." He turned to Fenimore.

Throughout this announcement, Ted continued to eat, studiously avoiding his father's eye.

"I'd be glad to look at the diary," Fenimore said neutrally, "if Ted agrees, that is."

Ted started to rise.

"No," Polly said. "Let Andrew finish his dinner. After dinner will be time enough."

Ted sat down. Ned, obeying a signal from his wife, changed the subject to a less emotional topic, the stock market.

"Do you have a busy practice?" Bernice asked Fenimore from across the table.

"Oh, perking along."

"I wondered if the new interest in home remedies was having any effect."

"I haven't noticed it. Oh, occasionally someone will want to substitute herb tea for a sedative, but I don't find patients staying away in droves, treating themselves with roots and weeds."

"I'm attempting an herb garden of my own," Bernice said, and a discussion of the attributes of herbs carried them through dessert.

After dessert, Polly trundled them back to the living room for coffee. When Fenimore had finished his, he asked to see the diary.

CHAPTER 17

LATER TUESDAY EVENING

Ted brought Fenimore the diary, and Polly led him to the small study where they had talked when he had first arrived. "Take as long as you like," she said and closed the door. For a moment he had the sensation that he was a prisoner rather than a guest.

He examined the diary. It was small, about five by seven inches, with no lock or clasp. A simple bound notebook. He opened it. The paper was lined. The first entry was dated July 20. Her handwriting was small but clear. He began to read.

> 7/20 T. and I drove to Cape May today. Perfect beach weather. After a swim and picnic on the beach, we went to the Marine Museum. Saw horrible examples of what we do to our marine life. A flounder suffocated in a plastic bag, etc. Will we never learn?
>
> 7/22 Dull day. Routine chores. Did wash. Cleaned. Paid bills. Never got around to weaving. Should start with weaving and let the rest wait.

The following entries were more of the same routine. Fenimore flipped through them. The next entry of interest was not
until August 1.

> 8/1 T. drove me out to meet his parents for the first
> time. Was overwhelmed by the size of their home. T.
> always played down their wealth. I'm afraid I wasn't
> dressed for the occasion—jeans, a sleeveless blouse,
> and sandals. I'd taken my cue from Ted. He was
> wearing a T-shirt and cutoff jeans. But they were *his*
> parents. Not mine. I was embarrassed. I caught his
> mother looking at me, and her expression was not
> approving! Dinner was a disaster. They asked politely
> about my family and when I told them I had only a
> brother, and we were no longer close, I don't think it
> went over too well. Family is very important in cer-
> tain Philadelphia suburbs. Not just your living rela-
> tives, but all the ones that came before, and how they
> got here. It's better to have come over on the
> *Mayflower* than the *Welcome*, for example, because
> the *Mayflower* came first. Of course, I could have
> told them about my peoples' trek across the Bering
> Strait fifteen thousand years ago!

Fenimore laughed aloud. Sweet Grass was emerging from
these pages, unfolding like a flower. Not a shrinking violet, either. More tiger lily. The next entry of interest was in September.

> 9/10 Had episode of rapid heartbeat. Went to see
> Dr. Robinson. She took an electrocardiogram and
> assured me there was nothing to worry about. Told
> me to take Inderal along with my digoxin. Two a day.
> And told me to call her if I had any more episodes.

Fenimore laid the diary aside, made a note of the medicines, and decided to see Robinson as soon as possible. Flipping through more routine entries, he paused at September 15.

9/15 Chose my wedding dress today. Mrs. H. insisted on coming with me, and it was a battle royal trying to find something not too expensive. There was one I liked, but it was much too high and she offered to pay half. I declined, not too graciously, I'm afraid. But Ted and I can't start off under any obligation to his family. If we do, it will never work out!

"Cheers," murmured Fenimore.

9/25 Went to see RW. No good. He still refuses to come to the wedding. Depressed.

10/1 Held my first weaving class. Nice group of women. Hope I'm not biting off more than I can chew before the wedding. But I've wanted to do this for such a long time. And the women are so eager. I'm really excited.

10/12 T.'s mother steamed in here tonight and started laying down the law—about the wedding, the honeymoon, and how to furnish our new house. She took me completely by surprise. I wasn't expecting an ambush. Her parting shot was, "I only hope you two know what you're doing." Now what the hell is that supposed to mean? Doris was here, in the next room, and heard the whole thing. She was shocked. When I told T., he just shrugged and said, "Mother likes to run things. She'll cool off after the wedding." She'd better.

10/13 Another episode of rapid heartbeat. Robinson took an electrocardiogram and upped the Inderal to three tablets a day. I asked if she thought it could have been caused by the excitement of getting married. She smiled and said, "Could be."

Fenimore harrumphed and turned the page.

10/14 Tragic news. Doris had a routine physical today and was told she needed surgery. A hysterectomy! I can't believe it. So young and no children? God, it's unfair. God damn. She's my maid of honor. I think we should postpone the wedding.

10/15 T. won't hear of a postponement. Neither will Doris. Her doctor assures her she will be well enough by November 15 to take part in the ceremony. The operation is 10/25.

As Fenimore read deeper into October, he began to grow apprehensive.

10/16 T.'s mother again. She called to check on the wording of the service. I told her we want to drop the "obey" and conclude the ceremony by reading an ancient Lenape prayer. She asked again if my brother was going to "give me away." (I haven't told her yet that he may not even come.) I explained that I didn't want to be "given away," like a package, from one man to another. Even if Roaring Wings comes, I don't want him to take part in the ceremony. I told her, "I want to walk down the aisle to Ted as free as a bird in the sky, a deer in the wood, a fish in the sea." She hung up on me.

Fenimore smiled. Maybe, at last, Polly had met her match. He frowned, remembering that the diarist had met hers.

> 10/17 T.'s sister called. The dark one. Lydia. She hinted that she would like to be part of the ceremony. Damn. I only want one attendant. Doris. I hardly know this woman. She seems nice enough, but if I have *her*, then I may have to have the other two!

Sensing hysteria building, Fenimore quickly turned the page.

> 10/18 Had blood tests today, for sexually transmitted diseases. What a joke. The only one they don't test for is AIDS.

> 10/19 A disturbing call from Kitty, the youngest sister. She said she was upset about being left out of the wedding. (What did I tell you?) I explained as reasonably as possible that Ted and I wanted a small wedding and we really couldn't add any more people at this late date. There was a long pause, and I thought I heard sniffling. Then she said, "You'll regret this," and hung up. I'm afraid to tell Ted. He'll be so upset. Maybe I better let her be in it. What's the difference? I just want it to be over.

> 10/20 Ted and I went to City Hall for the license. Shabby little office, full of lots of happy couples. One couple was making out on the bench in front of us. We thought they were going to have sex then and there. When you're getting married, you tend to think you're special. You're the only ones having this experience. This visit helped to put things in perspective. Still upset about Kitty. I think she may be a little unbalanced.

10/21 A call from Bernice, the eldest. She wanted us to come for dinner at her apartment. We went, even though there's so much to do! She's my favorite of the lot. Her apartment has a terrific view of the river and Boathouse Row. The boathouses, outlined in white lights, are cartoonlike. You almost expect Bugs Bunny or Donald Duck to pop out and go rowing up the Schuylkill, or over the waterfall. Inside, the apartment was a cross between a herbarium and a jungle. Plants everywhere—dried and living. Not common houseplants, either. Strange, exotic ones that require an expert's care and knowledge. Pots on the windowsills, baskets swinging from the ceilings and doorways, tucked into every nook and cranny. When Bernice disappeared into the kitchen, T. whispered, "Whenever I come here, I expect a headhunter to jump out at me." Dinner was delicious. She went to a lot of trouble. Indian curried chicken (Asian Indian, that is), rice, salad, and a fruit compote for dessert. A special wine too. She made only one reference to my "background." Asked if I ever cooked any native dishes. I told her I made *sapan*.

Fenimore grimaced. A kind of mush made from cooked corn, as he recalled.

Bernice made a face. But when I mentioned huckleberry bread, she asked me for the recipe. I promised to make her some. We talked about the diet of the Lenapes, when they lived off the land long ago in south Jersey. She was entranced by our word for strawberry—*w'tihim*, meaning "heart berry." She said, "How lovely. Of course it is shaped like a heart. But we cold-blooded Anglo-Saxons overlooked that entirely." I don't mind when people show a genuine interest in our people and their ways.

10/22 Another call from Kitty. This time she tried to disguise her voice. "Stay away from Ted, or else," she whispered. I really should tell T. She may need psychiatric help.

"Definitely." Fenimore read on.

10/23 T.'s father was here.

God, can't they leave her alone? Fenimore groaned.

His excuse for dropping by was the wedding present. He and Mrs. H. are giving us an oriental rug, and he wanted the dimensions of our living room in the new house. T. and I would rather have throw rugs and leave the floor exposed. We sanded and stained and polished it and it's very beautiful. But I gave him the dimensions to keep the peace. I was hoping he would leave, but instead he began to inquire, not too subtly, about my health. I told him about the tetralogy of Fallot and that I'm on digoxin. But I didn't bother to tell him about the episodes of rapid heartbeat. It's none of his business. He nodded, taking it all in. I hope I convinced him that his son isn't marrying an invalid. He also asked the name of my doctor.

What next? Are they going to ask to look at her teeth? Fenimore ground his own, as he turned the page.

10/24 Polly called. She asked me to call her that. It will be hard, but I'll try, for T.'s sake. She's planning a party for us, to introduce me to the rest of the family and some old friends.

To look her over, Fenimore grunted.

She said, "Nothing formal. Just a little barbecue with family and dear friends." I guess she's afraid to have a dinner party. After the way I was attired last time, I might show up in a tank top and jeans. God, will this never end? All I want is to be alone with T. The thought of our honeymoon is the only thing that keeps me going. T.'s parents think we're going to Bermuda and will stay at a luxury hotel. Actually, we've rented a shack in south Jersey, in the middle of a field. Nothing but field and sky and the scent of the bay. No one around but hawks and herons and an occasional deer. And nothing to do but walk the fields, sit by the fire and—oh, yes—make love. I hope I can last.

10/25 Doris had her operation today. They say it was a success. Some success. Last night she broke down. It took me three hours to calm her. It was the thought of no kids. At one point she was so distraught, she said she hated me because I could have kids. I know she didn't mean it. God, life can be hell!

A tap on the study door. Fenimore dragged himself up from the diary. "Yes?"

"How're you coming?" Polly's voice sounded hollow behind the door.

"Almost done." He glanced at his watch: after ten. "I'll be out in a minute." He could understand her curiosity. This document must never fall into her hands.

Her footsteps faded away.

10/26 Had fitting for dress. It is lovely, despite the expense. Very simple. Polly explained to me, "Simplicity has its price." I suppose she's right. I've always preferred plain things—like Shaker furniture. That's expensive too. Even their famous boxes. The smallest ones cost about fifty dollars. And why not? Each one takes days to make. I should know from my weaving. Sometimes the simplest patterns are the most difficult.

10/27 Gave quizzes to two freshman sections. Shopped. Early to bed for a change.

10/28 A.M. Marked quizzes. Paid bills. Worked at loom for two hours. Eureka! When I'm at the loom I forget everything, except the pattern I'm working on. I wonder if this was true of the Egyptian women, and my Lenape ancestors—my grandmother? If T. hadn't called, I might have worked through the night.

10/29 Went to see RW yesterday and stayed overnight. Tried to persuade him once more to come. Of course, he refused. "If I disapprove of the marriage," he said, "why should I come to the wedding?" Always so logical. He was like that even as a child. I guess that's why he's a good engineer, but not such a good brother. He gave me a wedding present, though. My grandmother's weaving shuttle. She carved it herself from very light pine. I know it will fly like a bird. I can't wait to try it. I would try it right now, but there's this damn party. I wish I could stay home. I wish RW would change his mind. I wish the wedding were over. I wish I were dead.

Nice thoughts for a bride-to-be. Fenimore's eye traveled down the page.

10/30

Beneath the date stretched blank paper, waiting for the next entry. Fenimore swallowed hard. Before he went to find Ted, he deliberately laid his pipe on the floor beside the chair.

CHAPTER 18

WEDNESDAY, NOVEMBER 2

The next day, Fenimore had some catching up to do. The first order of business was Mr. Liska. He checked in with Larry to make sure he had kept that aggressive cardiology team at bay during his absence. Then there were his other hospital patients and the paperwork that always accumulated when he missed even a day. But the diary haunted him. Snatches of it would come back to him as he walked the hospital corridors, filled out a chart, or wrote a prescription. The sane, clear sound of Sweet Grass's voice kept interrupting him.

It was after seven when he finally finished. He had already called off his dinner date at Jennifer's because of his backlog of work. She had taken the news in her stride. (Anyone romantically involved with a doctor/detective becomes inured to postponements.) He decided to end the day by performing one last unpleasant duty—informing Doris Bentley about the death of Sweet Grass. She should be strong enough to handle the news by now, and he wanted to tell her before she heard it casually from some other source.

Setting off on foot for Franklin Hospital, he had gone less

than a block when he regretted not taking his car. Walking in the city at night was no fun anymore. And his recent mugging had done nothing to improve his nerves. He was toying with the idea of taking a karate course or some other form of self-defense. He had to cross the street twice to avoid sinister-looking characters. Nostalgically he thought of the night walks he had taken as a medical student. At ten o'clock, when he had finished a bout of studying, he would set off from the university for center city fifteen blocks away to take in an old movie. Before the days of the VCR, you had to go out to find Greta Garbo or Ingrid Bergman. Then he would take the bus back up Market Street and hit the books again, or bed. Never once had he looked over his shoulder in fear for his wallet—or his life.

For some reason, the streetlamps were out on this block. He walked close to the curb, avoiding doorways and alleys where some mugger might be lurking. The street was quiet, but he couldn't shake the feeling that someone was following him. Like Lot, he refused to look back. Instead, he concentrated on walking faster. When he reached the cross street the light was green for him, but a car turned the corner, forcing him back. He knocked into someone and jumped out of his skin.

"Hi, Doc!"

"For God's sake!" Fenimore glowered at Horatio.

"Sorry. I followed you from the office. I wanted to tell you I didn't cop your slipper. That old broad—"

"Enough! I never thought you took it."

"Yeah?"

"No."

"You shouldn't be out alone at night, Doc."

"Thanks. Look who's talking."

"I can handle it."

"I see," said Fenimore. "You're impervious to weaponry?"

"Huh?"

"Your hide's too thick for knives and bullets?"

"I don't let 'em get that close."

"Really."

"I'm invisible."

Fenimore groaned. "Now I've got 'the Invisible Man' working for me?"

"You know him?"

"H. G. Wells—at his best."

"We read it in English class last year."

"Good choice." They were walking side by side now, toward the hospital.

"I've been invisible ever since."

Fenimore looked at him.

"Well, almost."

"How do you manage it?"

"Wear sneaks. Dark rags. Move quickly but don't make quick movements. Don't do anything to attract attention."

"I thought that was called 'street smarts.' "

"Yeah. But I've perfected it."

"So have I."

"Naah. Look at you. You're too dressy. (It was the first time Fenimore had ever been accused of that!) Take that tie. A dead giveaway to a fat wallet. And those shoes. They beat a tattoo you can hear all over town. You should wear sneaks."

Fenimore undid his tie, pulled it off, and stuffed it in his pocket as he walked. "Okay. What else?"

"That shirt. It glows in the dark."

He buttoned his suit coat and turned up the collar to hide his white shirt. "How's that?"

"Better. But you oughta wear black. Black T, black jeans, black sneaks."

His patients would love that—the only doctor in town who looked like a hood. The physician's dress code had lightened up in recent years, but not that much. "I'll take it under advisement."

"Where you headed?"

"Franklin Hospital. One more block."

"I'm goin' with you."

"Suit yourself."

Under the stark lights of the hospital entrance, they faced each other. Fenimore looked gray. Horatio's darker complexion took on a yellowish cast. They both looked like candidates for the ICU.

"How long you gonna be?"

"About half an hour."

"I'll wait."

"There's no need."

For answer, the boy moved into the lobby and stretched out on the nearest black vinyl sofa. Fenimore shrugged and made his way across the cavernous lobby to the bank of elevators. As he pressed the button, a husky man in a dark uniform approached him. "Visiting hours are over," he said.

"I'm a doctor."

The guard flicked his eyes over him. "And I'm Madonna."

Fenimore felt his neck. No tie. And his coat collar was still up. He pressed it down and pulled his tie from his jacket pocket. "I took it off for security purposes." He grinned. "Honest."

The elevator had arrived. The door stood open, but the guard had placed his finger on the button and continued to block his way. Fenimore fished in his pocket for his card and handed it to him.

After a cursory glance, he handed it back. "Sorry, Doc. We get a lot of odd characters this time of night. Especially when it starts gettin' chilly. Once we found a homeless guy asleep in a bed upstairs. Tucked in as cozy as you please. He would've gotten away with it, if it hadn't been for the smell."

"Isn't there a shelter near here?"

"Yeah, but they never use it."

As soon as Fenimore got off the elevator, he found a men's

room and checked out his appearance in the mirror. He took extra care knotting his tie, combing his hair, and removing all traces of lint from his suit. He was pleased to note that the left side of his face was beginning to match the right side again. When he left the bathroom, there was no chance of anyone mistaking him for a vagrant.

CHAPTER 19

LATER WEDNESDAY NIGHT

Fenimore broke the news as gently as possible, and Doris took it as well as could be expected. After she had recovered from the initial shock, she said, "When I first heard Sweet Grass was missing, I had a premonition that I'd never see her again." She wiped her eyes. "How is Ted taking it?"

"Badly. He's blaming everyone. Her brother. His family. Himself."

"Me?"

"No. You're the only one he can't blame. You were in here."

"I was awful to her the night before I came in." She stifled a sob.

"You were upset. She understood that."

"How do you know?"

"I read her diary."

She looked up. "She didn't hold it against me?"

He shook his head. "Not at all."

Her face relaxed. "How did you get hold of her diary?"

He knew she didn't mean it to sound like an accusation. "Ted found it. He asked me to read it. He has this idea she committed suicide and—"

"Oh, no. She would never do that. She had everything to live for."

"So it would appear."

"You sound doubtful. What else did her diary tell you?"

"That she was a thoughtful, generous, strong-minded young woman."

"Yes." She nodded. "She was all of those things." She fought back another sob.

"And she was under a great deal of stress from Ted's family."

She nodded again. "They're very difficult. That was the one thing I didn't envy. Ted's a sweet guy, but he has no control over his family. If it weren't for Sweet Grass, he'd still be completely under their thumb."

"How long had they known each other?"

"About three years. But they didn't start living together until last year. He wanted to, but Sweet Grass was more conventional. Ted was the stronger in that regard, and he finally convinced her."

Fenimore was afraid he was tiring her. "I'd better be going and let you get some rest."

"That's the one thing you get plenty of in here." She smiled.

A nurse's aide stuck her head in the door. "Sorry, I didn't know you had company."

"I was just leaving," Fenimore said. When he was just outside the door, he heard the aide speak to Doris. He paused to listen.

"Is your friend feeling better?"

"Friend?"

"You know, the one who took sick here last Saturday."

Fenimore went back in. "How did you know she was sick?" The aide was startled.

"He's a doctor," Doris explained. "And . . . a friend of mine."

"When she left here, she asked me how to get to the ER. She caused quite a fuss down there."

Someone pushing a trolley full of dirty dishes made a clatter in the corridor. Fenimore leaned forward, straining not to miss a word.

"What kind of fuss?"

"Well, they took a cardiogram on her, and it was pretty bad. They were about to admit her, but when they went to get her to sign the papers, she was gone!"

The trolley rattled on down the hall.

"How do you know all this?" Fenimore asked.

"My boyfriend's an orderly in the ER."

Fenimore asked his name.

"George Johnson," she said, "but he's not on tonight."

"Why didn't you tell me this before?" Doris asked.

"I took a few days off. You didn't miss me, I guess." Her tone was sulky.

"I was under sedation most of the time." Doris tried to make amends.

Mollified, the aide went about her work, plumping pillows, cranking the bed.

Fenimore left them, mulling over this new information.

On the way down the corridor, preoccupied, he passed the nurses' station without a glance. But when he came to room 208, on an impulse, he looked in.

"Doctor!" The frail, elderly woman was no longer buried in a blizzard of sheets and pillows. She was sitting up in a pale lavender bed jacket trimmed with lace, her white hair neatly combed, sipping from a water glass. "Come sit down." She waved him in. "I want to thank you for your help the other night. The nurses have treated me like a queen ever since." She smiled.

That smile must have won her countless swains when she

was young, Fenimore thought, as he approached her bed. "You're certainly looking well."

"Yes, they're letting me out tomorrow. That's why I'm celebrating. Won't you join me?" She waved her water glass under his nose and he was treated to a strong whiff of gin. "You look like the martini type." She began rummaging under the covers and brought out a large mason jar with pieces of lemon peel floating in it.

"Good grief! How did you manage that?"

"I have one nephew who isn't a complete fool. He does whatever I ask him. He smuggled this in here tonight. I think it's still chilled. There's another glass over there on the sink. Bring it here." She began unscrewing the cap. "Martinis are out of fashion now, I know. People have forgotten how to drink. Filling themselves up with all that insipid stuff—wine coolers, fruit punch. Why, they even pay for water, for heaven's sake! But gin will come back, like everything else. Short hair, long skirts, long hair, short skirts. I've lived long enough to see all the ups and downs. My name's Myra, by the way. Myra Henderson. What's yours?" She filled his glass to the brim.

"Fenimore. Andrew. Uh, Ms. Henderson, aren't you afraid someone may come in?" He glanced over his shoulder.

"Don't worry. They never come near me, unless I ring. Then they jump—thanks to you. And forget that Ms. stuff. It's *Mrs.* Henderson. My husband was a great man, and I never minded sharing his name. A judge. Been gone over twenty years. But I'm Myra to you."

Fenimore sipped his drink. "Tell me something. When you called out the other night, you called me Doctor. And when I asked how you knew, you said I looked like one. What did you mean by that?" He didn't tell her that he had just been mistaken for a vagrant and was suffering from an identity crisis.

"Well, you did. You do. In my day, all doctors had a kindly,

113

competent air, and you could recognize them right away. Now, it's different. They're always on the run. Who were you visiting?" she asked.

"A Ms. Bentley in two-one-four."

Her expression changed. "Poor child. I met her in the solarium the other day. Tried to cheer her up. Terrible thing, to be denied children. I never had any myself. Gerald and I were always too busy. On the go all the time. We liked it that way. But if you want them, you should have them."

"Well, I'm afraid I undid all your good work. I had to inform her of the death of a friend." It was good to talk about it, to someone who had no connection with the case.

"Oh, no." She put down her glass.

"Her roommate was missing for several days. She was found dead and was identified yesterday. She was to have been married this month." Fenimore felt the full impact of the tragedy again, mirrored in Mrs. Henderson's face. "I was afraid to tell Ms. Bentley until she had recovered her strength."

"Of course." The elderly woman shook her head. "What . . . what did the young woman die of?"

"Heart failure. At least that's the official cause."

She shot him a sharp glance. "There's some question?"

Why on earth had he said that? He eyed the tumbler. It was half empty. He set the glass down.

"Come on. Drink up. Indulge a sick old lady. Tell me all the gory details."

"You don't look sick or old." Indeed, she seemed to have shed at least ten years since he had come in.

"Flatterer. Well, tell me anyway."

To his consternation, he found himself confiding the whole story. When he came to the part about meeting Ned Hardwick in the PSPS herb garden, she stopped him.

"Neddie?"

"You know him?"

"Since he was knee-high. His mother and I were thick as thieves. The only thing we ever disagreed about was the way she raised him. Spoiled him rotten. But of course nobody ever listened to me on the subject of children, because I didn't have any. She always gave him everything he wanted. Now, that's not good training for anybody. He still calls me Aunt Myra. . . . Wait a minute." She pressed her hand to her mouth. "This woman who died. She isn't . . . ?"

They stared at each other.

When Mrs. Henderson spoke again, all trace of her former bantering tone had vanished. "Sweet Grass." She spoke the name tenderly. "A lovely name. A lovely young woman. I only met her a week ago. Polly gave a party for the youngsters, and I was invited."

"You mean you were at the barbecue?"

"Why, yes. As an old friend of the family, I was invited to meet Ted's"—she faltered—"bride-to-be."

Fenimore tried to control his excitement. Was he actually going to hear a firsthand account of that infamous barbecue? He allowed a decent interval to elapse before he asked, "Can you tell me a little about it? The party, I mean?"

"It was an awful party. Full of false gaiety and tension. I never could stand the Hardwicks' parties. The only *real* person there was Sweet Grass. I talked to her for some time."

Fenimore couldn't believe his good fortune. He leaned closer, hanging on every word.

"They had someone else picked out for Ted, of course."

"Oh?"

"Oh, yes. Ellen Potts. The two families brought the children up together with marriage in mind. But that never works, you know. Familiarity breeds . . . Ellen's parents had all the right credentials. Her mother went to Vassar. Her father was in the First City Troop and was a member of the Union League."

115

"What about Ellen?"

"She went to Vassar too."

"And now?"

"I think she's taking a few courses toward an M.A., still wait-ing and hoping. Ted's family never really believed in Sweet Grass, you see. They thought, like an unwelcome ache or a pain, eventually she would go away. Polly was very offhand about her. Take this barbecue, for example. Why a barbecue for such an important occasion? I thought it very odd at the time. And, by accident, I overheard Ted confronting his mother in the kitchen about the same thing. 'Why a barbecue, Mother? And in Octo-ber,' he said. 'Did you think Sweet Grass would feel more at home around a campfire? Or were you afraid she couldn't han-dle a knife and fork?' "

She was an excellent raconteur. Fenimore could see Ted, flushed and angry, accusing his mother.

"It was the first time I ever saw Polly at a loss," the older woman continued with relish. "After a pause, Polly mumbled, 'I thought nothing of the kind. I just thought it would be more re-laxing, and since the weather was so mild . . .'

" 'And at least at a barbecue,' Ted ranted, 'if Sweet Grass showed up wearing something out of line, no one would notice. Whereas at a dinner party, how your friends' tongues would clack.'

" 'Don't be ridiculous, darling,' she said. 'I'm sure Sweet Grass has a nice dress.'

" 'Oh, the hell with you!' he shouted. And he almost knocked me over as he stormed out of the kitchen."

"And?"

"At that point, I continued into the kitchen and asked if there was anything I could do to help—meaning with the food, of course. But Polly misinterpreted me and broke down completely. 'Oh, Aunt Myra, I'm such a wreck,' she said. 'Ted thinks we're against his marriage because she's an Ind . . . Native American.

116

But that's simply not true. We can handle her origins. It's her health that worries us. She was born with a heart defect. And from what Ned tells me, even if she's able to have children, she may not live long enough to see them grow up—' "

"There's no foundation for that," Fenimore interrupted.

"Well, I knew nothing about it. But I tried to reassure her. She was crashing around the kitchen, banging pots and pans. I was afraid she might hurt herself. Finally, I calmed her down and convinced her to go outside and join the others." She paused. "It was then that Lydia, the middle daughter, made her unfortunate remark."

To get any closer to Mrs. Henderson, Fenimore would have had to get in bed with her.

"As we came up to the group on the patio, Lydia was rattling on about the balmy October weather. 'This has been the longest Indian summer.' She stopped and looked embarrassedly at Sweet Grass. I could have spanked her. But Sweet Grass simply ignored her."

"I don't understand."

"Well, 'Indian summer' is a slur on the Native Americans. As you know, it refers to an unexpected warm spell in autumn, a sort of false alarm. The weather, like the Indian, is not to be trusted."

"I use that term all the time. Its implications never occurred to me."

"They occurred to Sweet Grass, I assure you. Another, similar slur is 'Indian giver.' "

"I remember that. That's what you called a child who gave you something and then took it back. But I never thought about its origin. It was just another form of name calling, like tattletale or fraidycat"—or Sitting Frog, thought Fenimore. "What happened next?" He steered Mrs. Henderson back to the picnic.

"Well, the afternoon wore on with the usual inane twaddle. Ned was at his most pompous and overbearing, bragging about his ancestors who came over on the *Mayflower*. At one point, he gave Sweet Grass that boyish grin (which wasn't particularly endearing, even when he was a boy) and said, 'Of course, *your* ancestors were already here to greet mine.' Sweet Grass ignored him. She was polite, but she wasn't meek. Finally Polly brought out the ingredients for the shish kebab, and we were all given a skewer made from a branch and whittled to a point. We were supposed to spear our own bits of food and grill them. I may be old-fashioned, Doctor, but I don't go for these do-it-yourself parties When I'm invited out, I like to be waited on."

Fenimore nodded.

"So we all filled up our skewers with bits of meat, tomatoes, mushrooms, and so forth, and—"

"Did everyone take these ingredients from the same bowl?"

"Well, actually, each ingredient was in a separate bowl. We helped ourselves from each one." She looked at him quizzically.

"Go on."

"Well, then we crowded around the barbecues—there were three. Whenever the wind changed, we'd end up coughing and sputtering. Horrid way to cook. What's the point of inventing things, if people insist on going back to the Stone Age? Anyway, I found myself standing next to Sweet Grass, and as we grilled, we talked. Something seemed to strike a chord between us. Despite the difference in our ages, we seemed to share a common bond."

Dislike of the rest of the company, perhaps, thought Fenimore.

"She told me about her passion for weaving. She had been taught the Lenape method by her grandmother when she was seven. Now she was teaching a class. Her work had been exhibited all over this area, and I wormed out of her that she had won a number of prizes. I told her I'd like to see her work, and she promised to send me an invitation the next time she had an exhibit. . . ." Her voice faded with the realization that there would be no more exhibits.

"And then . . ." Fenimore prompted gently.

"Oh, then Ned came around and checked everybody's skewer, to make sure the meat was done enough. Some of it was pork, he said. He's such a fusspot. And Polly sent us to a table under the trees where the rest of the food was laid out. There was a big bowl of potato salad, and another of pasta, and loaves of French bread oozing with butter and garlic. And wine. There was plenty of that."

"What about dessert?"

"Ice cream. Vanilla with chocolate sauce. Polly's meals always fall apart at dessert. I guess she doesn't care for sweets herself. Have another?" She proffered the mason jar.

"No, thanks. I really must be going. Just one more question. Did you see Sweet Grass again before she left?"

"Just in passing. Not to talk to. She left early. Said she had to visit a sick friend. I remember thinking it was a pretty lame excuse at the time. Now, of course, I know it was true." She shook her head sadly. "That poor child down the hall was the sick friend." The elderly woman slumped back into her pillows, looking her age again.

Fenimore patted her hand.

She smiled. "Sometimes we live too long and see too much, don't you think, Doctor?"

"Now, that's just the gin talking. You have a big day tomorrow. You're going home. You'd better turn off the light and get some sleep." He lifted the mason jar, took it over to the sink, and emptied it. The bits of lemon peel collected in the drain. He picked them out and tossed them in the wastebasket. When he had washed and dried the jar and the two glasses, he turned to say good-night. There was no answer. Mrs. Henderson was asleep.

119

As Fenimore passed through the dimly lit lobby, he noticed a familiar figure stretched out on a sofa. Oh, my God, Horatio.

When Fenimore had finished making his apologies, Horatio sniffed, "You've been drinking."

It seems he had acquired not only a bodyguard but also a nagging wife.

CHAPTER 20

STILL LATER WEDNESDAY NIGHT

Fenimore had been asleep no more than an hour when he was aware of a persistent ringing. The alarm? The phone? The doorbell. He staggered out of bed and stumbled barefoot down the stairs. Who the hell? He peered cautiously through the glass panel of the front door. First rule of city living—never open the door without checking first. The panel was frosted with a profusion of curlicues in the Victorian manner. All Fenimore could make out was the shadowy bulk of a man. He called out, "Who is it?"

"Officer Brown. Urgent message from Detective Rafferty."

Rafferty occasionally did send one of his men over with a message, if it was something he didn't want to communicate over the phone. Fenimore opened the door.

What happened next was so fast Fenimore had trouble remembering the details later. As soon as he took off the chain and turned the knob, the man on the doorstep pushed past him into the house. He was followed by another, shorter man. Neither man was in uniform and neither spoke. They alternately dragged and shoved Fenimore down the hall and into his office.

The first man held his arms twisted behind his back in a painful grip. The other began to slap him across the face—hard.

Between slaps, Fenimore caught sight of Sal. She edged out from under his desk where she had fled when the doorbell rang. The slapper spotted her too. He paused long enough to kick her.

"Hey." The fellow holding Fenimore spoke for the first time. "Cut that out. I like cats."

The slapper grunted and gave Fenimore another blow. Not with his open hand this time. With his fist. The cat lover released his grip and shoved Fenimore into a chair.

Fenimore fought for consciousness, but the comforting darkness, like a cloying syrup, kept drawing him down. He forced his eyes open.

The slapper was roughly pulling out drawers, throwing open cabinet and closet doors, rummaging through their contents, and hurling them on the floor.

Drugs, Fenimore thought hazily. Well, they won't find any here. He hadn't kept any powerful drugs here for over a decade. But the man was wrecking his office.

The cat lover wasn't much help to his partner. He had picked up Sal and was stroking her. "Nice kitty," he crooned. "Nice puss." He put his face down close to her ear. It was the moment she had been waiting for. Twisting in his arms, she made a horrid cat noise and scratched his face.

"Ow!" The man covered his face with his hands. Sal jumped free and ran.

The other man stopped his wrecking long enough to laugh.

"I'll kill her," the injured man cried.

"Come on. Help me trash this place."

The ex–cat lover, still holding his face, went to look in the mirror over the sink. "My eye," he cried. "She got me in the eye."

"Christ. You and that damned cat!" But the other man stopped his ransacking long enough to look at the eye.

"I gotta see a doctor," the injured one whimpered.

The slapper laughed again and looked down at Fenimore, still slumped in his chair. "Hey, Doc." There was menace in his voice. "Looks like you've got yourself a new patient."

Fenimore forced himself up through the syrupy darkness and tried to pay attention. His eyes were swollen. He could see only slits of light. And there was a buzzing in his ears. Although he could barely see or hear, there was nothing wrong with his sense of smell. There was an odor, strong and unpleasant, very near. Garlic. He forced one eye open. A face was close to his. It had two eyes, and blood was oozing from one of them. "Your lousy cat did this," the face said. "What are you gonna do about it?"

And if I don't help you, thought Fenimore, what will you do? Sue me? Fenimore groped at the chair arms and tried to pull himself up. The uninjured man helped him. Fenimore made it to the medicine cabinet, which for some reason they hadn't ransacked. Maybe they weren't after drugs. He found an eye cup. He filled it with a cleansing antiseptic and handed it to the man with the bad eye. Through lips now swollen to twice their size, he instructed his new patient how to wash his eye. The orders came out thickly.

The man went to the sink and tried.

People are funny about doctors, Fenimore thought fuzzily. They criticize them, insult them, even beat them. But when they need them, they turn around and place their health— even their lives—unquestioningly in their hands, with no fear of reprisal. And usually, their trust is not misplaced. It had something to do with that oath, framed and hanging on the wall, hanging crookedly now as a result of the ransacking.

The man at the sink was bungling. Most of the solution was

missing his eye and going down the drain. Fenimore went to his aid. When the eye was finally clear, Fenimore examined it with his ophthalmoscope, as well as he could with his own swollen eyes. Sal had left her mark. There was a scratch just missing the cornea.

Fenimore said, through swollen lips, "You have a nasty scratch, but it's shallow and the cornea isn't damaged." He felt more alert now, and the buzzing in his ears was beginning to fade. He took a tube from his doctor's bag, another thing they hadn't found and violated. "I'll put some ointment in your eye," he said, and squeezed it in. The hood winced. "But this is only a temporary measure." Fenimore turned to his partner. "You must get him to an ophthalmologist right away."

"Speak English, Doc."

Fenimore rooted through the mess they'd made of his desk until he came up with a prescription pad. Another search uncovered a pen. He wrote the name, address, and phone number of an ophthalmologist at a nearby hospital. "Take him there and ask to see this doctor." He ripped off the slip and handed it to the thug.

"You gotta go to the hospital," the man told his companion, as if he were deaf or not in the same room when Fenimore had given his instructions.

The patient clenched his fists. "Not 'til I get that cat," he hissed, scanning the room with his good eye.

Fenimore held his breath.

"No time for that." The other man took his arm and started to lead him out of the office.

Fenimore breathed again.

He stopped and turned back to Fenimore. "I almost forgot. We have a message." His eyes narrowed. "Lay off the Lenape."

Fenimore looked puzzled. "That wasn't from Rafferty."

"No, it's from . . ." The thug's face split into a grin. "Nice try,

124

Doc." He pushed his partner before him, through the front door.

As soon as Fenimore had slid the chain back into place, he felt Sal rub against his leg. Reaching down, he carried her into his office. There, he gave her the body rub of her life.

CHAPTER 21

THURSDAY, NOVEMBER 3, DAWN

Rosy-fingered dawn was filtering through the slats of the interior shutters of Fenimore's bedroom when the six aspirins and several shots of Scotch (he hadn't counted) finally took effect. With apologies to Homer, he fell asleep. At 7:00 A.M. he was jarred awake by the alarm clock. He had forgotten to reset it. For a split second he was blissfully unconscious of the previous night's events. But when he reached out to punch the button on the clock, a shock of pain charged up his arm, his shoulder, his neck, and came to rest directly behind his eyes. There it remained. Gritting his teeth, he reached for the button again, successfully silencing the instrument, and fell back exhausted on the bed.

As he lay there wondering which shades of the rainbow his face would assume today, Sal slid onto his chest. With her face a bare two inches from his, she gave a sharp staccato mew not unlike a bark. A reminder that it was breakfast time, or at least time for another body rub. Fenimore shoved her gently off his chest and sat up. He would like to loll around all day with her, sipping Scotch and staring at the TV, while he recovered. But

126

today he could not afford such luxuries. Today was not Sunday. Today was a workday, and he had lots of work to do. The least of which was finding out whom he had to thank for last night's free home entertainment. Cautiously, he reached for the phone.

It was 7:05 when the phone rang in Mrs. Doyle's apartment. She was standing at the kitchen counter, packing her lunch while watching the news on TV. She put down the knife she was using to spread egg salad (made with no-fat mayonnaise, of course) on a slice of whole-wheat bread and went into the hall to answer it. The receiver had a long cord so she could move back to the kitchen and continue watching her favorite programs while chatting with her callers. She did not do that with this caller, however. This caller demanded her full attention. When she hung up, she finished packing her lunch in record time. She turned off the TV and the overhead light and trotted briskly around the apartment gathering together the things she would need—from the top of her bureau, the medicine cabinet, and a duffel bag stowed in the back of her closet. She tucked all these items into a navy blue purse (which most people would have taken for an overnight bag) and grabbed a powder blue cardigan from a chair and her keys from the coffee table. She had one foot out the front door when she remembered her lunch.

One nice thing about Philadelphia is the public transportation system. There is hardly a corner in the city where a bus doesn't stop and take you where you want to go. Mrs. Doyle was especially grateful for this today because she had an errand to do in an obscure part of town before she went to the office. As the 32 bus peeped over the brow of the hill a block back, the five people at the bus stop moved toward the curb as if drawn by a single, invisible string. Mrs. Doyle was the first in line, her token ready.

"Nice day," the driver said. He was a stranger. She knew all the ones after 8:00 A.M., but today she was early. She settled into a seat, but instead of taking out her latest Harlequin romance, she thought about the doctor. He had downplayed the whole thing, of course. Told her two toughs had roughed him up a bit looking for drugs and could she come in a little early? She could imagine what they had done to him, if he needed her services. She shifted in her seat, evoking a grunt from the woman next to her. Well, she would fix him up. She'd done it before. And this time she had a special cure in mind. Three buses and forty-five minutes later, Mrs. Doyle pulled the overhead cord, signaling the driver to stop at the next corner. As she stepped off the bus, she picked out the sign at the end of a row of dilapidated shops: OTTO'S PHARMACY. Behind the dirty window was an arrangement of glass pharmaceutical jars filled with colored liquids— red, blue, amber, green, the standard pharmacy display, vintage 1920. Each jar bore a thick coat of dust. Stuck in the upper panel of the glass door was a small handwritten card: "Open for Business." She pushed on the door. It refused to budge. She looked around for a bell, found one, and pressed it. A buzz, like an angry hornet, brought Otto himself to the door.

CHAPTER 22

LATER THURSDAY MORNING

Fenimore was seated in a straight-backed chair next to Mrs. Doyle's desk, a lavender towel draped around his neck. Mrs. Doyle was taking the last of her assorted packages from her purse and arranging them in a row on her desk when the doorbell rang.

Fenimore flinched. "Don't answer it."

"Nonsense." Mrs. Doyle started down the hall. "You can't go through life not answering the door."

"I can try," he called after her.

Mrs. Doyle peered through the frosted glass pane. "It's Horatio," she called back.

"It can't be. He's not due 'til three. It's someone disguised as Horatio."

"Yo, man. Let me in." Horatio's familiar voice echoed down the hallway.

Mrs. Doyle opened the door. "What are you doing here?"

"It's a saint's day. I have off." He sidled in. "Thought I'd drop by. My mom sent me to early Mass, and if I go home now she'll have me scrubbin' floors and washin' windows all day. Filing's

129

easier. Besides, here I get paid. Holy Christopher!" He caught sight of the doctor.

"Your epithets have been tempered by your visit to the holy sanctuary," Fenimore said.

Horatio looked to Doyle for a translation. When none was forthcoming, he said, "What hit you?"

"Not what. Who. Two thugs looking for drugs." He wasn't ready to reveal the whole story yet.

"Hold still." Mrs. Doyle was trying to apply ointment to his cracked and swollen lips.

"Two hits in five days?" Horatio shook his head. "You better stay home, man."

"I *was* home."

Mrs. Doyle patted a scratch on Fenimore's forehead with something that stung. He winced.

"Better get out, then."

"I was *out* the first time, remember?"

"I mean outa town."

The doorbell.

"What is this? Grand Central Station?" Mrs. Doyle put down the jar of ointment, but Horatio was already at the door.

"Check who it is first, Rat," Fenimore cautioned.

"It's a dame."

"Woman, for God's sake. It's the nineties. What's she look like?"

"Small, dark . . . a babe."

"Oh, no. Get rid of her. I can't let her see me like this." He started to get up from the chair.

Mrs. Doyle pushed him down. "I told you to hold still." With a brush, she applied a coat of pancake makeup to his chin.

"The doctor's not in," he heard Horatio say.

"Who are you?" A female voice, faint but familiar.

"I'm his new employee."

"Well, I'm his *old* girlfriend," she said, not so faint.

130

The rasp of the chain being pulled back. Horatio opened the door a crack and leaned out. "By appointment only," he said and pointed to the sign in the window.

"That's a very old sign. I happen to know he has hours this morning."

The babe didn't look nearly as pretty with her eyes narrowed and her hands on her hips, Horatio decided. "What'll I do, Doc?" he called back.

"Let her in," he sighed.

Horatio came in, followed by Jennifer.

Jennifer didn't see him at first. Mrs. Doyle's ample back, in a white starched uniform, blocked her view.

"I brought a book on the Lenapes. . . ." She caught sight of the cluttered desk. With its assortment of bottles and tubes, tissues and powder puffs, it resembled the cosmetic counter at Saks when someone was undergoing a makeover. "What's all this?"

Mrs. Doyle stepped aside to get something from her purse and Jennifer let out a gasp, just like in the TV sit-coms.

"I didn't want to let you in," Fenimore said in an injured tone.

Jennifer paled as she contemplated his ravaged face.

"Next to me, Lon Chaney's a matinee idol." Fenimore tried to grin, but it turned into a grimace.

"What happened?" she murmured, her eyes moving to the ravaged office.

"A nocturnal visit from a couple of thugs."

"You told me your investigating was always done on a high intellectual plane." Her voice bordered on the hysterical.

"Yes, well, last night it dropped a few notches."

Doorbell.

"Bring out the music and the drinks," Fenimore said. "It's party time."

"No party," Mrs. Doyle said sternly. "I'm not finished with you yet."

Horatio had gone to the door again. There were male voices

in the hall. Fenimore froze. "What did I tell you," he whispered. "More guests." Warily, he watched the door to the hall until it was filled with Rafferty's reassuring frame.

"Well, well." The policeman surveyed the chaotic scene. "Are we party crashing?" His expression didn't match his jocular tone. "Is it just starting—or breaking up?" He glanced at his watch. "And how come I wasn't invited?"

"An oversight," Fenimore said. "Ouch." Mrs. Doyle had jerked his chin front and center.

A uniformed officer came in behind Rafferty, followed by Horatio. Horatio slunk quietly back to his filing cabinet. He was never completely at ease in the presence of officers of the law.

"Gentlemen," Mrs. Doyle turned on them, a powder puff in one hand and an atomizer in the other, "state your business and be on your way. As you can see, I'm caring for a patient."

"Yes, ma'am." Rafferty looked past her at the patient. "This is Officer Mario Santino." He indicated the man in blue. "Since you were mugged in that alley, I thought you could use some protection. I brought him over to keep an eye on the store, only to find the horse has already been stolen."

"This is not a store. I am not a horse. And you're mixing your metaphors."

"From now on, wherever you go, he goes," Rafferty said. "And wherever you stay, he stays. He'll make himself as inconspicuous as possible." Considering the officer's husky frame, thick neck, and protuberant ears, not to mention his uniform, this seemed highly dubious.

Mrs. Doyle looked impatient. Jennifer, anxious. Horatio, uneasy. Fenimore, annoyed.

"When Mrs. Doyle gives up trying to make you look like Clark Gable," Rafferty continued, "give me a call. I'd really like to hear the whole story—from the horse's mouth." He turned and walked out.

In the silence that followed, Officer Santino smiled apologetically and found a seat in the corner. Horatio continued filing. Jennifer laid the book she had been clutching on a corner of the desk. Fenimore picked it up and riffled through it. Mrs. Doyle took out another parcel from her purse. This one was small, wrapped in brown paper, and tied with string. She placed it on the desk. Fenimore looked up. "Ah." He recognized the wrapping instantly. "You've been to Otto's."

Mrs. Doyle removed the wrapping. At first Jennifer saw only an empty jar. But on closer inspection, she noticed some black things curled on the bottom. As she watched, one of the black things separated itself from the other and started to move up the side of the jar. It had no legs. Like the toy animals you see stuck to the rear windows of cars, it adhered to the glass by suction.

"Ugh." Jennifer shivered, as recognition dawned.

"Now, now," Mrs. Doyle admonished her, "the leech is a much maligned creature. Just like the bat. They both suffer from bad press." She picked up a pencil and placed it in the jar. They watched as the leech wrapped itself around it. As soon as she felt it was securely attached, Mrs. Doyle removed it and with a deft motion applied it to the outer edge of Fenimore's left eye.

"Doesn't it hurt?" Jennifer was horrified.

"Not a bit," Fenimore said.

"What does it feel like?"

"Like a light pinch," he said, shrugging.

Fascinated, Jennifer watched Mrs. Doyle draw out the second leech and apply it to the periphery of Fenimore's right eye.

"Now you watch. In no time that vivid purple will turn to a pale lavender and then fade away completely." The nurse patted her patient's arm.

To pass the time, Jennifer asked, "How are bats useful, Mrs. Doyle?"

"Insects, dear. If it weren't for bats, we'd be overrun with them—gnats, flies, mosquitoes, and the rest. Bats do their work at night, while we're asleep, so we don't appreciate them. Right, Doctor?"

He nodded. Like his two assailants, he thought bitterly.

The two women looked at him with concern. Slouched in his chair, still in rumpled pajamas, with a leech attached to each eye, he looked very forlorn and un-Fenimore-like.

Horatio, casting a cautious glance at the officer in the corner, left his filing cabinet to come inspect Mrs. Doyle's handiwork. "Whew," he whistled. "Where'd you get those suckers?" He was the first to wake up to the fact that leeches don't grow on trees. Nor are they available in the average supermarket.

"A little drugstore on the other side of town," Mrs. Doyle said enigmatically. She wasn't about to give out her trade secrets. If there was a run on leeches, they might not be available the next time she needed them.

Officer Santino coughed discreetly from his corner.

"Oh, Officer, would you like a cup of coffee or tea?" Having finished her work as a cosmetologist, Mrs. Doyle became the gracious hostess.

"That would be nice. Tea, please."

"I think we could all use a cup," she said. "Jennifer? Doctor?"

"I'll help," Jennifer said, heading for the kitchen.

"Make mine java," Horatio said over his shoulder.

While the women toiled in the kitchen in a very politically incorrect fashion, Fenimore chatted with Officer Santino. "It was my own fault. I opened the door."

"Why did you?"

"They said they had a message from Rafferty."

"Um." Santino shifted on his chair. "After drugs?"

"No. They ransacked the place to make it look like a robbery, but they didn't take anything."

"A warning?"

Fenimore paused. He would have to tell Rafferty anyway. He nodded.

Conversation lagged until the women came back with the drinks. "It's almost gone!" Jennifer stopped midway as she was handing Fenimore his tea.

"What?"

"The purple. Look, Mrs. Doyle."

Mrs. Doyle sniffed, unexcited. She passed a pocket mirror to Fenimore.

"Bravo, Doyle. You've done it again," he crowed. "That stint of yours in the theater has stood you in good stead."

"Theater?" Things were moving too fast for Jennifer.

"Mrs. Doyle was once a member of Plays and Players," Fenimore explained.

Horatio came to inspect. "Not bad." He sent Mrs. Doyle a grudging look of admiration. "They could use you at the rings."

"Rings?"

"Boxing, Doyle," Fenimore explained. "Would you like to leave my services and patch up boxers after their fights? The pay's probably much better."

Mrs. Doyle sniffed again.

"How do you get those suckers off?" Horatio was staring at the leeches.

For the answer, Mrs. Doyle drew the last surprise from her purse—a saltcellar. She sprinkled a little of its contents on each leech. They let go and fell into her palm. She returned them to the glass jar.

"I don't care how you *look*," Jennifer said fervently. "How do you *feel*?"

"Fine. Right as rain. A-OK."

She shook her head. "What happens to those?" She nodded at the leeches.

"Oh, they go in the refrigerator," Fenimore said.

Jennifer suppressed a shudder, envisaging them between the mustard and the ketchup.

"Then back to the store," Fenimore added.

"You mean they get recycled?"

"Well, I have no more use for them. And," he lowered his voice, "with Hercules over there, I don't expect to."

Jennifer shook her head again. "There must be something I can do for you."

"Not a thing. This book you brought will keep me occupied for hours." He tapped the cover of *The Lenape,* by Herbert C. Kraft. "It just happens to be a definitive work on the Lenape Indians."

"Well . . ." She hesitated, wanting to kiss him but intimidated by the audience: a nurse, a policeman, a file clerk, and a cat. Sal had suddenly emerged from under the radiator, a puff of dust clinging to her tail. Jennifer blew Fenimore a kiss instead.

As soon as she had gone, Fenimore was out of his chair. "I've got to get to work."

"Work?" Mrs. Doyle was startled. "Shouldn't you go back to bed?"

"Surely you don't think I put you to all this trouble"—he waved at the cluttered desk—"to send me back to bed." He was halfway up the stairs. "My public awaits." He bowed deeply to his audience of four and scurried up the rest of the stairs.

CHAPTER 23

STILL LATER THURSDAY MORNING

Despite the delay for cosmetic surgery, Fenimore arrived at the emergency room of Franklin Hospital at 10:00 A.M. But not alone. Officer Santino stood in the hallway, watching him through the glass door of the ER. The young woman at the desk, cradling a cup of steaming coffee, glanced up. She registered nothing when she saw his face. Three cheers for Mrs. Doyle.

"I'd like to see the records of Joanne Field." (He had almost forgotten her Anglicized name.) "She was here on Saturday, October 29th—in the late afternoon, around 4:30. But she left before she could be admitted." He showed her his identification.

The nurse blinked. "I think I was on duty, Doctor. Was she a Native American?"

"Yes." Another eyewitness? He could hardly believe his good fortune.

"I'll get the file." She disappeared between a pair of sliding glass doors.

He watched her walk over to a desk and boot up a computer.

The scent of the coffee she had left behind reached him. In his convalescent mode, he had wanted tea. In his recovery mode, he wanted coffee. He looked around for the coffeepot. He spotted it in a corner, complete with packets of sugar, milk, and Styrofoam cups. ER employees, apparently, were undaunted by warnings about high cholesterol and recycling. Helping himself, he went back to the reception desk. He had scalded his mouth twice before the nurse came back and handed him a printout.

"It was quiet here that day, Doctor," she said. "That's why I remember her. Later on it was a zoo. We had an apartment fire, a three-car accident, and a stabbing. But when your patient walked in, it was as quiet as a church."

"Tell me what you remember."

"Well, the thing I remember about her is that after a very short time, she walked out. And a few minutes later Dr. Sheehab, two nurses, and an orderly came rushing after her."

"What did they say?"

"The doctor said, 'That woman who just left is an MVA case. Is there any way we can get her back?' I said, 'Her home number must be on her chart.' And he said—I remember this distinctly—'She may not *make* it home.' "

MVA stood for malignant ventricular arrythmia, a condition known in the popular medical vernacular as "the Pearly Gates syndrome." If you had it, and it was untreated, that's where you were headed.

Fenimore glanced at the file. "Anything else?"

"No. Except she looked terrible. I almost stopped her myself. But she was moving so fast and looked so determined. . . ." She shrugged.

Fenimore thanked her and, still studying the file, felt his way to an empty chair. When he came to the electrocardiograms, he let out a low whistle. No wonder they had run after her. After scanning the computer printout of her SMA 20 blood test, he laid the file aside to consider.

The report held the following significant facts: distinct abnormalities in her electrocardiograms—heart block, ventricular tachycardia, and MVA. Such irregularities could occur years after complete repair of tetralogy of Fallot. But the presence of another factor altered this conclusion. Her SMA 20 blood test revealed a potassium level of 7. Very high. Top normal was 5. These two results taken together pointed to a different diagnosis altogether: digitalis toxicity. In order to verify this, he must have the blood test of her digoxin level. He riffled through the file. Where was it? Surely they had done one. He went back to the desk.

"I'm sure it was done, Doctor. Some blood serum is always put in a separate tube with a lab slip requesting a digoxin level."

"Then why isn't it here?"

She frowned. "I don't know."

A pretty poor show. Fenimore thought that *his* hospital staff was sloppy, but he had never known them to lose a blood test. Disgruntled, he returned to his chair. As he read on, he discovered that Dr. Sheehab had shared his suspicions. At the end of the file, he had scrawled in his own hand, "Test results suggest possible dig toxicity. Staff prepared to administer FAB to patient, but despite strong recommendations to be admitted to the hospital, she left of her own volition." He was also covering himself, in case of a lawsuit.

"FAB," Fenimore murmured. Fragments of antigen binding. He was familiar with the treatment. Derived from sheep, it was an antibody which, if administered in time, was capable of rendering digoxin inactive. If Sweet Grass had not signed herself out—if she had stuck around long enough to receive this treatment—she might still be alive today. He rubbed his eyes and reached for his coffee.

If Sweet Grass had been suffering from dig toxicity, he had three questions: (1) When was the lethal dose administered? (2) How? and (3) By whom?

It might have been administered shortly before her attack, at the picnic. Did one of the picnickers lace her potato salad with powdered digoxin tablets? But Mrs. Henderson had told him that they all had helped themselves from the same serving dishes. If any of them had been seasoned with digitalis, some of the other guests would have developed symptoms.

Fenimore chucked his Styrofoam cup into the nearest wastebasket. Of course, Sweet Grass might have received the dose earlier, during her visit with Roaring Wings. A little digoxin could easily go unnoticed in a cup of strong herb tea. It was hard to know how fast these drugs would work. It depended on many factors: age, weight, how tired you were, how long it had been since you had last eaten ... Then again, Sweet Grass, feeling despondent after the picnic, could have increased her own dose of digoxin. He returned the file to the nurse.

"I don't suppose there's any hope that this patient's blood serum sample is still lying around the lab."

She shook her head. "That's disposed of right away, especially if the patient checks out before being admitted."

He nodded. His own hospital followed the same procedure. But, in order to prove digitalis toxicity, he had to have a sample of that serum. He thanked her and was about to leave when he remembered something. "Uh, one more favor. Could you call George Johnson out here."

"The orderly?"

He nodded.

She paged him on the intercom. Johnson appeared in a few minutes. A lanky black man with a friendly grin, he was glad to help. Unfortunately, he couldn't add much to what Fenimore had already gleaned from Johnson's girlfriend.

"I don't know, Doc. It all happened so fast. She was in and out before any of us could blink an eye. It's not often someone with Pearly Gates takes off. We were all kind of in shock. Even the doc. But there was no stoppin' her. She was determined." The same word the nurse had used.

Fenimore nodded. "Well, thanks anyway."

It was a brisk morning. Autumn had finally given Indian summer a swift kick in the pants. Fenimore turned up his collar and buried his hands in his pockets. It was that chilly. Absorbed in his thoughts, he forgot about his shadow, Officer Santino, hovering a few yards behind. He passed a fruit vendor flipping chunks of pineapple, cantaloupe, and strawberries into plastic containers for the lunch crowd. A pigeon abandoned a prize chunk of pretzel to make way for Fenimore, and a homeless man blocked his way to ask for a quarter. He dug into his pocket and came up with one. While his mind was registering these details on one level, it was churning rapidly away on another.

Sweet Grass had been born with tetralogy of Fallot. The defect had been surgically corrected when she was a child, but she still required a daily regimen of digitalis. Under stress from her pending wedding, she had experienced two episodes of rapid heartbeat. According to her diary, her doctor had prescribed a small dose of Inderal in addition to her regular digoxin, but no increase in her dig regimen. He made a mental note to visit Dr. Robinson later that day.

As he turned the corner, he kicked a soda can into the gutter, a sure sign that he was preoccupied. Normally, he would have lobbed it into a trash can. (Santino did so.) Sweet Grass had complained to Doris of nausea, headache, and dizziness— all symptoms of simple food poisoning. But she had felt bad enough to seek out the ER. There, they had taken several electrocardiograms. The results were alarming, and she had been strongly urged to admit herself to the hospital. Instead, she walked out. Of course, this denial of her illness could be explained by her pending wedding. She couldn't face the prospect of an illness that might cause a delay. (Having never been on the brink of matrimony, it was clever of Fenimore to deduce this.)

Red light. He waited at the curb, oblivious to the other pedestrians elbow to elbow on either side of him. He would feel better if he could absolutely establish the cause of death. But he couldn't do that without the blood serum sample. Once the cause was established, he could go on to whether it was accidental or deliberate. And, if the latter, who was to blame.

Green light. He crossed. Facing him was the hospital. Without realizing it, he had circled the block. He decided to go back in and bother the nurse for one more look at the report. Maybe he'd missed something.

As the nurse handed him the folder, she said, "I just thought of something."

He looked up.

"That blood serum you asked for . . ."

"Yes?" His heart rose.

"It may still be around. There's a doctor here doing research on MVA. There's the memo." She pointed to a notice attached to the corkboard over her desk. "We're supposed to send a sample of blood serum from all MVA cases to his lab. You might find what you want there."

His heart leaped. "What's his name?"

"Applethorn."

His heart sank. He knew him. The most suspicious research doctor in all of researchdom. If he asked Applethorn for one of his blood samples, he would immediately suspect Fenimore of trying to steal a jump on his research. Applethorn slunk around the hospital corridors looking over his shoulder even more than the doctors who were on the lamb from the IRS. Nevertheless, Fenimore would have to give it a try. "Thanks. I'll look into it." She *had* been helpful. How was she to know that Applethorn was paranoid?

CHAPTER 24

THURSDAY AFTERNOON

Deciding that a personal visit would produce better results than a phone call, Fenimore scanned the list of names on the board beside the elevators. Applethorn and his lab were located on the fifth floor.

Fenimore stepped into the elevator, quickly followed by Officer Santino. "I had a little shadow . . ." Fenimore muttered to himself.

Applethorn's office was protected from the rest of the hospital by a heavy glass door. When Fenimore pulled it open, he was met with a hush usually reserved for church sanctuaries. In the tones of a church usher, a jittery receptionist informed him that the doctor would see him presently. Between phone calls, she kept glancing over her shoulder at the door behind her as if the Furies were about to descend on her. The turnover in this job, he suspected, must be fairly high.

His last encounter with Dr. Applethorn had been at a cardiology conference in Boston. Fenimore traveled there each October to catch up on the latest innovations in his field. The topics that year had been especially erudite and impractical, and

144

Applethorn had been reading one of the principal papers. During the question-and-answer period, Fenimore had asked a question that had cast some doubt on the premise on which Applethorn's entire research project was based. At the cocktail party afterward, he had caught the research man staring at him once or twice, in a manner that could only be described as malevolent. But that was more than four years ago. He hoped, by now, the doctor had forgotten the incident.

Fenimore's ruminations were interrupted by the receptionist speaking to him in a tone usually reserved for introductions to royalty or the pope.

"Dr. Applethorn will see you now." She glanced at Officer Santino.

"Oh, he stays out here," Fenimore said.

Santino looked up from his magazine and smiled broadly.

Relieved, she hurriedly ushered Fenimore into the inner office.

The center of the room was occupied by an enormous teakwood desk, devoid of clutter. Its only ornaments were a lamp, a telephone, and a pristine blotter in a bilious shade of green. Fenimore deduced that all the paperwork in Applethorn's department was performed by underlings in less elegant quarters. His energies must be preserved for more important matters—such as selecting the expensive furniture that surrounded him.

The figure behind the desk peered at him through dark-rimmed glasses, reminding Fenimore of a certain small rodent he had seen on a recent trip to the zoo. The name escaped him at the moment, but . . .

"Ah, Fenimore." A tic began near Applethorn's left nostril, and Fenimore knew he had not forgotten their encounter four years ago.

Fenimore plowed ahead with his request. As he was outlining his reasons for requiring the sample of Joanne Field's blood serum, the telephone rang. Applethorn snatched up the receiver.

"Two milliliters, you say?" Without apology, he dropped the phone and darted through a door that must have been connected to his laboratory.

Fenimore, left alone, practiced the climax to his plea. When the research man returned, he looked flushed but satisfied.

"False alarm," he said. "New man misread some results." He wiped his forehead with a handkerchief, which looked as if it was used often for this purpose. "Where were we?"

Fenimore concluded his request, careful to emphasize that it had absolutely nothing to do with research.

There was a pause before Applethorn said, "Doing any research these days, Fenimore?"

"No indeed." Fenimore shook his head vehemently. "Not my line, I'm afraid. I leave that end of medicine to the brainier fellows, like yourself."

"Come, come, Fenimore, it's never too late to begin. I find that most of my colleagues like to take a turn at it, at least once in their careers."

"Not this one." Fenimore spoke emphatically. "Practice takes up all my time." Jerboa, that was it, the small rodent Applethorn reminded him of.

"You're still on your own, I understand."

Fenimore nodded.

"And you have your own lab?"

"Uh, yes, but it's very small, strictly for simple blood tests and urinalyses."

Applethorn turned in his expensive Swedish swivel chair to gaze out the window. His view, unlike Fenimore's brick wall, was a lovely panorama of the city. After a moment's reflection, he turned back. "I'd like to help you, Fenimore . . ."

Over my dead body, translated Fenimore.

". . . but the work I'm involved in is so sensitive, and . . ."

. . . and your ego is so fragile that you're petrified I'll steal your work and publish first, Fenimore finished silently.

"... so near completion that I can't risk the slightest disruption. I'm sure you understand." The tic had subsided, and the eyes behind the dark-rimmed lenses held a triumphant gleam.

Fenimore rose. He was sure the little doctor had expected him to grovel and was disappointed when he merely thanked him for his time and left. As he came out of the inner office, the receptionist cast him a furtive glance and scurried in to receive her next command.

Later that evening, as Fenimore tidied up his desk for the night, he noticed a pink message slip that Mrs. Doyle had neglected to tell him about. From Polly Hardwick, the message read: "Found your pipe. All at ballet tonight. If you want to stop by for it, the maid will let you in." On the surface, hardly an urgent message. How was Mrs. Doyle to know that it was the one message he had been waiting for?

When Fenimore rang the bell, the maid answered the door. She was small, delicately made, her skin the color of amber. "They are at the ballet." She spoke with a faint Spanish accent.

"I know. I've come for my pipe."

"Oh, yes." Her smile was quick and bright. "I'll get it."

He followed her into the hall and waited. When she reappeared bearing his pipe, he resisted checking it for scratches. He shuffled and said haltingly, "I wonder if I might use your facilities. I've been making house calls all day, and ..."

"Of course, Doctor. Down the hall and to the left." She pointed the way to the powder room. "You may let yourself out." Another quick smile and she disappeared into the back recesses of the house.

He stood, holding his pipe, until her footsteps died away. Quickly and silently, he made his way up the broad central staircase.

There were three aspects to private-eyeing that Fenimore detested: snooping, lying, and eavesdropping. No matter how often he told himself that the end justified the means, whenever he indulged in these activities he felt guilty. Fortunately, like alcoholics whose desire for that first drink always outweighs the memory of their last hangover, Fenimore's desire to know the truth always outweighed his memory of the awkward consequences of his last snoop.

Pausing at the top of the stairs, he looked down the long polished hallway with doors leading off to rooms on either side. He plunged into the first room on his left. He didn't know exactly what he was looking for, but he felt certain that anything he learned about the weird sisters and their mother (Lady Macbeth?) would bring him closer to discovering how—and why—Sweet Grass had died.

This wasn't a bona fide search, of course. He had no warrant, no right to rummage through drawers or closets. Just a brief self-guided tour. And it must be brief. He would have to take in everything with the blink of an eye and sort out the details later.

The first room he entered was obviously the master bedroom. An elephantine four-poster, more than large enough to accommodate the two elder Hardwicks, dominated the center of the room. All the furniture was large and mahogany and reeked of antique. There were no traces of its inhabitants. No breath of perfume. No hint of aftershave. No evidence of recent habitation of any kind. The furnishings were so impersonal they might have just arrived from the showroom of a department store that afternoon. Either the owners had nothing to hide—or everything. The next room was even less revealing. A twin bed, a bureau, a dressing table. Not a single book, picture, or gewgaw to give the owner away. A guest room, no doubt, with no guest in residence. Perhaps it had been Bernice's room before she had moved to an apartment downtown. On the third try, he was rewarded. This room had obviously been recently occupied and abandoned in haste. It was a mess—bedspread rumpled, dressing table lamps left on, and books everywhere. In addition to

148

three bookcases crammed to capacity, there was a pile on the floor by the bed and two more untidy piles flowing around an easy chair by the window. Lydia had not exaggerated her passion for reading. The maid must have strict orders not to disturb this literary sanctuary. Fenimore went over to the chair and picked up a book that rested spread-eagle over one arm. *The Confidence Man* by Herman Melville. He remembered it vaguely—a dark, sardonic tale. He turned it over. In the margin, the reader had scribbled, "Are God and the devil one?" Carefully, he replaced it. The only other thing that caught his eye was a picture on the bureau—a single, silver-framed photograph of a man. Curious to see what sort of man would attract Lydia, he moved closer. Her brother, Ted.

The door to the next room was shut but not locked. Cautiously, he opened it. His heart stopped. A small, anxious-looking man stared back at him. It was a split second before he recognized his own reflection in a long mirror. Some cardboard cartons, a sewing machine, and an ironing board completed the furnishings of what was obviously a storeroom.

Fenimore closed the door and hurried to the last room at the end of the hall. It seemed to be a child's room. What child? Colored posters of Garfield and Winnie-the-Pooh hung on the walls. The window seat was covered with an assortment of teddy bears and dolls. A bunch of limp balloons drooped from a bed-post. A pair of pink bedroom slippers with bunny ears and faces peeked out from under the bed. On the windowsill was an aquarium. Smaller than the one downstairs, it was filled with tropical fish of many hues. Kitty. From her appearance, Fenimore had guessed her age to be about twenty, but her room was that of a child of ten. The fish peered back at him. He went over to the window seat and picked up a doll that was different from the others. Instead of painted plastic, it was made of cloth and stuffed with cotton. "Ouch!" He watched a spot of blood grow on the ball of his thumb. He sucked it dry and examined the doll again. More than a dozen pins were sticking into various parts of its body. Wrapped around its head was a wide rubber band with three pigeon feathers tucked inside it—a crude attempt at an Indian headdress. He carefully replaced the doll among the others.

When he first heard the Labrador bark, Fenimore thought he was barking at something outside. Then he heard the click of the dog's toenails on the polished wooden stairs. These were followed by quick, feminine footsteps. They were coming down the hall, when he emerged from the room.

"Uh, I couldn't find the bathroom. . . ."

Despite her diminutive size, the young woman managed to hold onto the Lab's collar as he strained to get at Fenimore. She said nothing as she followed him with the dog along the hall, down the stairs, and to the front door. As he looked back, the tiny woman was still hanging onto the big Lab. She had no bright smile of farewell for him. (And dogs never smile. They just bare their teeth.) He closed the door and wondered what she would tell her mistress.

As he drove home, Fenimore kept repeating to himself, "The end justifies the means. The end . . ." It was no use. He would never make a good communist.

CHAPTER 25

FRIDAY, NOVEMBER 4

"Good morning, Mr. Liska."

The gaunt man in the bed turned to look at Fenimore.

"How are you feeling?" Fenimore drew up a chair to the side of the bed and began taking his patient's pulse. It was rapid and his color was bad. "Is anything wrong?"

"They're going to catheterize me," the man whispered.

"What?"

"They were in this morning. Four doctors—all in white. They said it was the only thing to do. They've got me down for Monday morning at ten o'clock."

Fenimore went to the end of his bed and looked at the chart. There it was: "Catheterization. 11-7, 10:00 A.M."

"I don't want it, Doctor." His voice was high and peevish. "I'm eighty-six years old. I've lived my life. Why won't they let me be?"

"Don't worry." Fenimore came back to the bedside and patted his hand. "I'll take care of it." He completed his examination of Mr. Liska and hurried out.

"Larry?" He was calling from a pay phone in the lobby. The

151

hospital phones were too open and public for this type of private conversation. "Liska's going to be cathed Monday. . . . Yeah . . . Four of them ambushed him this morning. Bullied him to agree. We have to act fast. Meet me in the doctors' lounge. No, make it the coffee shop around the corner—less conspicuous—in ten minutes." As he left the hospital, Fenimore's mouth was set in a grim line. It was still a free country, by God. And if someone wanted to die in peace . . . Besides, there was a good chance Mr. Liska would be around longer without the cath.

Larry added some cream to his coffee and stirred. "It was all settled. He was going home tomorrow. His niece was coming for him."

"Well, it's all *un*settled," Fenimore said.

"They gave it one last try." Larry emptied half his cup in one gulp.

"Niece, you said?"

He nodded.

"You've met her?"

"Yes. She's in and out. Seems attached to the old boy—and it must be for real, 'cause he hasn't got a dime."

"What's her name?"

Larry concentrated. "Martinelli . . . Florence."

Fenimore jumped up, snapping his fingers.

"What the hell?" Larry stared at him.

"Do you have her number?"

"Whose?"

"Florence's?"

"She's over sixty years old, for God's sake."

"I'll see you later."

"So you don't need my valuable services after all?" Larry looked crushed.

"Sorry. Did I drag you away from something critical?"

"Yeah. A patient chewing me out for prescribing a drug that saved her life but gave her mild indigestion."

"Then you owe *me* one," said Fenimore.

"Who's your friend?" Larry whispered, catching sight of Officer Santino rising from a nearby table to join them.

Fenimore blushed. "Oh, a poor relation in need of a job."

It took Fenimore a while to reach the niece. After playing phone tag for a few hours, he finally caught up with her and explained the situation. Larry had been right. She *was* fond of her uncle and more than happy to cooperate.

"This is what I want you to do. . . ." Fenimore outlined his plan.

She followed his instructions.

A few minutes later, the phone rang in the offices of Aggressive Cardiology, Inc., Thomas, Gilbert, Morris, and Lazarus. After reciting the names of the doctors, the receptionist asked whom the caller wished to speak to. Florence picked the first name on the list.

"Dr. Thomas is performing an angioplasty right now."

"Then Dr. Gilbert?"

"She's on vacation."

"Morris?"

"It's his golf day."

"What about Lazarus?"

"I'll connect you."

There was a long pause while they raised Lazarus. When he came on the phone, his voice was brusk and businesslike. "How may I help you?"

Florence had barely begun when Dr. Lazarus jerked the receiver away from his ear as if it were hot or contaminated. He spoke abruptly into the mouthpiece. "Of course. We'll take care of it. We'll cancel the procedure immediately."

When Fenimore reported this news to Larry, Larry asked, "What did she say to him?"

"She said, 'Lay off my uncle or I'll see you in court.'"

"But that's just an empty threat. She couldn't back it up."

"Oh, I forgot to mention, she prefaced her remark by telling him where she was employed."

"Where?"

"The district attorney's office." Fenimore grinned. "Florence Martinelli is one of our assistant DAs."

"How the hell did you know that?"

"I read the papers, my dear boy, instead of watching television. It pays to keep abreast of politics, outside the hospital as well as in!"

It was noon when Fenimore finally got back to his office. He headed straight for the kitchen and returned with a sandwich, a slice of bologna slapped between two pieces of rye bread, slathered with mustard, which he proceeded to wash down with a Coke.

"How can you swallow that stuff and call yourself a doctor?" Mrs. Doyle shook her head and began her own tidy, balanced meal: pasta salad, yogurt, and a peach. Later she would make herself a cup of tea.

"Tastes differ, Doyle."

She pricked up her ears. "Doyle?" Was she back in his good graces? Maybe he had forgiven her for the spat with his new protégé over that slipper. Perhaps it was her cosmetic treatment. Dare she venture to ask him about the case? Nothing ventured, nothing gained. Doyle was a great one for homilies. "Anything new on that Indian girl?"

Still exhilarated from his morning's success with Mr. Liska, Fenimore was brought down to earth with a jolt. The Sweet Grass case had reached a stalemate.

"Do you suspect foul play?" Mrs. Doyle liked to dramatize things, the result of a steady diet of romance novels and TV daytime drama. (She taped her favorite soaps during the day and watched them when she got home at night.)

"Perhaps." Fenimore was preparing a pipe for his afternoon smoke.

She brightened.

Between puffs, he told her about the ER report and his interview with Applethorn. He watched her digest this information. From experience, he expected her to come up with some useful suggestions. If not now, at some future date. When he had finished, Mrs. Doyle went back to her typing and Fenimore opened the *Textbook of Cardiology*. Leafing through the index of this formidable tome (it weighed close to ten pounds), he came to "Digitalis Intoxication, 1024." He turned to that page.

"Although digitalis is one of the cornerstones of the treatment for heart failure, it is a two-edged sword. . . ." He continued to read to the end of the article, the gist of which was it is easy to upset the balance of digitalis in a patient. A few milligrams in excess can cause irregularities of the heartbeat—arrhythmias, fibrillation, syncope, and ultimately death. He knew all this but wanted to make sure that no new knowledge had been added during the past year that he had missed in the journals. He reached for the phone and dialed. "Raff?"

"I thought things were too quiet."

He told him of his findings in the ER report—Sweet Grass's death was probably caused by digitalis toxicity—and of his subsequent visit to Applethorn.

"Could she have accidentally taken an overdose?" Rafferty asked.

"Not likely. She'd been taking dig for years."

"On purpose, then?"

"Sure. And buried herself, Lenape style, afterward."

"She could have killed herself and left instructions for her brother to bury her."

"Then why would she go to the ER to be cured?"

"She might have had second thoughts after taking the overdose. What have I done . . . ?" Rafferty enjoyed playing the devil's advocate, especially with Fenimore.

Fenimore pondered this. "It's a possibility. But I've read her diary and she didn't strike me as the suicidal type. She was the kind of person who dealt directly with a problem. Attacked it head on. If she thought her marriage couldn't weather Ted's family, she would've broken it off and gone on. Not done away with herself."

"Is this opinion based on your seasoned experience in matters of the heart?"

Fenimore winced.

"Well, I hate to admit it," Rafferty admitted, "but some evidence has come in that supports your theory. When we searched Sweet Grass's apartment, we found the bottle of her most recently acquired supply of digoxin tablets."

"And?"

"There were a lot left. I'd say she hadn't taken more than she was supposed to."

"There's only one other possibility, then," Fenimore said.

"Right. Shall we review the suspects?" the homicide detective was eager to get down to the business of murder.

Fenimore obliged. "Her brother strongly disapproved of the marriage, and he would be the logical one to bury her in the traditional Lenape manner. He also is the only one who would benefit financially from her death—by the life insurance. On the other hand, the burial could have been arranged by someone else, to throw suspicion on Roaring Wings." Fenimore paused, thinking. "Then there are the Hardwicks. None of the family wholeheartedly supported the marriage. They were all against it for one reason or another. Even her roommate, Doris Bentley, wasn't totally enthusiastic."

"There are easier ways to prevent a marriage than by killing one of the partners-to-be," Rafferty put in.

"True," Fenimore said, "but I think they had all been tried—and failed."

"Who's your favorite suspect?" prodded Rafferty.

"I'd rather not say."

"Don't be coy."

"Seriously, it's just a hunch."

"Her brother? The groom's mother, father, sisters? Her roommate? Take your pick. More than one, if you like. But it would help to whittle the gang down a bit."

"Sorry, Raff."

A sigh, reminiscent of the steam engine, puffed down the wire. "Okay. You've helped us—coming up with the cause of death. But we need to see that ER report. You can probably get it faster than we can."

Rafferty was under the misapprehension that the medical community was one big friendly family in which all knowledge was joyfully shared. The days of getting a patient's report without a legal hassle were over. "I'll give it a try," Fenimore said. But he thought, What I'd really like to get hold of is Sweet Grass's blood serum sample, but I can't see Rafferty getting me a court order for that.

"By the way," Rafferty said suddenly, "you never submitted a report on that break-in the other night."

"I don't want to make an official complaint."

"Off the record, then. What did they want?"

"Two hoods were sent to rough me up as a warning. Their parting words were, 'Lay off the Lenape.'"

"Huh."

When Horatio arrived that afternoon, he was in good spirits. A truce seemed to have been reached between Fenimore's employees. The boy and the nurse spoke civilly to each other and went about their business. For this, Fenimore was extremely grateful. It had been hard for him to believe that Mrs. Doyle had turned into a bigoted monster overnight or that Horatio had maliciously copped one of his favorite slippers. The real cause of their peculiar behavior had dawned on him gradually: simple jealousy. His two staff members were jealous of his attentions. He supposed he should be flattered, but he would have preferred that they be indifferent to him and have a more harmonious office. He was grateful that today, at least, there was an armistice. Afraid of reigniting the contest, he waited until Mrs. Doyle disappeared to the lavatory before approaching Horatio with his proposal.

"Are you free tonight?"

The boy looked up from the file drawer.

"Could you meet me in the parking lot behind Franklin Hospital after dark?"

His eyes widened, but he nodded.

"Do you know anything about locks?"

He gave a slow grin.

"Fine. Bring the necessary tools."

"Right, Doc," he said cheerfully. His eyes slid over his employer. "You're not comin' with me like that."

Fenimore glanced down at his shirt, tie, pants, and oxfords.

"You and me are going shopping first," Horatio said.

"What are you two up to?" Mrs. Doyle was back.

Fenimore grabbed a folder from Horatio's stack. "Just checking a file." He carried it over to his desk and buried his nose in it. He hoped she hadn't noticed the name. It belonged to a patient who had died fifteen years ago.

Later that afternoon, Fenimore called Dr. Robinson. She was brisk and businesslike on the phone, but when he arrived at her office, which was only a few blocks away, she seemed glad to see him and genuinely disturbed by the death of her patient.

"It's a complete mystery to me, Dr. Fenimore. I saw her two weeks ago in connection with an episode of rapid heartbeat. But I wasn't particularly alarmed. She had had similar episodes before, and people who aren't suffering from tetralogy of Fallot often have episodes of this kind before something as stressful as a wedding. And I understand her situation was an especially stressful one."

"Yes, her future in-laws were, shall we say, difficult. Could you tell me what medication you prescribed?" If Dr. Robinson had prescribed digitalis in some other form—in addition to digoxin tablets—Sweet Grass could have taken it and disposed of the container, and a case could still be made for suicide.

"I prescribed twenty milligrams of Inderal two times a day and later upped it to three. I advised her to continue her regular regimen of digoxin."

Fenimore laid the suicide theory permanently to rest. "Exactly what I would have prescribed," he said. "There are factors involved here that have nothing to do with her previous medical history."

"Oh?" She had no knowledge of Fenimore's avocation.

"We're examining them carefully."

"Well, I hope you'll keep me informed."

"Of course."

Her slightly stiff professional manner relaxed. "I've been in practice more than ten years, but I still find it hard to accept a young person's death."

"Don't expect that to change. I've been in practice twice as long, and cases like this still rock me," he confessed. "I don't suppose you could let me have a copy of her records?"

"Not without permission from her next of kin." Her professional manner was back. "Do you know who that is?"

"Yes. Forget it."

"Very well." She walked him to the door.

"Thank you for your help."

"If I can do anything more, please call." She shook his hand warmly.

Unfortunately, there was nothing more she could do. She had closed one door in the investigation. It was up to him to open another.

Back at the office, Fenimore placed a call to Rafferty. Officer Santino was sipping yet another cup of tea in the outer office. In a low tone, Fenimore spoke to his friend. "Could you call off your watchdog tonight? I have a heavy date."

"Jennifer?"

"Who else?"

Ever the romantic, Rafferty agreed. "But he'll be back at his post first thing in the morning."

"Right." Gleefully, Fenimore went to relieve the watchdog of his duties.

CHAPTER 26

Friday Evening

Fenimore was no stranger to thrift shops. Whereas most of his colleagues headed for Brooks Brothers for their wardrobes, Fenimore preferred the more relaxed atmosphere of second-hand shops. He could afford better clothes, but it was a matter of principle. Why spend two hundred dollars for a jacket, when you could get a slightly used one for twenty? It was the same with his car. He got a bigger bang out of keeping his battered '89 Chevy alive than from buying a new BMW or a Lexus. (Jennifer called it "inverted snobbery.") One of Fenimore's favorite secondhand emporiums was the Salvation Army outlet on Market Street. Over the years, this store had supplied him with a variety of handsome, barely worn tweed jackets, raincoats, and overcoats. It had even supplied him with a cat. During one shopping expedition, while passing the bin provided for bundles of cast-off clothing, he had heard mewing inside. Peering in, he saw a pair of amber eyes peering back. Assuming she had been cast off along with some old clothes, he scooped her out, took her home, and christened her Sal, after his favorite haberdashery.

Even though Fenimore preferred secondhand clothing, his taste ran along more conservative lines than Horatio's. His employee preferred black leather to tweed, and sneakers to oxfords.

The two thrift shop volunteers watched their new customers suspiciously. The older man stood in front of the only full-length mirror, eyeing himself critically. He had removed all his clothes, except for his underwear. They lay in a heap on the floor of the broom closet that served as a dressing room. His younger companion kept pulling clothes off the racks and flinging them at him. Clad now in a dark blue turtleneck, jeans, and a black leather jacket, the older one seemed satisfied. But the younger one wasn't. He kept shaking his head, rummaging through the racks, and ransacking the shelves.

At one point, he brought Fenimore a cap with a visor. Fenimore put it on, visor in front. With a quick flip, Horatio turned it to the back. The transformation was amazing. Mrs. Henderson would never have called out "Doctor," to him now, in her hour of need. On the contrary, she would have probably crossed the street to avoid him.

Horatio looked at Fenimore's brown oxfords. "Shoe size?"

"Nine B."

He disappeared to the back of the store where assorted shoes lined the wall in pairs. He came back hugging three pairs of sneakers, one black and two brown. Fenimore sat on the floor (there were no chairs) and tried on each pair.

The younger volunteer stifled a giggle. The more seasoned one frowned at her.

The black pair was a perfect fit. He stood up.

"Cool." Horatio gave the outfit his highest recommendation.

Unaccountably pleased with himself, Fenimore gathered up the clothes he had worn when he came in and carried them over to the cash register.

"You're wearing those home?" Even the seasoned volunteer failed to hide her astonishment.

He nodded. Her helper murmured, "I'll get a bag for your things," and turned quickly away.

The vintage volunteer came out from behind the counter to check the price tags on the clothes he was buying. For the price of the sneakers, she asked him to raise one foot: $1.50 was scrawled across the sole with a magic marker.

Horatio was fooling with some trinkets in a dish on the counter. Finding one he liked—a heavy metal cross on a chain—he paid a dollar for it. Vastly overpriced, Fenimore thought. Funny how quickly your values changed in a thrift shop. Twenty dollars, the sale price for a shirt in a department store, seemed exorbitant after thumbing through a rack of shirts for $2.50 each.

When Fenimore had paid for his things, the assistant handed him a large shopping bag. Inside, his original clothes lay neatly folded on top of his shoes. Fenimore said, "Thank you very much. That was very kind—"

Horatio hustled him out before he could finish. On the sidewalk, he chastised him. "When you're dressed in rags like this, you can't talk like that."

"You mean, I can't say thank you?"

"That's right."

"What should I say?"

"Just grunt. Uh," Horatio grunted.

"Uh. Like that?"

"You gotta work on it. And your walk—it's terrible. You walk like some working dude. Watch me. Get behind me and do what I do."

Fenimore followed, observing Horatio. The boy hunched his shoulders, swung his hips slightly, and looked from side to side at regular intervals. About every half block, he glanced over his shoulder. Fenimore imitated him.

Horatio stopped and turned. "Now get in front of me."

Fenimore obeyed.

163

Horatio observed him. "Better. But it still needs work. You gotta act. Pretend you're in a movie and you're playing the part of the hood."

It worked. All of a sudden Fenimore felt relaxed. He slouched. He swung his body easily. "Uh," he grunted.

A banker type, rushing home from work, cast a nervous glance at him and quickened his pace. Horatio looked approvingly at Fenimore. "You'll do," he said.

It was too early to go to the hospital. Darkness was settling in, but there was still a streak of orange in the sky. Fenimore was hungry. "How 'bout a hamburger?"

Horatio nodded. They turned into Market Street and entered the first fast-food place. Fenimore chose a table toward the back and let Horatio do the ordering. He was still uneasy with his new persona in public. While they ate, Fenimore filled Horatio in on the job.

"The lab's on the fifth floor. There's a fire escape on the wall right outside. One of those metal ones with the hanging steps. You can go up and try the window, while I keep watch down below. If I see anyone coming, I'll hoot like an owl."

Horatio looked at him. "This is the city, Doc. Better coo like a pigeon."

"Right. Hoots are out."

"If someone comes, you beat it and I'll take care of myself," Horatio said.

Fenimore looked doubtful.

"What's so special about this serum, anyway?" He squeezed a blob of ketchup on his bun.

"We're trying to find out if this woman's death was caused by an overdose of digoxin."

"A druggie, huh?"

"No. It might have been an accident, or someone may have increased her dose deliberately."

164

Horatio stopped chewing and looked up.

"If only she'd stayed at the hospital and let them give her FAB."

"Like in fabulous?"

Fenimore shook his head. "It's a medicine, antigen binding fragments."

At this point, most people's eyes would have glazed over, but Horatio's were alert and curious. Fenimore felt obliged to explain the procedure to him. "FAB is an antibody that combines with the antigen or poison—in this case digoxin—in the body and inactivates it, making it harmless. We use antibodies all the time. Take tetanus, for example. If you step on a rusty nail, the doctor immediately prescribes a tetanus shot. That shot is full of antibodies that inactivate the tetanus and keep you from getting lockjaw. The same is true of rabies." That ought to satisfy him. Fenimore bent to his burger.

"Where do antibodies come from?"

Fenimore took a deep breath. "Antibodies are made in the bodies of animals and humans, to fight infections and poisons." Carefully, Fenimore explained how digoxin was injected into sheep, and the sheep, in turn, produced antibodies to fight against it. "These antibodies are then taken from the sheep's blood and purified. Then they're given to people who, for one reason or another, have too much digoxin in their systems."

"How do the sheep make the antibodies?"

"Whew!" Fenimore held up his hand. "You'd need a year's course in immunology to answer that one."

Reluctantly, Horatio returned to his food, and Fenimore was struck by a strange thought. Could he possibly be sitting across from a potential med student?

"Let's go." Horatio swallowed the last of his soda. He grabbed Fenimore's trash and his own and stuffed it all into the overflowing can.

As they were leaving, Fenimore caught sight of a tough-looking hood in a cap with the visor turned to the back, staring at him in the mirrored wall. He tensed, ready to fight, but Horatio grabbed his arm.

"Quit admiring yourself," he said and hurried him out the door.

Twilight was over. The street was dark except for the glow of streetlamps and neon signs in rainbow hues. They headed for the hospital. The parking lot was half empty. Fenimore glanced at his watch. Visiting hours had ended. The cars that remained must belong to the night staff and security personnel. They surveyed the back wall of the building. Lights glowed in a few windows, belonging to patients who were either TV addicts or suffering from pain or insomnia. But the row of four windows of the laboratory on the fifth floor was black. He pointed them out to Horatio.

The boy nodded, his eyes on the fire escape. It was metal all right, and it hung on the outside of the building. "How d'we get the ladder down?" Horatio asked.

"Shoot!" Fenimore's curses were not up to his new attire.

Horatio's eye fell on the shopping bag. Fenimore had set it down next to the Dumpster that partially shielded them from the parking lot. Quickly, he began rummaging through the bag. He pulled out the shirt and tie, and tied one shirtsleeve to one end of the tie. Reaching in again, he drew out the pants. He attached the end of one pant leg to the remaining shirtsleeve. When he had finished, he gave each knot a yank to test it. Stepping back, he gripped one end of the makeshift rope and hurled the other end at the fire escape. It grazed the bottom rung and fell to the ground. He tried again. Same thing.

Fenimore looked nervously around. No one in sight. He reached into the bag and came up with one of his shoes. Grabbing the rope, he attached the shoe to one end by a shoelace and heaved it at the fire escape. The rope slipped over the bottom rung, and stayed there, shoe dangling.

166

"Cool, Doc."

"It just needed some ballast."

Horatio had no time for the laws of physics. He lowered the shoe end of the rope until it met the end he was holding, then caught them together and slowly hauled down the steps. They had barely touched the ground when he began to scramble up them. Fenimore looked on, while the french fries he had eaten earlier congealed into a hard knot. When the boy reached the fifth floor, he turned and waved.

"Careful," Fenimore started to yell but caught himself. Silently, he watched Horatio test the window within his reach. It refused to budge. The boy took a penknife from his hip pocket, put it into the crack, and fiddled with the catch. Seconds later, the window rose and he climbed inside.

The next few minutes seemed interminable. Fenimore alternately looked over his shoulder and up at the window. Thoughts of losing his medical license and ruining the life of a minor filled his mind. By the time Horatio reappeared at the window, Fenimore was furnishing a twin cell for the two of them at Graterford State Prison. Horatio beckoned. Fortunately, Fenimore had remembered to keep his foot firmly planted on the bottom rung. Otherwise, he would have had to repeat the whole lassoing routine. He mounted the steps. Halfway up, he glanced down and saw the makeshift rope and shopping bag. What if a security guard came by and spotted them? Cautiously retracing his steps, he gathered up the rope. Careful to keep his foot on the bottom rung, he reached for the shopping bag. With an awkward lunge, he managed to throw the bag and the rope over the side of the Dumpster without letting go of the fire escape.

"What took so long?" Horatio helped him over the sill.

Fenimore explained.

"But what about your clothes?" Horatio was appalled at such waste.

"I'll pick them up on our way out."

167

Inside, the room was completely dark, and the only sounds were a series of scurries and squeaks. The smell of animal feces mingled with the usual chemical odors of a medical laboratory. Horatio, whose eyes had had time to adjust to the dark, led Fenimore through a maze of counters and tables covered with equipment and cages. He stopped abruptly before a tall, bulky object. Like a blind man, Fenimore ran his hands over it. The surface was smooth and cool, interrupted here and there by what felt like links of thick metal chain. As his hands moved on, there seemed to be more than one chain. Slowly regaining his vision, he discerned a huge refrigerator wrapped snugly in several layers of chain, fastened with padlocks ranging in size from a pocket watch to a large alarm clock.

At least they had found the right lab. Only Applethorn would indulge in such prehistoric security measures. His peculiar brand of paranoia could not be satisfied by an invisible electronic system. He needed something more tangible, something he could touch and see. Lucky for them. Horatio had had more experience with padlocks than with sophisticated electronic security systems.

Horatio had already begun to work on the most formidable of the locks. With a heartening click, it snapped open. He moved on to the next. Convinced that Horatio had the situation in hand, Fenimore passed the time by moseying around the laboratory. He examined equipment and peered into cages. The first two cages were filled with mice, each with an electrode attached to its side. In the next, he found a white rat making its way easily through a plastic maze. The last two cages—the source of the loudest squeaks—held half a dozen small monkeys. Engrossed in their quaint antics, he was startled by a loud hiss from Horatio. The monkeys, startled too, began rushing frantically around their cages, screeching and chattering.

"What's up?"

The boy was standing by the open window, looking down.

Fenimore joined him. What he saw was not reassuring. Two men, dressed in security officer uniforms, were staring up at the window. Fenimore's eyes flicked to the refrigerator. One chain remained intact. Horatio went back to work. When the chain clanked to the floor, Fenimore opened the door. Inside the lighted interior were racks of tubes in neat rows. Fenimore removed the top rack. By the light from the refrigerator he checked the dates on the labels. The top rack held the most recent samples. He began scanning the names.

Horatio returned to his post at the window. Careful to keep well out of sight, he watched the action below. There was only one man now. Could the other one be on his way up to the lab?

"Step on it, Doc," he whispered.

Farmer. Fedder. Field . . . Fenimore grabbed the tube. Taking an empty tube from his pocket, he removed the plastic cap. He took the cap off Applethorn's tube and tipped it, intending to transfer some of its contents into his tube. Nothing happened. He peered into the tube. Frozen solid. What he had assumed was a refrigerator was actually a freezer. Now what? He didn't dare steal the whole tube. Applethorn, or one of his assistants, would surely notice that it was missing and send up an alarm the next morning.

"What's the matter?"

He told him.

"No sweat," He came over and offered him a cigarette lighter. "You smoke?"

"Nah. But it's cool to carry one."

"Sorry. It won't help. The tube's plastic. It'll melt or burn. But I have an idea." He went over to one of the stainless steel sinks and turned on the hot water. He added some cold to make it lukewarm. If it was too hot, it might upset the delicate chemical balance of the blood serum. He let the stream of water play on the tube. It would take longer this way, but eventually it would defrost. The seconds ticked by. The only sounds were of the water running and the animals scurrying to and fro. Anxious, Horatio went back to the window.

The guard below seemed restless. He kept glancing up at the window. Horatio was afraid he might try to climb the fire escape. "Hurry, Doc!"

Gradually, frustratingly slowly, the serum finally dissolved. Fenimore poured a small amount into his tube, capped both tubes, returned Applethorn's to its place in the rack, and slipped the other into his pocket. He shut the freezer door. Horatio gave up his surveillance and came to help rebind the freezer. They were snapping the last padlock in place when they heard footsteps. They looked around. The room had three doors. Fenimore tried the one nearest him. Locked. It probably led to Applethorn's office. The second door opened. In the glow of Horatio's lighter, they made out a closet full of antique scientific equipment, battered science textbooks, and a skeleton. It was only a teaching chart, but the way it gleamed in the flickering flame . . . He closed that door and tried the third one. It opened into the hall. The footsteps grew louder. Horatio, who until now had been breathing down his neck, ran over to one of the cages and fiddled with the door. Before Fenimore realized what he was up to, there were monkeys everywhere—climbing, jumping, swinging, running, and chattering. Horatio shoved Fenimore out the door and down the hall, away from the footsteps.

They ran until they came to a fire door. Fenimore yanked it open. Horatio darted ahead of him, seeming hell-bent on going all the way to the ground floor. A hoarse command from Fenimore stopped him. "There may be a guard at the bottom. We'd better get out on another floor and lie low for a while."

Horatio retraced his steps, and they crept out a door marked with a big black 3. The corridor was empty. They turned the corner, and for once Fenimore was grateful for the party in the nurses' station. As they passed, no one even looked up. Fenimore and Horatio glanced longingly at the bank of elevators but kept going. If there was a guard at the bottom of the fire stairs, there would certainly be one at the bottom of the elevators. Fenimore peered into a room. One patient asleep, the other glued to the television screen. He looked in the next. Empty. He pulled Horatio in after him. There was only one bed, neatly made up, awaiting a new patient. The chances of one coming in at this hour were slim. He sat down on the edge of the bed. Horatio slumped in a chair. The only sound was their quick breathing. While Fenimore caught his breath, he had time to think about Horatio's daring deed. He would never have thought of letting the monkeys out. His scientific training was too strong. He had too much respect for the trials of academic research. Although the chances of Applethorn coming up with anything of scientific significance were doubtful, those monkeys may have gone through months, even years, of painstaking preparations. And it would take many more years to ready more monkeys for whatever experiments he had in mind. Horatio, of course, had no way of knowing this. And his act *had* helped them escape. He decided not to waste any more sympathy on Applethorn—or his monkeys.

"Did you hear that?" Horatio was sitting bolt upright.

Fenimore listened. A tiny scratching sound. "Must be a mouse."

"I thought hospitals were clean."

Fenimore didn't enlighten him on that point.

More scratching.

The noise led Fenimore to the adjoining bathroom. He stepped inside. Afraid to turn on the light, he stood still, listening. It seemed to be coming from the bathtub. He stared into its depths.

"*Cheetcheetcheetcheetcheet.*" The shrill cry sent him careening backward into Horatio. Without a thought about being seen or caught, they fled. There had been something primeval in that cry, something harking back to the jungle, before civilization, to an earlier, more primitive time. Fenimore was still shuddering when he reached the fire door. Horatio was right behind him. As he yanked it open, something skittered between their legs. Before dashing down the stairs, the monkey turned and jeered at them.

On the way home, Fenimore puzzled over how that monkey got from the fifth floor to the third ahead of them. There was only one answer. He must have taken the elevator.

CHAPTER 27

SATURDAY, NOVEMBER 5
(GUY FAWKES DAY)

Fenimore arrived a few minutes late at the office. He had gone to the hospital early, to see Mr. Liska off. His niece had arrived well in advance of the appointed time for his release, and they had spent an enjoyable half hour trading political jokes. Fenimore had come away with the impression that the assistant district attorney was a thoroughly nice woman and that he was leaving Mr. Liska in very good hands.

As he entered the office, Mrs. Doyle nodded toward the waiting room. Gracing an old, beat-up easy chair from the Salvation Army was Roaring Wings. He stood up and announced, "I've come for my sister."

"Come in." Fenimore waved him into his inner office.

When the man with the piercing eyes was seated on a straight-backed chair facing Fenimore, he said, "I came to you first, before the police. You are more courteous."

"Were they rough on you?" Fenimore's hackles rose.

Roaring Wings held up his hand. "I am used to them. Since I was a boy, when they would stop me in the street for no rea-

173

son, I learned how to handle them. Never fight fire with fire. Always fight fire with water."

"Water?"

"Courtesy. When you are polite to a policeman, he becomes all thumbs. It is like a bucket of cold water. Have you never noticed?"

"No," Fenimore said, "but it's an interesting theory. I'll try it next time I run a red light." He couldn't wait to share this theory with Rafferty.

Roaring Wings was silent, fixing Fenimore with his eyes.

Fenimore rearranged some things on his desk. Two pens, a saucer full of paper clips, and a prescription pad changed places.

"I stayed away three days," Roaring Wings spoke finally, "time enough for their investigations. Now I am here."

"I'll call Rafferty and tell him." He reached for the phone. Before dialing, he asked, "Er, have you made arrangements for the removal . . . ?"

"Not yet. Later."

Fenimore dialed. "Raff? I have Roaring Wings here. Ms. Field's brother. He would like to collect his sister's body." Fenimore nodded to Roaring Wings, to let him know that everything was okay. "I'll send him right over." He hung up. "You may collect the body anytime."

" 'Collect'?" Roaring Wings repeated, shaking his head. "The English language." He waved his hand, dismissing it. "For removing a loved one to her final resting place, the Lenape would say, *Lap a Gishelamukaong.*"

Fenimore waited for the translation.

" 'Once more to the Creator.' "

"Much more suitable." Fenimore nodded. "The English language has more appropriate words for such a move too. 'In my father's house there are many mansions,' " he quoted.

174

"Mansions?" Roaring Wings's tone was derisive.

"Well, in the newer version 'mansions' has been changed to 'rooms.'"

"Better." He nodded.

Fenimore disagreed. He thought the new version reduced heaven to a kind of seedy boardinghouse. But he refrained from saying so.

The phone rang. Fenimore let Mrs. Doyle answer it. Cupping her hand over the mouthpiece, she called, "It's young Hardwick."

Fenimore lifted the receiver. "Yes, Ted?" As he listened, he glanced warily at Roaring Wings. "Well, there may be some complications. Your fiancée's brother, Roaring Wings, is here with me now. He's come for Sweet Grass too."

Roaring Wings sat impassively.

After a minute, Fenimore said, "All right. I'll tell him," and replaced the receiver.

"What is it?"

"Ted Hardwick wants to talk to you about the burial. He asked if you would please wait. He's coming right over from the university."

Roaring Wings's eyes swiveled around the room once, before coming to rest on Fenimore. "She's my sister. I'm the next of kin. It is my right to bury her the way I choose." His eyes burned into Fenimore's. "He had his chance—and bungled it."

"There's no proof of that." He paused. "And Ted loved your sister. It's only common courtesy to talk to him. Perhaps you could have two ceremonies."

The Lenape made an unpleasant noise in the back of his throat, something between a laugh and a grunt.

For the first time, Fenimore disliked him. "Will you wait?"

He shrugged.

Fenimore rose, indicating that their discussion was over and he should return to the waiting room. He did. Fenimore busied himself with desk work and phone calls.

When Ted arrived, Fenimore offered the two men his office to confer in. Suddenly he felt the need of fresh air. He told Mrs. Doyle he was going for a short walk. Even though it was Guy Fawkes Day, he had no desire to witness any fireworks. When Officer Santino got up from his seat in the corner to follow him, Fenimore wanted to scream. There had been no more threats, no incidents of violence for several days. He must speak to Rafferty tonight about relieving Santino of his post. Surely there were more important duties for such an able policeman to attend to. When Fenimore returned, Roaring Wings had left but Ted was still there. From his dejected countenance, it was obvious who had won the contest.

"How'd it go?"

He looked up. "I let him have his way."

"Which was?"

"He'll take care of all the arrangements. But my family and I and a few friends are welcome to attend the ceremony."

"Damned generous," Fenimore snorted. "When is it?"

"Tomorrow at ten."

He showed his surprise.

"Well, it's already been six days, and . . ."

"Of course," Fenimore said hastily.

Ted got to his feet. "Thanks for your office." His face showed the strain of the recent interview. "I'll see you tomorrow, then?"

"Certainly."

He started for the door.

"And Ted . . ."

He turned.

Fenimore ached to restore Sweet Grass to him, alive and well. "You did the right thing," he said lamely.

Fenimore sat down and went through his mail. An envelope

from the lab. It had been delivered by messenger, as he had requested. The results of Sweet Grass's blood serum analysis. A
glance told him what he wanted to know. There was enough
digoxin in her blood to knock off two horses.

CHAPTER 28

SUNDAY, NOVEMBER 6, 10:00 A.M.

Fenimore arrived unaccompanied at the gate to Camp Lenape. After a lengthy discussion, he had managed to convince Rafferty that there was no immediate danger to his life or limb. Officer Santino had been given a new assignment, and Fenimore felt a lightness of being he hadn't experienced since he was a child and was allowed to walk to a friend's house two blocks away without his mother.

This morning the imposing iron gate stood open, and several cars were already parked along the drive. One was a glossy limousine the color of onyx. A man in a maroon chauffeur's livery lounged against the fender, smoking. Fenimore parked his car and nodded to the chauffeur. As he made his way up the drive, he noticed a small female figure ahead of him. She was moving slowly but determinedly. He caught up with her. It was Myra Henderson, manipulating an aluminum walker.

"Good morning," he greeted her.

She glanced up. "Oh, Doctor. I hate this damned thing!" She shook the shiny implement. "I can't wait to get back to my cane."

"It was brave of you to come. Shouldn't your chauffeur be helping you? Or at least have driven you nearer?"

"Charles? I told him not to. Can't stand anyone hanging on to me. And I didn't want to show up in that ostentatious car. Only keep the damned thing because Charles likes it. Only keep Charles because I can't drive myself with this damned arthritis." She shook the walker again, as if it were to blame. She would have toppled if Fenimore hadn't grabbed her.

The driveway seemed endless, creeping at this snail's pace. Fenimore was afraid the ceremony might begin without them. As if reading his thoughts, Mrs. Henderson said gruffly, "You go on. No use both of us being late." She had barely finished speaking when they rounded the bend and caught sight of the barn.

"We're almost there," he soothed, "and nothing's started yet. Look at all the people."

There were a number of people standing around in clusters eyeing each other awkwardly, the way people do at funerals when the only thing they have in common is the deceased. The Hardwick family formed the largest cluster. Polly spotted them right away and hurried toward them.

"Oh, you dear thing." Polly took the elderly woman's arm, leaving Fenimore to look after the walker. "Isn't she amazing?" she spoke to him over her shoulder. "Imagine coming all this way with a new hip and barely out of the hospital."

Fenimore agreed, looking around for a place to stash the walker. He finally settled on carrying it over one arm. As he approached, he sized up the other guests. The older ones were professorial types, probably colleagues of Sweet Grass and Ted from the university. The younger ones looked like students. Doris was there, looking frail and sad.

"I say, Fenimore," Ned hailed him in a hushed tone. "Another accident?" he nodded at the walker.

Fenimore flushed, remembering his former lie about falling down stairs. "No. I'm guarding it for Mrs. Henderson."

"You know Aunt Myra?"

The socially prominent were always surprised when someone outside their circle knew someone inside their circle. Not bothering to answer, Fenimore tucked the walker into a corner beside the door to the bungalow, just as Roaring Wings emerged in full ceremonial regalia. He was an impressive figure. The guests stared unabashedly. His fringed jacket, leggings, and moccasins were made of deer hide. But it was his headdress that caught the eye—a crest of deer hair dyed bright orange, set into bands of deer hide. The bands were decorated with intricate geometric designs in many colors, and when Roaring Wings turned to greet someone, Fenimore saw that his jacket bore a turtle, a sign of the Lenape clan. Later he would learn that this complex design had been painstakingly made out of porcupine quills that had been flattened between the teeth and then dyed many colors.

As Roaring Wings gravely greeted the guests, a group of Lenape people appeared around the corner of the house. Four of them were dressed like Roaring Wings, with a little less decoration. A fifth was a wrinkled old man, with no headdress, wearing a colorful cape of turkey feathers. Around his neck was suspended a drum. At a signal from Roaring Wings he began to beat the drum very softly. *Tum, tum, tum, tum.* The other four Lenape men disappeared behind the house and immediately reappeared bearing a litter high above their heads. *Tum, tum, tum, tum.*

Fenimore was just able to make out a slight figure, lying on the litter, knees bent. Slowly the procession wound past the bungalow, the barn, and out into the field. The guests looked at one another and hesitantly fell in behind.

The field was still crusty from the morning frost. The only sounds were the crunch of their feet and the drum. Fenimore stayed toward the rear of the procession to better observe the guests. Mrs. Henderson was being propelled along by Polly on one side and Ned on the other. At one point she cast him a desperate look, but there was little he could do. The three Hardwick sisters, Bernice, Lydia, and Kitty, walked together, looking suitably depressed. Ted walked behind them, in a daze. Roaring Wings came last, carrying a cloth sack.

Fenimore looked at the vast expanse of field and sky and tried to forget why he was there.

Tum, tum, tum, tum.

When they came to the far edge of the field, the drumming stopped. The silence was startling. The procession halted automatically. At the edge of the field there was a deep hole, lined with bark and surrounded by mounds of earth. With deliberate gentleness, the four men lowered the litter and laid it on the ground beside the grave.

Fenimore had decided early on that the only way to get through funerals was to think about anything but the deceased or the bereaved. He forced his mind away from Sweet Grass; away from Ted. Instead, he thought of that other grave—in the city burial ground—and tried to determine which of the assembled guests would have been capable of digging such a large hole and lifting a body into it. Ned and Polly would have no trouble, with their broad shoulders and strong backs. Bernice, although shorter than her parents, had a solid frame that was more muscle than fat. Lydia, although of a more delicate build, might, under the right circumstances and with the necessary amount of adrenaline, manage it. Kitty, on the other hand, was too slight—not only of figure but also of intellect. He found it hard to believe that her childish mind could devise a murder scheme of any complexity, let alone carry it out. Of course, she could have had help. Then there was Doris. Standing on the other side of the grave, a handkerchief to her face, she was about the same build as Lydia. But she had been in the hospital—the perfect alibi. But Sweet Grass had visited her the afternoon she died. Doris was the last person to see her alive, before she went to the emergency room. Could she have slipped her something fatal during her bedside visit? As her roommate, she knew her medical history and was familiar with her medicines. An accomplice could have buried the body. But what was the motive? Temporary insanity because she couldn't have children, and Sweet Grass could? Fantasy material, Fenimore. You might as well suspect Myra Henderson. She too was in the hospital. But not until the day after Sweet Grass died. She had attended the picnic. She also had Charles. He had seen his muscles swelling under his chauffeur's uniform. Carrying out such a burial would be child's play for him. But for what motive? Who knew what network of subterranean passions motivated members of old Philadelphia society? No one but the members themselves. And their lips were sealed, as in any exclusive fraternity or club.

And any one of them could have imitated the Lenape method of burial. This information was readily available in a number of historical societies.

One of the first rules of detecting, Fenimore believed, was to suspect everyone, especially the least obvious. His doctrine was the exact opposite of that of his friend Rafferty, who believed that in 99 percent of cases the most obvious suspect turned out to be the right one. It was that other 1 percent that Fenimore worried about.

One of the Lenape pallbearers adjusted the litter in preparation for lowering it into the grave. For the first time Fenimore saw Sweet Grass clearly. Her features were small and delicately formed. Her skin was the shade of a certain autumn leaf, pale brown with an underlying hint of coral. (No trace of cyanosis there.) Each cheek had been decorated with a deep red spot. She lay on her side, knees drawn up, like a sleeping child. Her dark hair was arranged in a plait that curved down over one shoulder. Her hands were hidden in the folds of her long white dress. The dress was embroidered with cream oval shells that made the embroidery on Roaring Wings's jacket seem almost coarse. On her feet were moccasins no bigger than a child's.

Fenimore scanned the group for Ted. He was standing a little apart, his eyes fixed on Sweet Grass. A shadow passed over her face. Fenimore looked up. A hawk. He watched it glide, borne solely by the wind, to another part of the field.

Tum, tum, tum, tum.

Roaring Wings raised his hand, and the drummer was still. He took his place at the head of the grave and began to speak—or rather, to chant, in Algonquian, the original Lenni-Lenape tongue. The words meant nothing to Fenimore, but they had a lilt to them, like poetry, and were easy on the ear. The chanting lasted only a few minutes, not long enough for even the most impatient guest to grow restless. When he had finished, he gave a terse command to the four bearers, and they took their places at the four corners of the litter. With the same deliberate care they had demonstrated before, they lowered it into the grave.

Roaring Wings bent down and carefully arranged Sweet Grass. He placed her in a flexed position, knees drawn up, her back resting against the inside wall of the grave. He adjusted her head so her chin rested on her knees. Of course, she was facing east. He opened the cloth sack he had brought with him. From it he drew a shawl decorated with beads and shells, a round loaf of bread, and the wooden shuttle that had been found in her first grave. Carefully, he wrapped the shawl around her entire body, to prevent the earth from touching her. Then he lay the bread at her feet and placed the shuttle in her right hand.

For the first time, Fenimore noticed two piles next to the mounds of earth beside the grave—one of stones, the other of ashes. In a whisper, he asked the Lenape woman next to him about them. She told him that the stones were collected from the Wisamek River by the Lenapes to keep the wolves away. (He wondered when a wolf had last been sighted in south Jersey.) The ashes were brought from the hearths of the Lenapes to make the deceased feel at home. As she finished speaking, Roaring Wings and the four bearers began to line the grave with the stones. When that was done, each took a handful of ashes and threw them in the grave. When there was only one handful left, Roaring Wings placed it in Ted's hand. The young man moved forward as if in a trance. The other men stepped aside to make room for him. Blindly, he hurled the ashes. They missed the grave and soiled the skirt of a woman standing on the other side. With a sob, which seemed to come from the bottom of a well, he turned and ran across the field.

Fenimore paid close attention to the faces of the Hardwick family members. Polly's wore a look of anguish as she moved to follow her son. Ned's remained impassive as he placed a restraining hand on his wife's arm. The expressions of the three sisters ranged from concerned (Bernice), to embarrassed (Lydia), to surprised (Kitty). Fenimore switched his gaze back to Roaring Wings. His face wore the same expression of controlled gravity it had worn since the ceremony had begun.

Tum, tum, tum, tum.

At a sign from Roaring Wings, the oddly assorted group began the return pilgrimage across the field. The drummer was in the lead, closely followed by the litter bearers. This time the litter was borne by one man, and the ground, no longer frost covered, made no sound under their feet.

Fenimore, like Lot's wife, felt compelled to look back. One litter bearer had remained behind to fill in the grave. Fenimore's eyes swept the field and the woods edging it. No sign of Ted. The only sign of life were two buzzards, hovering high above the grave, vainly awaiting their chance.

CHAPTER 29

LATER SUNDAY MORNING

Roaring Wings had arranged, on very short notice, to serve refreshments to the funeral guests. The interior of the bungalow was as attractive and immaculate as Fenimore remembered it. But today it seemed smaller, because it was filled with extra tables and chairs and some flower arrangements. The tables consisted of a long picnic table and several card tables. The chairs were an unmatched hodgepodge, probably collected from various kitchens and porches of friends by pickup truck earlier that morning. The flowers, Fenimore learned, were from mutual friends of Ted and Sweet Grass who, for one reason or another, could not attend. It was not the Lenape custom to send flowers to a funeral or to bring them to a grave—or to mark the grave in any way, the Lenape woman confided to Fenimore. They simply planted grass on top and kept it neatly trimmed.

The picnic table had been placed in the center of the room and was covered with a brightly woven cloth. Gracing it were two electric pots, one containing hot water for tea, the other containing coffee. They were surrounded by an assortment of cups and saucers, containers of sugar and cream, and a pile of plastic spoons. The cookies, resting on paper plates, were standard supermarket fare.

As the room filled with people, its size diminished accordingly. Conversation came uneasily for everyone but the Hardwicks. Adroitly balancing their cups, they made small talk with the ease of Olympic champions. (And why not? They, like those athletes, had been trained in the art since birth.) All except Ted, who was still missing.

As the somber mood of the ceremony began to wear off, the guests became more animated. They admired the woven wall hangings, the plants, and the pottery. Fenimore spotted Doris Bentley and Myra Henderson in conversation near the window. He joined them. Doris's face bore signs of weeping. Mrs. Henderson's attempt at a spritely greeting fell flat, and she succeeded only in looking downcast. Fenimore drew their attention to the string of dried herbs hanging above the window frame. Doris, it turned out, was a gourmet cook and could identify most of them.

"Rosemary, oregano, thyme, parsley, but . . . I'm not sure about that one."

Fenimore recognized the leaves immediately. He had seen them often enough on his trips to the herb garden at PSPS. "Foxglove," he said.

Roaring Wings appeared in their midst, offering a plate of cookies.

"Delicious tea," Mrs. Henderson said. "May I ask the brand?"

"It's a blend of herbs. I grow them myself."

Fenimore chewed his cookie thoughtfully. "Would this be the tea you served Sweet Grass?"

All three looked at him, surprised that he would bring up her name in such an abrupt manner. Fenimore had more important things on his mind than social protocol as he waited for his answer.

"Yes. It was her favorite."

Fenimore watched him move away to serve his other guests. "Doctor?" Mrs. Henderson jogged his attention back to her. "I wonder if you would mind getting me another cup of tea."

"Of course." He took her cup and started for the table.

"Sugar and lemon," she called after him.

Observing the volume of tea being consumed around him, Fenimore had a pang of guilt over Officer Santino. He would have enjoyed this affair immensely.

The Hardwick family members were beginning to take their leave. Roaring Wings was giving each of them a stiff handshake. Polly caught sight of Fenimore and drew him aside. She spoke in a low tone, "I'm worried about Ted. He hasn't come in yet, and Ned has to get back to the hospital. I hate to ask, but could you stay until he comes back and give him a ride home with you?"

"Certainly. I was planning to hang around awhile anyway. Don't worry."

She gave him a grateful smile and, bending slightly (she really was a large woman), pecked his cheek.

When he returned with the tea, Mrs. Henderson was saying, "And do you plan to keep the apartment?"

"Oh, yes," Doris answered. "It was mine to begin with. Sweet Grass was only staying with me temporarily, until she . . ." she faltered.

"Yes, of course." The elderly woman took the tea from Fenimore and thanked him.

After a moment, Fenimore excused himself. "I'm going to look for Ted."

They nodded sympathetically as he left.

The cold air and open sweep of sky were welcome after the stuffy, overcrowded room. Roaring Wings's bungalow was not built for major social gatherings. He had no doubt where he would find Ted. He strode across the field. The smell of smoke reached him before he saw the fire. It was small and flickered low over the grave. This custom was probably left over from a

187

time when it was necessary to protect the dead from wild animals (those wolves). The litter bearer who had remained behind to fill in the grave had probably made the fire. Ted was kneeling with his back to him. Fenimore made no attempt to quiet his footsteps. He wanted to give him plenty of notice. The young man turned. When he saw who it was, he looked relieved. "I'm ready," he said. And when he stood up, he seemed composed.

"Fine. Your parents had to leave. I'll drive you home."

"Thanks."

They didn't speak again until they reached the house. Fenimore handed Ted his keys. "Go wait in the car. I'll say your good-byes."

With a grateful look, Ted took the keys and went on.

The room, now nearly empty, had almost returned to its normal size. Doris and Mrs. Henderson were at the door, saying good-bye to Roaring Wings. Two young women, probably students of Sweet Grass, stood behind them, waiting their turn. Everyone else had gone. Fenimore took his place behind the students. When his turn came, he said sincerely, "It was a beautiful ceremony."

Roaring Wings said, "It is over one thousand years old."

"There is no need to change some things." Fenimore was thinking of the burial service in his own church and how it had been changed beyond recognition.

The Lenape looked at Fenimore with new respect. "That's true," he said. "Of course we omitted the feasting and the dancing. I didn't think the Hardwicks . . ." He spread his hands. "We'll have that another time, for our own people."

"That was wise." Fenimore started to leave but turned back. "By the way, what herbs did you use in that tea?"

He raised his eyebrows. "Would you like the recipe?"

"Very much."

He went over to the desk. While he was rummaging in a

drawer for paper and pen, Fenimore reached up and tore a few leaves of foxglove from the string of herbs above the window. He slipped them into his breast pocket, just as Roaring Wings turned and handed him the slip of paper with the recipe.

Fenimore folded it carefully and slid it into his breast pocket next to the leaves.

"I'll walk you to your car." Roaring Wings had suddenly become the congenial host, after Fenimore had showed an interest in his tea.

"No." Fenimore had no desire to bring fiancé and brother together again. "You have all this to clean up." He waved at the collection of dirty cups and saucers and crumpled paper napkins.

The Lenape looked at the debris and made a face, the first really human thing Fenimore had seen him do.

As Fenimore walked to the car, he took the recipe from his pocket. As he had expected, foxglove was one of the ingredients.

CHAPTER 30

Fenimore awoke depressed. It was more than a week since Sweet Grass's body had been found. Now it was twice buried, and he was no nearer a solution. After downing his usual dose of "swill," he decided to return to the original burial site, hoping that something significant would come to him. It was one of those freakish warm days that sometimes crop up in November, bringing fog. The street was a blank. The only cars visible were those parked directly in front of the house. The occasional passing car, headlights on full, floated briefly into view and was swallowed up again. Walking east on Walnut toward the river, he felt like the last man on earth after the bomb.

Instead of red, the traffic light glowed a hazy pink. When it glowed a hazy green, he crossed. At Watts Street, he turned in. The cobblestones were slippery and led to nothing but a pocket of fog. The only tangible thing in the small space was the hard surface under his feet. As he stood there, something fluttered to the ground nearby. He could barely make out the familiar shape. He took a step toward it. With a rush of wings, it took off. The incident triggered his memory of another pigeon. Another day. And a gray van with the unusual license tag SAL123.

He slipped and slid on the cobblestones. Crossed Broad before the light changed. And fumbled with his keys on the front step. As soon as he got inside, he called Rafferty.

"It's a little early, even for you—"

Fenimore was in no mood for their usual banter.

Yes, Rafferty could get him the information from Harrisburg. Did Fenimore want to hold, or call back?

Hold. In a few minutes, Fenimore was jotting down: Budget Rent-a-Car, 614 N. Broad St., Phone: 555-6667. Henry Wendkos, manager. "Thanks." He slammed down the receiver. On an impulse, he decided to don the thrift shop togs he had recently bought.

Mr. Wendkos was a wisp of a man in a shiny blue suit, pink shirt, and wild tie (pink water lilies floating on a maroon pond). When Fenimore came in, the manager was nursing a paper cup of coffee large enough to keep three Eagle linebackers awake.

"Yeah, that's one of my vans."

"Would you have a record of who rented it on October 29th?"

"I might." His eyes flicked over Fenimore.

Whoops. Wrong dress code. "Uh, I'm an undercover man for Detective Rafferty, Homicide Division."

The man tipped the white cup to his mouth. Fenimore watched his Adam's apple jerk up and down. "What's his number?"

Had he worn his customary suit and tie, he never would have had this trouble. Silently he cursed Horatio and gave the man Rafferty's number.

While the man was making the call, Fenimore glanced around the office. Two yellow vinyl-covered chairs, repaired here and there with utility tape, a coffee table with a smeary plastic top, a pile of dog-eared *Popular Mechanics,* and an ashtray the size of a Frisbee with a nude woman decorating the bottom. When you looked at her a certain way, she swiveled her hips and winked at you. Rafferty's cantankerous early morning squawk drew his attention back to the phone. Mr. Wendkos covered the mouthpiece and looked at Fenimore. "Name?"

He told him.

"Fenimore," the man said into the phone.

More squawks. But they must have contained an affirmative somewhere, because the man hung up and went over to his filing cabinet. "My girl usually does this," he said over his shoulder, "but she's always late."

To convey his sympathy for all employers with delinquent employees, Fenimore tried out one of Horatio's grunts, "Uh." It seemed to do the trick.

"Here it is." He pulled three copies of a form, one white, one yellow, one pink, from a folder and squinted at the name. Carbon copies like that would soon be as obsolete as his father's old medical apparatus, Fenimore noted. "I remember this one," Wendkos said. "It was that homeless fellow from across the street." He nodded at a ragged little park on the other side of Broad street. "Normally I wouldn't have rented it to him. But he paid cash, and these days you can't be too picky." He referred gloomily to the state of the economy.

Fenimore saw "CASH" scrawled across the bottom of the top sheet but was unable to read anything else. "What's his name?"

"It says here Joe Smith." He shrugged.

"What's he look like?"

"Tall. Skinny. Long hair. Dirty beard. Dirty brown sweatshirt. Black jeans. Sneaks." Noticing Fenimore's expression, he laughed. "Don't worry, they never change their clothes." He took a big slug of coffee. "He'll be easy to spot. As you go into the park, he's always on the first bench to the right."

Fenimore dropped a ten-dollar bill on his desk. "Thanks for your trouble."

"No trouble." He quickly pocketed the ten.

Fenimore crossed Broad Street at the light and entered the park. The first bench on the right was empty. But the second one to the left was occupied. Wrapped in several layers of sweaters, blankets, and scarves, it was impossible to determine the figure's real size, shape, or sex. From the shoes he surmised it was female. He took a seat on a bench nearby and stared at a bed of ivy full of discarded beer cans, fast-food cartons, and empty cigarette packs. He glanced again at the figure on the next bench. Two shopping bags bulged at her feet. Another rested on the bench against her side. From the corner of his eye he watched her reach under the filthy yellow blanket, which served as a shawl, and draw out a small paper bag. She sprinkled some of its contents on the ground. Popcorn. From nowhere, pigeons came, surrounding her feet.

"Excuse me, ma'am." Even though he was several yards away, the stench of stale beer and urine was overpowering. "Where is the fellow who usually sits over there?" He pointed to the bench on the right.

The woman looked at him but seemed to be focused on something inside her head.

"Do you know where he went?" The popcorn was all gone. Two pigeons continued to peck hopefully around her feet. He could see a bare toe poking out of a hole in one of her shoes.

He tried again. "The fella over there. Have you seen him lately?"

She looked at the empty bench and shook her head.

"Where did he go?"

She shrugged.

Who invented the shrug? Some caveman? Or cavewoman?

When her husband asked her what she thought of his latest cave painting, had she shrugged? And the age of noncommunication was launched?

"How long has he been gone?"

Another shrug.

"A day, a month, a year?" If she shrugged again, he'd shake her.

She produced more popcorn from under the layers of blanket and scattered it. More pigeons came. (Or were they the same ones?)

Beaten, he stood up and turned to leave.

"About a week."

He swiveled around.

"He was sick." She pointed to the flagstones in front of the empty bench. He looked down and saw stains. They could have been vomit. "I looked for a cop. But there's never one when you want 'em."

"What happened then?"

"He conked out."

"For how long?"

The pigeons absorbed all her attention.

"How long was he out?" Please, lady, he prayed.

" 'Til the cops came."

"And when was that?"

"I dunno. I don't have no watch." She spat on the flagstones, and the pigeons scattered.

"Did they take him away?"

She nodded, peeking into her little paper bag. Finding it empty, she crumpled it and tossed it under the bench.

"Did you know he rented a car?"

She stared. "He didn't have no car."

"Sorry. I meant a van. A gray van."

"He never had one."

"Not even for a day?"

She shook her head.

He tried a different tack. "Did he ever go over there?" He pointed across the street to the pink fluorescent sign blinking BUDGET RENT-A-CAR in big block letters.

"Sure."

"He did?"

"The manager useta buy him coffee." Her tone was resentful. "Sometimes he'd give me some." She groped in one of her shopping bags and pulled out a filthy plastic cup.

Fenimore took the hint. Before heading for the police station, he stopped at the nearest fast-food place. He ordered a sausage burger, a large coffee with sugar and cream, and a large bag of popcorn. When he delivered these items to the woman on the bench, she accepted them as her due.

To gain the cooperation of the sergeant at the Ninth Precinct, Fenimore was once again forced to call on Rafferty's services. This time the detective's ire rose to a fever pitch. Nonetheless, Fenimore came away with the following report:

> On the evening of Saturday, October 29, a homeless man was found unconscious in Randolph Park and taken to Franklin Hospital. Severe food poisoning and MVA were diagnosed. He died a few hours later. There was no identification and no inquiries were made about him. He was buried in the pauper's cemetery with full religious rites performed by Father O'Hare, a local priest who volunteers for such services.

Fenimore considered this information carefully, before calling Rafferty from a pay phone. The voice that greeted him was not reassuring. He persevered, requesting an exhumation of Joe Smith, an autopsy of Joe Smith, and that a copy of the report on Joe Smith be sent to him as soon as possible.

"You'd better be on to something, Fenimore. These routines you're asking for aren't cheap." (His department was economizing that month.)

"I assure you, this information is vital to the solution of the case," he answered, adopting his most formal manner.

"I've let you have a pretty free hand, Fenimore, because the Hardwicks are such a prominent family," Rafferty said. "But we've already put more time and money into this case than usual."

"Oh? And what line of inquiry are you planning to pursue?"

"The obvious one, the one we coarse policemen usually blunder along with and come up with the right solution ninety-nine percent of the time."

"And who's your obvious suspect this time?"

"The brother, of course. He's the beneficiary and the only one who would know about that burial ground."

"I knew about it."

"Should we make you a suspect?"

"Give me another twenty-four hours, Raff, and I'll prove this case falls into that one percent category."

Rafferty acquiesced with a grunt.

On the way home, Fenimore saw a pompous medical colleague approaching. Seeing no way out, he paused to greet him. The man, visibly startled, hurried on. At first, Fenimore was offended. Then, remembering his attire, he grinned. This new identity would come in handy. Think of all the boring encounters he could avoid. As he let himself into his vestibule, he was whistling.

"That you, Doctor?" Mrs. Doyle called out.

"I'll be there in a minute." He ducked up the front stairs to his bedroom to change. Perhaps some day he'd become adept enough to change in a phone booth.

CHAPTER 31

MONDAY AFTERNOON

"D*umdeedumdeedum*," Fenimore hummed as he worked the mortar and pestle that had once belonged to his grandfather. He had known it would come in handy someday. That's why he hung on to these old things that people were always nagging him to get rid of. His grandfather had been a strong believer in the efficacy of herbal cures.

The herb that Fenimore was busily pulverizing was foxglove, the leaves he had snitched from Roaring Wings's bungalow. The Lenape's recipe for tea had also called for marjoram, anise, and cinnamon, all of which his spice cabinet supplied.

He glared at the uncooperative kettle as Mrs. Doyle came in to make herself a cup of tea. "Boil, damn it!"

"Now, Doctor, a watched kettle . . ."

Damn the woman and her homilies. He turned his back on the kettle. It immediately began to boil.

Pouring the steaming liquid over his mixture of herbs and spices, he stirred and sniffed with pleasure. Mrs. Doyle watched him take a sip. "Delicious," he pronounced. "Want some?"

"No, thanks. I'll take a beer, though." She had noticed several bottles on the back of the refrigerator door. Beer was the only exception Mrs. Doyle made to her healthful diet.

Fenimore tut-tutted primly.

"Spoilsport." She dunked her tea bag. Suddenly she looked up. "What a pity Officer Santini isn't here to sample your brew. Shall I call him?"

Surprised by the vehemence of the doctor's negative response, she returned to her desk to tackle the latest accumulation of Medicare forms.

He made another cup of tea, exactly like the first, and, with infinite care, poured an ounce into a plastic tube. He sealed it, labeled it, and gave it to Mrs. Doyle. "Call the lab and have them pick it up—express. And tell them to get the report to me today."

"Aye, aye, sir." Unable to hide her curiosity, she asked, "Testing for arsenic?"

"No. Glycosides."

She knew she shouldn't ask. "What's a glycoside?"

Her reward was exactly what she had feared—an in-depth lecture on the chemistry of plants. When he had finished, she had learned that a glycoside was a compound that, when mixed with water, usually gives off sugar. Different plants contain different types of glycosides. She called the lab.

When the report came back a few hours later, Fenimore grabbed it and disappeared with it into his inner office.

Preparing to leave for the day, Mrs. Doyle was stopped in her tracks by an explosion.

"That lets him out!"

"Did you say something, Doctor?"

He burst from his office, waving the lab report. "Look at this, Doyle." He showed her the results of some tests that were totally incomprehensible to her. "This may let Roaring Wings off the hook."

"Of course." She nodded politely.

"He made his tea from foxglove, *Digitalis purpurea,* which is the usual kind of dig grown in this country, and the glycosides it produces are dig*itoxin* glycosides. But the glycosides found in Sweet Grass's blood serum were different—they were dig*oxin* glycosides, the same kind found in her medicine. Digoxin is produced from a species of digitalis rarely found in this country: *Digitalis lanata.* It has white flowers instead of purple and is found mostly in the Balkans. There were no dig*itoxin* glyco-sides present in her serum sample, only dig*oxin* glycosides." He waited for her congratulations.

"Brilliant, Doctor."

He smiled with satisfaction. "Yes, actually, it is. I've got to call Raff." He went back to his inner office to make the call.

Mrs. Doyle stood beside her desk with her coat on, thinking. She was afraid this case was beyond her. She couldn't seem to get hold of it. Usually, by now, she would have come up with some helpful suggestions. The best she could do was hang around and offer moral support. She decided to stay until Fenimore had finished with Rafferty. She sat down at her desk, pretending to attend to some last-minute details. She was glad she did. When he came out, his ebullient mood had vanished.

"What did he say?"

" 'You're a busy little bee, Fenimore,' " he quoted Rafferty. " 'First you present us with another body. Then you throw doubt on our prime suspect. Why don't you behave like a normal doc-tor and play golf!' "

CHAPTER 32

MONDAY EVENING

Fenimore hurried down Walnut Street to Nicholson's Books. It was gratifying, he thought, after reneging on two dinner invitations, that the Nicholsons still wanted to see him. They must value his company, he decided, because he shared their interest in history and old books. Jennifer, he hoped, valued him for something more. She did not discourage easily, he knew. Her willingness to put up with his idiosyncrasies over the past two years without any commitment from him had convinced him of this. When it came to important things, Jennifer could be very patient. She was in no hurry to marry; she enjoyed her work and had her father to look after. And she wasn't anxious to start a family early. Her mother had been forty-one when Jennifer was born, and she hadn't turned out too bad, she had told him wryly. Well, at least her father liked her, she assured him.

Father and daughter shared an apartment over their bookstore. It was one of the last independent bookstores in Philadelphia. The front of the store was devoted to contemporary stock, best-sellers, and so on, but the rabbit warren of smaller rooms in the back housed a collection of rare books that was sought out by scholars, young and old. Professors and students came there in search of books that were either unavailable in the libraries or too expensive for their pocketbooks. Sometimes these scholars turned Nicholson's Books into a research library. But the bookseller and his daughter overlooked how often they came and how long they stayed, without making a purchase. Mr. Nicholson was a scholar in his own right but without the benefit of degrees. His knowledge of classical and medieval history was legend, and it had been acquired not at a university but by devouring and remembering the contents of the books that passed through his store. And, unlike certain university scholars, he was happy to share his knowledge with anyone who happened to wander in.

Fenimore followed Jennifer up the narrow stairs, inhaling the delicious cooking aromas filtering down from above. The spaciousness of the apartment always took him by surprise. Built in the twenties, it had high ceilings and wide windows, carved cornices and fine moldings. His favorite room was the library, where they always gathered before and after dinner. This was where Jennifer deposited him now, among the glass-fronted bookcases and stained-glass reading lamps, in the squashy easy chair that was always reserved for him. When Mr. Nicholson handed him a martini made exactly to his specifications, the stresses and strains of a doctor/detective's life melted away, and he basked in this little bit of heaven.

After their initial greeting, the doctor and bookman shared a few minutes of contented silence, sipping their drinks, while Jennifer finished whatever she was doing in the kitchen. When she rejoined them, with a glass of Chablis, Fenimore thought she looked especially well. Her fair skin and dark hair made a striking contrast, and her face was flushed, as if with excitement (at seeing him, or from the heat of the stove she had probably been slaving over all day?).

"We're having a cold dinner tonight," she said. "We were very busy in the store today and I didn't have time to cook."

"Where are all those enticing smells coming from, then?" asked Fenimore.

"From the apartment above. We rented it to a bachelor who's a gourmet cook." Fenimore didn't know which he resented more, the fact of the bachelor living in such close proximity to Jennifer, or the fact that he wasn't going to have the chance to sample his cooking. He must have looked crestfallen, because Jennifer said quickly, "Never mind. We're having shrimp salad and corn muffins. I defrosted a batch. And for dessert, apple cobbler with whipped cream."

Fenimore relaxed. All three dishes were favorites of his. He'd worry about the bachelor later.

Unable to contain himself any longer, Mr. Nicholson said, "I've made a few acquisitions since you were here last, Doctor."

Fenimore turned reluctantly. Usually fascinated by the older gentleman's rare book finds, tonight he would have preferred simply to sit and enjoy Jennifer. He hadn't seen her for a while, and the last time had been under rather constrained circumstances. But the bookman was handing him a heavy, dusty tome, and there was nothing to do but put down his martini and lift it into his lap.

As he opened to the title page, the odor of must and mildew obliterated all the tantalizing aromas from above.

MATERIA MEDICO
An Herbaria
By
Dioscorides
The Properties Of Six Hundred Medicinal Plants

The words wandered down the page in the fashion of medieval manuscripts.

"Dioscorides was a Greek who traveled with the Roman army in the first century A.D.," Mr. Nicholson explained, "and the first person to establish botany as an applied science."

"Dad, maybe Andrew just wants to relax tonight," Jennifer said. She had noticed that he had looked tired when he came in.

"No, that's quite all right." In spite of himself, Fenimore was becoming interested. Cautiously, he turned the page. The paper was so old and brittle that one false move would crumble it. He thought of Polly Hardwick's Roman garden. Here were enough specimens to furnish her entire exhibit. He paused to admire an intricate drawing of a familiar plant. Each bell-like blossom, down to the individual grains of pollen on every stamen, had been carefully rendered by hand. The only thing missing was the color, that delicate purple shade from which it drew its botanical name—*Digitalis purpurea*. And on the facing page was an illustration of another variety—*Digitalis lanata*, a shorter plant with a smaller, white blossom. It was rarely found in America. Below this drawing was an equally delicate rendering of belladonna, more commonly known as deadly nightshade.

Mr. Nicholson, curious to see what was absorbing his guest's attention, came to look over his shoulder. " 'Foxglove and nightshade, side by side, / Emblems of punishment and pride,' " the bookseller quoted.

Fenimore looked up.

"Scott. 'Lady of the Lake.' "

Fenimore was reminded of the poisonous potential of foxglove. Like most things in this world, it could be used for good or evil. "A two-edged sword," the *Textbook of Cardiology* had described it. Dioscorides must have known this. Otherwise he wouldn't have grouped it in his text with other poisonous plants.

"You look awfully serious," Jennifer said. "There's only one cure for that. Let's eat. Dinner's ready." She drained her Chablis and led them into the dining room.

During dinner, Mr. Nicholson entertained them with poisonous plant lore.

"Hellebore was a good one to have on hand. The Greeks used it to pollute their enemies' water supply. Their foes grew so weak from purging, it was a cinch to conquer them. Can't you see all those Trojans rushing for the men's room."

"Nice dinner table talk, Dad."

He laughed. "And think of all those kings who were done in by one herb or another."

"And philosophers," put in Fenimore.

" 'Roote of Hemlocke, digg'd i' th' darke,' " recited Jennifer.

"Of course, there was a positive side to that," the bookseller said.

Fenimore and Jennifer looked puzzled.

"It decreased unemployment. Enter the poison taster! No king or queen dared be without one. The medieval classifieds must have been bursting with ads placed by them. Of course, the positions were usually temporary, and their résumés weren't expected to be very long. Good taste buds and a suicidal tendency were the only requirements." He paused to cautiously chew a bit of corn muffin, as if testing for deadly ingredients.

"I read somewhere that Richelieu was too cheap to hire a taster," Jennifer said, "but he kept lots of cats around and never ate anything without trying it out on one of them first."

Fenimore wondered what Sal would have to say about that.

"Arsenic was the favorite poison in those days," Mr. Nicholson said. "It was easy to get hold of in the form of rat poison, and every pantry had a good supply. Sometimes the lady of the house put it to other uses. The infamous Madame LaFarge bumped off several husbands that way. And one grande dame, the marquise de Brinvilliers, did away with her father and two brothers because they stood in the way of the family fortune."

"Not all poisoners were women, Dad," Jennifer admonished him. "Maybe Andrew should have brought Sal along to sample his dinner," she added.

"I'm afraid that wouldn't have worked out."

"Why not?"

"She doesn't care for corn muffins."

Jennifer plucked one from the basket and threw it at him, knocking over his wineglass in the process. Fortunately it was empty.

Mr. Nicholson righted the glass, filled it, and continued. "Did you know that the symptoms of arsenic poisoning are almost the same as the symptoms of cholera, Doctor?"

Fenimore shook his head. He was comparing this dinner to the dinner he had recently had with the Hardwicks. Did those people ever have any fun?

"Cholera was very prevalent in those days, and deaths by poison often went undetected because the cause was attributed to that disease. Frequently the poisoner got off scot-free."

"The heyday for poisoners." Fenimore laughed.

"What fascinates me," said Jennifer, "are the ingenious ways poisons were administered. Have you ever heard of 'poison rings'?"

They looked dumb.

"These rings looked ordinary enough, but they had a cavity behind the stone with a barb attached. You filled the cavity with arsenic, or some other deadly poison, and the next time you ran into your enemy, you gave him or her a friendly handshake, and—presto—you administered the fatal scratch."

"Never heard of that one," Mr. Nicholson said, "but I've heard of kings who poisoned the points of their scepters. If the king took a sudden dislike to a servant or subject, he just gave him or her a little tap on the head."

"I prefer more straightforward methods," Fenimore said. "The poisoned cup or sword, like in *Hamlet*."

"There was nothing straightforward about the way Hamlet's father died," Jennifer said, and recited,

205

"With juice of cursed hebenon in a vial,
And in the porches of my ears did pour
the leperous distilment . . . "

Fenimore clapped, suitably impressed.

She flushed.

"How about the Lenapes." Fenimore had just finished the book Jennifer had brought him. "They used to crush the green balls of walnut trees and throw them into the river to make the fish sleepy and easier to catch."

"That doesn't sound quite cricket," Jennifer said.

"No worse than our custom of tranquilizing cattle before corralling them and slaughtering them," Fenimore said.

"They also poisoned the tips of their spears and arrows, didn't they?" said Mr. Nicholson.

"Actually, that's a misconception," Fenimore said. "Many Indians who we thought died of poisoned arrows died of tetanus. That green, gummy substance on the arrows that we thought was poison was nothing more than an animal glue made from hide or hooves to hold the arrowhead in place."

Mr. Nicholson looked dismayed. "If they keep revising history at this rate, my books will soon be worthless."

"Don't worry, there will always be readers who'll want to laugh at the quaint beliefs of their predecessors. Your books will become priceless collectors' items," Fenimore assured him.

Jennifer appeared, bearing the apple cobbler and whipped cream. For the first time that evening, silence fell on the table.

It was their custom, after dinner, to go back to the library for coffee and watch an old movie on the VCR.

"What'll it be tonight?" Fenimore asked, reclaiming his favorite chair. *Arsenic and Old Lace?*

Jennifer showed him the cassette she had in mind, *Notorious.*

"Good choice," he said.

Before she put the cassette in the machine, Jennifer placed

two books in his lap. *The Big Sleep* and *The Long Goodbye* by Raymond Chandler. "You can't read them now," she said as he opened the first volume. "Take them home. They're yours."

"To keep?"

She nodded. "Although I can't imagine why you'd want to read such violent books after your recent experience. I'd think a nice cozy mystery would be more relaxing."

Fenimore closed the book in his lap and, with a smile of deep satisfaction, settled back to watch Ingrid Bergman being slowly poisoned to death, secure in the knowledge that Cary Grant would arrive at the eleventh hour to save her.

On the way home, Fenimore's step was light. All traces of his former exhaustion had vanished. After recovering from Jennifer's good-night kiss, he reviewed their dinner table conversation. Something Jennifer had said stuck in his mind. "What fascinates me are the ingenious ways poisons were administered." It was no mystery now that Sweet Grass had died of digitalis toxicity. But how had it been administered? He had discarded his original idea, that someone had dumped ground-up digoxin tablets in her food or drink, because everyone at the picnic had eaten and drunk from the same source. He stopped for the light. Maybe he was under some misconception, like those historians who had jumped to the wrong conclusion about the Indians and their poisoned arrows. He crossed the street. But how was it done? There were no swords or scepters at the Hardwicks' picnic. . . .

He paused in midstride.

CHAPTER 33

TUESDAY, NOVEMBER 8

It was 4:00 P.M. The last patient had left the office. Mrs. Doyle had also vanished, a new paperback romance tucked under her arm. She was looking forward to an enjoyable evening in the company of Amanda Grey, the beautiful young heiress, and Henry Davenport, the penniless lord who was ruthlessly pursuing Amanda for her money while feigning undying love. Fenimore was surprised at Mrs. Doyle's apparent lack of interest in the Sweet Grass case. It was very unusual. By now, she should have come forward with at least half a dozen useful suggestions. He hoped she wasn't still miffed over his having increased his office staff.

Horatio was still there, affixing stamps to the weekly bills. He had just received his first paycheck from Mrs. Doyle, but he seemed in no hurry to spend it.

Fenimore said, "When you're done, Rat, come with me. I want to show you something."

He looked up warily, remembering the last time he had accompanied his employer. Unpleasant visions of mice, monkeys, and security guards flashed through his head. But he finished the bills quickly and followed Fenimore to the door.

"Where are we going?" he asked after they had gone several blocks.

"You'll see."

Fenimore turned left at Eighteenth Street. Midblock he passed through a pair of wrought-iron gates and led Horatio up the marble steps of an imposing brick building.

The boy halted on the threshold. "This some kind of palace?"

Fenimore saw the scene through his eyes—the acre of parquet floor, the towering classic columns, and the row of "distinguished" personages in gold frames staring down at them. A hush prevailed.

Fenimore shook his head. "But I see what you mean. These fellas," he waved at the portraits, "take themselves pretty seriously."

"Who are they?"

"Doctors. But their accomplishments lay more in the realm of politics than science, I'm afraid. Come on." He hurried him along. "They aren't the reason I brought you here."

The boy followed him, past the vacant front desk (the receptionist must have left for the day) and over the polished floor.

Click, click, click.

"What's that?" Fenimore turned.

"My cleats."

He groaned. "They'll throw us out."

"How come? It's not a gym, is it?"

"Try to keep them quiet."

They passed between two pillars the size of redwood trees (Horatio on tiptoe), ducked around a majestic staircase, and paused before an ordinary wooden door bearing a small sign: THE WINTERBERRY MUSEUM. HOURS: 9:00 TO 5:00, TUES.–SAT.

"This is it." Fenimore opened the door, and Horatio wrinkled his nose.

"Formaldehyde," Fenimore explained the unpleasant odor. "Preserves the specimens. You'll get used to it."

The room they entered was the opposite of the one they had just left. It was cramped and cluttered. Three walls were lined with glass-fronted wooden cabinets stuffed with medical curiosities—from a fingernail a foot long to a two-headed fetus. More display cases of a similar character occupied the center of the room. At the back, separated from the rest of the room by a frayed rope, was the replica of a doctor's office, vintage 1890.

"Hey, that looks like your office, Doc."

Fenimore had to acknowledge that there was a resemblance. He too had a microscope with brass attachments that was covered by a bell jar in need of dusting. It had belonged to his grandfather, who had also been a doctor. Occasionally Fenimore used it to examine simple slides. He was rather proud of it. He also had a centrifuge, like the one on the table, which had belonged to his father. He used it now and then to spin down blood and urine samples. Why not, if it still worked? And those antique bottles lining the shelf over the sink did look like some that he had in his own medicine cabinet. He never used them, but he liked to look at them and couldn't bear to throw them away.

"Cool, man." Horatio had turned from the doctor's office to a tall glass case that contained two human skeletons, one about eight feet tall, the other less than four feet. The placard read, "Giant and Dwarf."

Then something else drew his attention. "Look here, Doc." He was peering at the two-headed fetus in a jar. "This is better than that stuff at the circus."

The comparison drew Fenimore up short. He had never connected the esteemed Winterberry Museum with the circus.

210

"There is a difference, Horatio. The audience here comes to study and learn, not to laugh and gawk."

A laugh came from across the room where a group of first-year medical students were gawking at a display of a megacolon. The giant colon (a papier-mâché copy of the original) was six inches in diameter. Its former owner had been a victim of Hirschsprung's disease and, according to the placard, the poor man had been able to defecate only every forty-two days.

"The purpose of this museum," Fenimore continued huffily, "is to acquaint interns and medical students with unnatural physical phenomena, in order to cure them." He paused, suddenly aware of his pompous tone. This place did have a way of getting to you.

"Why would that big guy want to be cured?" Horatio nodded at the skeleton of the giant. "The Sixers would've loved to get their hands on him. He'd be rich and famous. And that little dude next to him, he'd make a terrific second-story man. He could rip off any jewelry store in town." He turned his dark eyes on Fenimore. "Why do we all hafta be alike?"

Fenimore hesitated. "I guess it makes us feel more comfortable."

"Comfortable, shit! I'd rather be in the Hall of Fame." He turned back to admire the eight-foot skeleton. "I'll bet that guy could have made Best Basketball Player of All Time."

Horatio passed quickly by the heart-lung machine invented by a prominent Philadelphian but lingered over the bronchoscope exhibit. He was fascinated by the drawers full of small objects that had been extricated from people's windpipes and lungs. He pulled out drawer after drawer of buttons, fish bones, needles, and pins. There was even a Sunday school pin inscribed, "For Perfect Attendance." But the most common objects inhaled were jacks, those six-pointed metal toys every girl played with, bouncing a rubber ball on the front steps. Fenimore ex-

211

plained that it was the practice to hold the jacks in your mouth while playing. And in the heat of the game, sometimes one would slip down the windpipe.

Horatio shook his head, like a disapproving parent.

They had reached a glass case that stretched the full length of one wall. It housed three rows of human skulls. According to the fly-specked card, the collection had been purchased from a European doctor who had obtained them from the graveyards of convicts and paupers in the eighteen hundreds.

"In those days it was hard to get hold of skulls legally," Fenimore said. "You had to smuggle them out, sometimes in the middle of the night."

"You mean dig 'em up?"

He nodded. "But it was for a good cause. You could learn a lot from them. Look at that fella." He pointed to a skull with indentations on the surface of its crown. "Those dents were caused by TB. And that one there belonged to someone who had the sailor's malady, scurvy."

"How can you tell?"

"See the erosion around the teeth. It develops due to lack of vitamin C. They didn't get enough fruit and vegetables on board ship."

Sure enough, the placard below read, "Sailor. Died at sea, 1894."

"No problem telling what finished him off." Fenimore indicated a skull with a hole in it the size of a Ping-Pong ball. The card beneath read, "Robber. Shot while trying to escape prison. Madrid, 1879."

Horatio's eyes were wide.

"Shall we go?" asked Fenimore.

The boy, mesmerized by a series of photographs of Siamese twins, didn't answer.

Fenimore looked at his watch. "Tell you what, I have some

work to do upstairs in the library. You stay here and have a look around, and I'll come back for you when I'm done."

The library was the most attractive part of the building. Tall arched windows lined one wall, admitting luminous shafts of light. The other walls were lined with bookshelves and wooden filing cabinets. The rest of the room was occupied by freestanding shelves interspersed with long, polished oak tables. The tables were equipped with freshly sharpened pencils and pads, paper cups, and thermoslike pitchers containing water that was always chilled. And the chairs, unlike those in most libraries, were comfortable. They had rounded backs with arms, and each was supplied with a back pad and seat cushion, proving that the pursuit of scholarship need not be synonymous with a sore bottom.

Fenimore went over to the filing cabinets, pulled out the drawer marked P-O, and fingered through the cards until he came to the category "Poisonous Plants." A further search produced three titles: *Deadly Plants, Weeds, and Flowers; Herbs That Kill and Cure;* and *Poisonous Plants of the United States and Canada.* He filled out the call slips and presented them to the librarian. He had barely sat down to wait when the three volumes appeared on the counter. This was the main reason Fenimore retained his membership in the society. After the librarian had verified his membership card, he tucked the books under his arm and went to collect Horatio.

Fenimore found the boy engrossed by a brain floating in a jar. According to the placard, it had once belonged to a murderer hanged in Upper Darby in 1892.

CHAPTER 34

Tuesday Evening

It was after 10:00 P.M. when Fenimore put the chain on the front door, turned the key in the vestibule lock, and made his way up the steep, narrow stairs to his bedroom. His encounter with the two thugs a few nights ago was already becoming a foggy memory. Sal was way ahead of him, curled at the foot of the bed on the blue comforter, sound asleep (or pretending to be). She looked bigger than usual. She would be having her kittens soon. Before getting undressed, he set his briefcase on the bureau and opened it. Inside lay the three books he had taken out of the PSPS library. He looked at them with the eager anticipation that most people reserved for a good mystery or, in Mrs. Doyle's case, for a romance novel.

He put on his pajamas and his worn tartan bathrobe, but not his slippers (one was still missing), and settled into the chair by his bed with the good reading lamp.

Deadly Plants, Weeds, and Flowers was profusely illustrated with colored photographs and was obviously written by a layman. (How this had found its way into the PSPS library, he had no idea.) If he had wanted to learn to identify plants for Polly's

214

garden club, this would be the book for him. He laid it aside. *Herbs That Kill and Cure* was more academic. The first part was filled with dire warnings about everything from toadstools to poison ivy. The second part was devoted to the remedies you should apply if you failed to heed the warnings in the first part. He placed it with the first book. *Poisonous Plants of the United States and Canada,* although bearing the least-intriguing title, was well organized and well written.

The contents were divided into "helpful" and "harmful" plants. The harmful plants were then subdivided into various classes. He scanned the subdivisions, searching for the specific kind of harmful plant he had in mind. It must contain cardiac glycosides like those in digoxin, which, if taken internally, would induce symptoms similar to those induced by digitalis toxicity—nausea, dizziness, blurred vision or yellow halos, tachycardia, arrhythmia, syncope, and—ultimately—death. He found the entry for cardiac glycosides.

Poisonous Plants Containing Cardiac Glycosides

Scientific Name	Common Name
Adonis spp.	pheasant's-eye
Apocynum spp.	dogbane
Convallaria majalis	lily of the valley
Digitalis purpurea	foxglove
Digitalis lanata	
Nerium oleander	oleander
Thevetia peruviana	be-still tree
Urginea maritima	squill

There they were, eight of them, taken in easily at a glance. Fenimore tore a piece of paper from the pad on his bedside table (the one he reserved for jotting down bright ideas that come in the night) and copied the list. Next to "foxglove" he wrote "dig-itoxin glycosides," and beside several of the others he wrote "digoxin glycosides." Mission accomplished, he was now wide-awake. Sal opened one eye, looked at him, made a half-turn on the comforter, and slipped back to sleep. If only he could do the same.

CHAPTER 35

WEDNESDAY MORNING, NOVEMBER 9

The first call Fenimore made the next morning was to Myra Henderson.

"Doctor, I was just thinking about you. I was wondering if you would care to come to dinner and keep an old lady company. I make a mean martini."

He laughed, touched that she would ask him. "I remember your martinis, and I'd be delighted another time. But right now I'm up to my neck in the Sweet Grass case."

"So it is a case."

"I'm afraid so. I know I can trust you not to mention—"

"Of course."

"I need some specific information, which I thought you might provide."

"I'll do my best."

"You said that at the picnic, you and the other guests grilled your shish kebabs on skewers."

"Yes, the old-fashioned kind, made from branches and whittled to a point. The Hardwicks were getting back to nature that day, in honor of Sweet Grass, I suppose."

"Now think carefully," he said. "Did you choose your skewer from a bundle, or did someone hand it to you?"

She was silent, trying to remember. "We were each handed one."

"Sweet Grass, too?"

"I think so. She was right next to me."

"Who handed them to you?"

Another silence. "I'm sorry, I was talking to Sweet Grass and wasn't paying attention."

"Polly, Ned, one of the girls . . . ?"

"I *am* sorry. I just can't remember."

"Never mind." Fenimore sighed. "What about later on? You said Ned was worried that the meat wasn't done enough, because some of it was pork."

"Yes, that's right. Oh, Doctor, you don't think she died of trichinosis, do you?"

Fenimore coughed. "No."

He was silent for so long that Mrs. Henderson finally asked, "Are you still there?"

"Yes . . ." He sounded far away.

"Was I any help?"

"You've been a great help." He said quickly, "I hope you'll give me a rain check on that dinner invitation."

"You have a standing invitation, Doctor."

Later that morning, one of Rafferty's personal deputies hand-delivered the autopsy report on Joe Smith. The results were disappointing. Nothing new had been uncovered that would contradict the original cause of death, food poisoning. Fenimore rummaged through his desk for his notes on the homeless man. He found what he was looking for. Joe Smith had been taken to Franklin Hospital, and he too had suffered from MVA, the "Pearly Gates syndrome." Therefore, a sample of his blood serum must have ended up in Applethorn's lab, and he could

check it out for digoxin glycosides. If some were present, chances were he had been poisoned by the same means and by the same hand as Sweet Grass. But this time, he and Horatio would not have to steal the blood serum. He would have enough evidence to get it by a court order.

CHAPTER 36

WEDNESDAY, AROUND NOON

Polly Hardwick met Fenimore at the door with a strained expression.

When he had called that morning to invite himself to lunch, she had been eager. But when he had requested that the entire family be present and said he would like to talk to each member individually, she had become uneasy.

"I'll try, Andrew," she said, "but Bernice is downtown, and I don't know what Ned's schedule is."

"Do your best," he urged.

She led him past the small study in which he had learned the secrets of Sweet Grass's diary—the door was closed today—and straight on to the spacious living room. The late morning sun sifted through the gauzy curtains, lending the room an ethereal glow. A bowl of yellow chrysanthemums rested in a pool of light on the piano, and a taller vase of rusty mums decorated the mantel. Access to fresh-cut flowers on a daily basis was one of the few things Fenimore envied the rich.

"The girls are waiting in their rooms. The men are puttering in the garden. I told them I'd call them when you wanted them.

Oh, and Bernice telephoned to say she'd be late. Shall I call Lydia first?"

"Please."

Lydia entered unhurriedly, dressed in a jade sweater and black pants, her dark hair tied back with a matching jade ribbon. She had a paperback book in one hand. (In case the interview grew too boring?) The cover was turned in, preventing him from seeing the title.

When Polly left them, Fenimore began without preamble. "What did you think of Sweet Grass?"

She shifted in her chair and turned the rings on one finger. "I hardly knew her. I'd met her only a few times, before, before she er . . ."

"Did you think she was a good choice for Ted?"

She sighed. "I suppose. She was earthy and arty, two attributes he admires. You know the type—torn jeans, wheat germ, and in her case the art thing was weaving."

"She was quite good at it, I understand."

"I haven't the foggiest." She waved a lethargic, meticulously manicured hand. "I never saw any of her work."

"On the day of the picnic, did you think she looked unwell?"

She frowned. "Now that you mention it, she did look a bit peaked. But I thought she was just worn out from all the wedding preparations. Mother had her jumping through hoops, you know."

"Did you know that after she left here, she ended up in an emergency room with food poisoning?" Fenimore watched Lydia's reaction to this fabrication of his.

Her eyes widened. "But I thought she died of heart failure, from that childhood disease. Tet . . . whatever it's called."

"That was the preliminary diagnosis. Since then we've learned that she took something internally, probably at the picnic, that caused her illness."

"If that were the case, why didn't the rest of us become ill?" Her face was open, inquiring.

When Fenimore didn't answer, her face suddenly closed into a mask.

"Do you have any ideas?" he asked.

Avoiding his eyes, she said, "I'm sure with all your diagnostic expertise, you'll be able to come up with the answer, Doctor."

Damn. By moving too fast, he'd lost Lydia.

"If you're finished with me . . ." She started to rise.

Reluctantly, he nodded. He watched her exit by the French door that opened onto the terrace. To read her paperback in the sun, while waiting for lunch to be served? He wondered fleetingly what it would be like to lead such a life of leisure.

"Next?" Kitty poked her bright head around the door.

"Come in, Kitty. I won't keep you long."

"Oh, I don't mind. I have nothing to do." She settled into a chair opposite him and smiled like a happy child waiting for her favorite TV show to begin.

"On the day of the picnic, the one celebrating your brother's engagement, did you notice anything unusual?"

"Well, it was very warm for October."

"No, I mean about the people."

She began to chew on her fingernail, "No. They were all Mother and Daddy's friends. That old Mrs. Henderson was complaining about the smoke and having to cook her own food."

"What about your mother and father. Did they seem themselves?"

"Oh, sure. Daddy was bragging to everybody about his ancestors, and Mother was running around like Chicken Little crying, 'The sky is falling.' "

"Not really."

She giggled. "Well, she looked like a big chicken and she seemed upset about something."

"Did you like Sweet Grass?"

Her smile vanished. "No."

"Why not?"

"She wouldn't let me be in the wedding." She stuck out her lower lip. "I know Ted would have let me. And I had such a pretty dress picked out. It was sky blue." She smiled at the memory of it.

"That's too bad."

She stood up and stamped her foot. "I hated her."

"Now, I'm sure you don't mean . . ."

"But now there isn't going to be any wedding," she said, a little smile creeping about her lips.

"Does that please you?"

She looked at him. "Oh, yes." And after a second's pause, she added, "Now we have Ted back again."

Polly was in the doorway. She must have been hovering nearby and overheard her daughter's outburst.

"Thank you, Kitty," Fenimore said.

She gave her abbreviated curtsy, brushed by her mother without a glance, and joined Lydia on the terrace.

Polly looked worriedly after her, then back at Fenimore. "What was that all about?"

"Kitty didn't care much for Sweet Grass."

"That's not surprising. She's crazy about her brother." She came into the room. "Is it my turn now?"

He nodded.

"Sherry?"

"Yes, thanks."

Polly went over to a polished wooden lowboy with a marble top and took out two small glasses and a decanter. The glasses, which she filled with gold liquid, were dainty and etched with a delicate vinelike pattern. She brought one to Fenimore.

He accepted it, wishing that his errand could match the glass in delicacy.

She settled into a corner of the sofa and took a sip of sherry.

Despite her size and age, Polly was a striking woman. Today she was wearing a green wool suit and a plaid scarf of matching shades fastened at her neck with a topaz pin. Her hair, once a ruddy blond, was muted now by streaks of gray and arranged in a becoming chignon. She used the minimum of makeup. Her mouth was colored a faint coral.

"How does your Roman garden grow?" he asked. He was determined to take a slower approach this time.

As always, at the mention of her favorite hobby, she brightened. "Everything's coming together. All the plants have been ordered. Some have even arrived. Would you like to see them?"

"Very much."

She led him to the greenhouse that opened off the living room. When she opened the glass-paneled door, the change in temperature was startling, from comfortable cool to jungle hot. He followed her down the aisle between two walls of thick greenery.

"There's an olive tree." She pointed to a slender tree with gray-green leaves in a terra-cotta pot. Fenimore recognized a tree he had seen by the hundreds dotting the hillsides near Florence. "And there's the oleander. That came a while ago."

He bent to examine its long stems and glossy leaves.

"And there's some hibiscus. It's not flowering now, but it will be in time for the show."

Fenimore's shirt was sticking to his back and his forehead was beading.

"We better get you out of here before you melt away," she laughed.

Back in the living room, Polly's manner changed. "But surely you didn't come here to discuss my hibiscus, Andrew?"

He shook his head. " 'Fraid not." Fenimore began obliquely. "Do you have any lily of the valley around?"

Puzzled, Polly said slowly, "Not cut, but we have a few beds on the shady side of the house."

"What about squill?"

"Sea onion." She nodded. "By the terrace. I have one or two plants."

"Dogbane?"

"What is this, Andrew? Are you starting a garden? I didn't think you had a green thumb."

He sighed and put down his sherry, careful to locate a coaster. "I'd like you to think back to the day of the picnic," he said.

Her brows knit.

"Do you remember how Sweet Grass looked that day?"

"Well, she was wearing—"

"No, I mean her face. Did she look pale or unwell?"

She shook her head. "To be perfectly honest, Andrew, I was so upset that day, she could have been naked and I wouldn't have noticed."

"Why were you upset?"

"Oh, about the wedding and everything." She put her glass down. "It's not what you're thinking. The fact that she was a Native American had nothing to do with it. It was her health. I couldn't stand the thought of my only son marrying someone who might not live long enough to raise his children."

Fenimore blinked. "That's unfair. Many women with her condition live to bring up families."

Her eyebrows shot up. "Well, she did die!"

"Yes, but not from natural causes."

If he had handed her a rattlesnake, she could not have recoiled more violently.

"Sweet Grass was born with a serious heart defect," he went on, giving her time to recover her equilibrium, "which was corrected surgically when she was a child. She was on a daily regimen of digoxin to alleviate a minor side effect caused by that surgery. But her life expectancy was almost the same as any woman her age, with or without childbearing."

"Then what did she die of?"

"Digoxin toxicity—the result of an overdose of the medicine she had been taking for years."

"Then it *was* suicide?" She was full of hope. The suicide theory had suddenly become vastly preferable to its alternative.

He looked at her carefully. "That might explain the overdose, but not the burial."

"Her brother," she said quickly. "He's the only one who knew the Lenape burial customs and the location of that old burial ground. He must have found her dead in her apartment and taken it upon himself to bury her. The Lenapes probably consider suicide a disgrace, and he wanted to cover it up. It wouldn't have occurred to him to notify Ted—or us."

Fenimore happened to know that the Lenape didn't consider suicide a disgrace. He merely said, "But he denied it."

Her shrug implied what she thought his word was worth.

"Actually," Fenimore spoke deliberately, "anyone who can read could find out about those burial customs. There are plenty of books on the Lenni-Lenape in the American Philosophical Society and at the university museum. And as for the burial ground, its location is public knowledge. The deed is registered in the Department of Records at City Hall."

She was watching him keenly now. "What are you getting at?"

It was Fenimore's turn to shrug.

"Are you implying . . . ?" She was on her feet.

"I'm not implying anything. I'm trying to find out the truth."

She towered over him, like an indignant goddess. "The truth? The truth is she was an unhealthy, unhappy girl, who did away with herself."

Fenimore rose to meet her furious gaze. "On the contrary, she was a healthy, happy young woman looking forward to spending the rest of her life with the man she loved."

"What's going on?" Ned Hardwick was in the doorway, flushed and muddy from the garden. "I heard voices."

226

Fenimore looked at Polly.

She looked away. "Don't come in here with those muddy boots." She spoke mechanically to her husband.

He glanced at his feet. "I'll be right back." Turning, he disappeared into the mudroom.

Polly returned to her place on the sofa and stared mutely at the oriental rug. Fenimore remained standing, not wanting to be caught at a disadvantage again, stuck deep in a chair. They kept their silence until Ned returned.

He was wearing a pair of L. L. Bean moccasins, Fenimore noted. They looked brand new and in need of breaking in. Fenimore thought fondly of his own worn slippers, then remembered that one was still missing. Strange, how irrelevant thoughts come to you during moments of stress.

"Now, are you going to tell me what's going on here?" Ned looked from one to the other as he made his way toward the sherry decanter.

Polly threw back her head like a great lioness. "Your so-called friend here has just implied that one of us is responsible for Sweet Grass's death."

Never overly quick, except in surgical matters, Ned took his time. "How's that?"

"According to Sherlock here, one of us did her in." Polly had not looked at Fenimore once since he had divulged his suspicions. As far as she was concerned, he no longer existed. A single remark had placed him outside the magic circle, in that vast gray void to which everyone not in the Hardwicks' social set was automatically consigned.

Ned examined his moccasins.

"What's all the commotion?" Lydia reappeared from the terrace.

"Oh, nothing, darling. We've just been accused of murder, that's all. Come in and join the fun." Polly beckoned to her.

Lydia was barely seated, eyeing Fenimore quizzically, when

227

Kitty flitted in. After pausing briefly, she darted to the fish tank and shook a blizzard of food into the water.

"Don't overfeed them," Polly spoke sharply.

Her daughter turned with an odd smile and crooned in a sing-song voice, "Lunchtime."

"Dr. Fenimore won't be staying for lunch," her mother said.

"Oh? Too bad," Kitty said. "We're having my favorites. Shepherd's pie and raspberry Jell-O with whipped cream." She clapped her hands.

Lydia looked amused.

Polly looked away.

"I must be going." Fenimore moved toward the door.

The surgeon followed him. "I'll see you out."

In the hallway, his host spoke in a low voice. "You mustn't mind Polly. I'm sure it's all a misunderstanding. She gets carried away at times, especially with anything concerning the family. She's like a lioness with her cubs," he said, half proudly. "She'd do anything to protect us."

Anything? thought Fenimore. "I understand," he said.

"Say, Fenimore, how about coming to PSPS tomorrow afternoon. We're having a little reception in honor of the Winterberry Museum. It's the hundredth anniversary, you know. Be my guest. Show there's no hard feelings. What d'ya say?" He lightly punched his arm.

"I'll check my calendar and give you a call." Fenimore stepped out the front door into bright sunlight.

As he walked to his car, he caught sight of Ted pruning a hedge. The young man waved and started toward him. Fenimore waited, his hand on the door handle.

"Thought you were staying to lunch," he said.

"Change of plans."

"An emergency?"

"Sort of."

"Well, I'd better let you go." He looked down at the shears in his hand.

"Where are you going to dump all those hedge clippings?" Fenimore asked.

"There's a compost heap over there." He nodded toward a grove of trees halfway down the driveway.

Fenimore got in his car and turned the key. Ted stepped back. As he drove away, he watched the solitary figure in the rearview mirror move slowly toward the house.

CHAPTER 37

WEDNESDAY AFTERNOON

At the foot of the driveway, Fenimore pulled over and waited. When he judged that the Hardwicks were well into their lunch, he got out and began walking back up the drive toward the grove of trees. For most of the way, he was screened from the house by a high, thick hedge of rhododendron and boxwood. But when he reached the grove, a vista opened up between the trees, and he could see the house and lawn. The lawn was empty, the terrace was vacant, and the hedge clippers were silent. Lunch must be in progress. Cautiously, he moved into the grove. The compost pile wasn't hard to find—he fell into it. His foot sank into the soft mass of decaying matter. When he withdrew it, bits of grass clung to his pants. He didn't bother to brush them off. He would be covered with them before he was finished. The pit was filled almost to the brim with grass cuttings, twigs, and hedge clippings, the accumulation of a summer's refuse on a well-run estate. He turned over a pile of grass with his foot. The blades were yellowish brown and shriveled. He probed again. More of the same. Keeping the house in his line of vision, he picked up a nearby trowel and dug. There was something. He pulled out a branch about two and a half feet long. One end was whittled to a point and charred. He examined the rest of it. Although no tree expert, it looked to him like a common variety, walnut or maple. He dug again and came up with two more. Both were pointed and charred and from the same tree. A crow cawed overhead, as if voicing outrage at his investigations. If only he had asked Mrs. Henderson how many people had been at the picnic, then he would know how many skewers to look for. Another probe uncovered three more. He wondered how long a Hardwick lunch lasted. He knew how long a Hardwick dinner lasted. Interminably. He glanced at his watch. They'd been at it about ten minutes. They must be well into the shepherd's pie. He dug again. Two more, identical to the others. He examined the trees nearest him. Maples, primarily. Comparing their branches with the cut ones, he decided they could very well have come from them. Another few minutes and he had come up with four more. He was perspiring. Between probes he cast anxious glances at the house. When he had unearthed sixteen identical branches he was ready to quit. One more try. He rummaged still deeper into the pile and pulled out number seventeen. Right away, he felt that it was different. Smooth instead of rough. And it wasn't stiff like the others. When he held it out, it drooped slightly. It had probably made a poor skewer.

He brushed the grass off his pants, collected the sticks under one arm, and headed down the drive back to his car. He was rounding the last rhododendron bush when he caught sight of something shiny gleaming in the sun. A car bumper. And not belonging to his car.

"Hi, Doctor." Bernice waved from her red Jaguar. "I was afraid I'd missed you, but as I came in I saw your car." She was smiling in such a friendly manner, it was obvious she had not been in touch with her family. She knew nothing about the recent brouhaha.

"I was just on my way out. Have to get to the hospital. If you

231

hurry, you'll be in time for the raspberry Jell-O." If only she doesn't ask about the sticks.

"Collecting firewood?" She nodded at the sticks.

"Well, actually, I did snitch a few twigs." He smiled, shamefacedly. "I've got a fireplace at home, and Philadelphia sidewalks don't abound with kindling."

"Help yourself. We're drowning in it. You'll save the gardener a lot of bother. Sorry I missed you." She smiled and started the motor.

"Wait." He moved up to the car window. "I did have a question for you. It's kind of technical, but being a botanist, I thought you might know."

She turned off the motor.

"Which plants have cardiac glycosides?"

"Wow," she blinked, "that's worthy of a Ph.D dissertation." She considered. "I can think of a few—foxglove, of course, and lily of the valley, and dogbane . . ." She grimaced. "Sorry. It's been a while since I studied this. What's it all about?" She seemed honestly curious.

"A colleague of mine is doing research on the effects of digoxin and wanted to know which plants have a similar chemistry."

"I can look them up for you when I get home."

"I'd appreciate that."

She took off with a wave.

If Bernice was faking her lack of knowledge about cardiac glycosides, she was a very good actor, Fenimore decided.

Back in the city, Fenimore's first stop was Penn Bot, otherwise known as the Pennsylvania Botanical Society. He double-parked, to the consternation of other motorists, and dashed in the door brandishing a stick. The dignified dowager at the front desk looked up in terror.

"Quick. I'll give a donation to the first person who can identify this twig for me."

232

"Well, I . . ."

"What is it, Ethel?" a chirrupy voice called from the next room.

"There's a 'gentleman' here with a question."

The owner of the chirrupy voice appeared. "Can I help you?"

"Yes. What's this?" He waved the stick under her nose.

"Well, I can't identify it if you keep waving it about."

"Oh, sorry." He held it still. A cacophony of car horns rent the air.

"Ethel, would you see what that awful racket is about?" She was studying the stick carefully, turning it from side to side, feeling the bark. "You don't have any leaves, do you?" She looked at him reproachfully.

"Sorry."

"Just a minute." She left the room and came back consulting a book.

"There's a car double-parked, blocking traffic," Ethel informed them.

"Oh, I wish they wouldn't do that. So thoughtless." She was pondering a photograph. "Yes," she said finally, "I'm sure this is it." She showed him the picture.

He read the caption underneath. "Thank you very much." He grabbed the stick and was almost out the door when he remembered his promise. Turning back, he scrawled out a check for twenty-five dollars.

"What a strange man," said Ethel, staring at the check in her hand.

The other woman nodded. "You never know what's going to walk in that door."

His next stop was the Police Administration Building. Deciding not to double-park there, he found a space a few blocks away. When he entered Rafferty's office, he was out of breath.

The policeman peered at him over a mountain of paperwork.
"To what do I owe——?"
Fenimore tossed the stick on top of the mountain.
"What's this?"
Fenimore told him.
"I'll be. We can make an arrest, then."
"Not quite. Give me 'til tomorrow. I think I can get a full confession."
"That's dangerous."
"I can manage it."
"You'd better have some backup."
"I'll call you if I need any."
"I don't like this."
"So long." He was out the door.
Rafferty studied the stick Fenimore had left behind. When he had satisfied his curiosity, he placed it carefully in a bag and labeled it. When the case came to trial, it would undoubtedly be Exhibit A.

That night, after a very full day, Fenimore would have liked to fall right to sleep. But he had some bedtime reading still to do in *Poisonous Plants of the United States and Canada.* He found oleander:

> Oleander (*NeriumOleander*) is an ornamental ever-green shrub or bush, up to 20 feet tall, which has been introduced from the Mediterranean region . . .

Fenimore's eye moved quickly down the page:

> Oleander is extremely toxic in all parts, green or dry, to all classes of livestock and to the human being. Leaves have been shown deadly at as little as 0.005 percent of the animals weight in horses and cat-

tle.... A single leaf is considered potentially lethal to the human being. Loss of human life, sometimes involving large numbers of persons during military operations, has repeatedly occurred when meat was roasted while skewered on oleander branches. . . .

CHAPTER 38

THURSDAY, NOVEMBER 10, 6:00 P.M.

The door to the Winterberry Museum was closed and gave no hint of the transformation that had taken place on the other side. It was so quiet that Fenimore thought he must have the wrong day. Cautiously, he turned the knob and was met with a rush of high-pitched chatter and a mixture of scents that had nothing to do with science. Toasted cheese and mushrooms vied with bay rum and Chanel. Expensively clad guests filled every available space, and flowers decorated every available surface. Chrysanthemums sprouted from the heart-lung machine, zinnias sprang from the megacolon display case, and ornamental shrubs surrounded the bronchoscopy exhibit. The women's committee had been working overtime. Gone was the pungent odor of formaldehyde, the respectful library hush, and the dust. Everything had been vacuumed and polished. The only thing that wasn't sparkling was the conversation: "I had no idea she was married again . . ."; "I hear they appointed Watson chief of staff . . ."; "So you finally threw caution to the winds and bought that boat. . . ."

Fenimore anxiously scanned the room for the bar. He located

it in the Victorian doctor's office. Efficient, white-jacketed bartenders were serving drinks from behind the mahogany examining table. He moved toward it with as much alacrity as the crowd would allow. As he approached, he spotted the broad back of Ned Hardwick. The surgeon turned and greeted him. "Ah, there you are, Fenimore. I was afraid you'd forgotten. What will you have? I'm on the wagon tonight. A little stomach upset," he explained, displaying a glass of Perrier with a twist of lemon.

"Scotch and water, please."

Ned gave the order to the bartender.

"Quite a crowd," Fenimore observed. "Are the receptions always this well attended?"

"Well, this is kind of special—the museum's hundredth birthday and all. And of course we don't usually hold 'em in here. Normally we gather in the front hall. But we usually have a pretty good turnout. You should come more often."

"The flowers are impressive."

"Yes, the women's committee went all out. Polly's the president this year."

"I thought I recognized her hand. Where is she?"

"Er, she was down here at the crack of dawn, arranging things, but I'm afraid she overdid it. When she came home, she collapsed and went to bed. . . ." His eyes shifted slightly, and Fenimore knew that Polly had stayed away on account of him.

"I'm sorry." He took a deep swallow of Scotch.

An exuberant young couple advanced on Ned. "Dr. Hardwick, I want you to meet my wife, Nancy."

Nancy grabbed his hand. "Oh, Dr. Hardwick, I've heard so much about you."

Fenimore excused himself (unnecessarily, as his departure went unnoticed) and grabbed a cucumber sandwich from a passing tray. Young men in white coats darted everywhere, offering glasses of champagne and trays of succulent hors d'oeuvres. While Fenimore sipped and munched, he scanned the room for

237

a familiar face. Ah, he glimpsed a fellow classmate from medical school, leaning against the heart-lung machine. He looked as out of place and ill at ease as Fenimore felt. Dodging guests, waiters, and busboys, he edged over to him. "Pete?" He placed a hand on his arm.

"Andy?" He grabbed Fenimore's hand as if it were a life raft, and the two men happily embarked on a sea of reminiscences while consuming alcohol and cucumber sandwiches at an alarming rate.

Later, back at the office, Mrs. Doyle was still working late when Horatio rushed in. "Where's the doc?"

"Who wants to know?"

He glowered. He had just spotted a pink message slip in the doctor's in tray, and he was in no mood to be trifled with. It read: "Call Dr. Applethorn. Re: Serum. Urgent."

Mrs. Doyle glanced at her calendar. "At the moment, he's attending a very fancy party at the Philadelphia Society of Physicians and Surgeons."

"Where's that?"

"Eighteenth and Walnut."

"Oh, yeah. I know the place."

"You do?" Mrs. Doyle was surprised.

Horatio slammed the file drawer he had been working in and reached for his leather jacket.

"You're not going there?"

"I hafta see him."

"But he left specific instructions that he wasn't to be disturbed except for an emergency."

"This *is* an emergency."

"You're not sick?" She flashed him a quick look of concern.

He shook his head and sprinted for the door.

"Wait . . ."

But he was gone.

The large, round academic clock read 8:15. It was the one thing the decorators had been unable to disguise with flowers or ferns for the party. Fenimore, on his third Scotch and his fifth cucumber sandwich, was regaling his companion with an escapade he and some other medical students had taken part in, something to do with throwing water-filled balloons at trolley cars at Forty-second and Woodland. He was nearing the climax, when yet another white-jacketed waiter shoved a tray under his nose and strongly urged him to try the single watercress sandwich that remained. Although it looked a trifle world-weary and worn around the edges, by this time Fenimore was relaxed, hungry, and easily subject to suggestion. He popped it in his mouth. As he did so, he noticed Ned staring intently at him from across the room. Was he behaving improperly? It *had* been some time since he had attended such a formal affair. He straightened up from his lounging position against the heart-lung machine and felt his neck to make sure his tie was in place. He concluded the anecdote he had been relating with a little less animation than before. But his companion's appreciation was undampened and his enthusiasm encouraged him to launch into another tale. He was two sentences into his new story when he stopped, staring at a busboy who was hovering nearby. He bore such a marked resemblance to Horatio that he could have been his twin. Warily, Fenimore eyed his drink and put down the glass. Once before he had drunk too much and seen double. He had been on his way home after an especially wild fraternity party and he had seen two moons. He had diagnosed the phenomenon as due to the influence of excessive alcohol on the brain stem. But to see the double of someone who wasn't even there? And who was coming toward him with some urgency?

"Doc, I've gotta talk to you."

"How the hell did you get in here?"

Fenimore's friend politely excused himself.

"And where did you find that getup?" He was referring to the white jacket.

"I stole it."

"That's nice."

Horatio glanced behind him. "I've gotta talk to you."

Fenimore felt a hand on his shoulder. "The crowd seems to be thinning out," Ned said, ignoring Horatio.

Fenimore looked around. The room was less crowded. The bartenders were beginning to stow their half-empty bottles in cartons. The waiters and other busboys were retrieving soiled glasses from odd corners of the room and stacking plates. All except Horatio.

"I want to show you something." Ned, his hand still on Fenimore, steered him across the room toward the long glass case filled with rows of human skulls. It was illuminated tonight, in honor of the occasion. Horatio followed them. Ned turned on him abruptly. "Don't you have work to do?"

Horatio gave him one of his looks, but it was lost on the surgeon. He had already turned back to the display case. "Look here." He pointed out a skull with very few teeth and read aloud from the placard underneath: " 'Sailor. Died of dagger thrust off Malta, 1816.' And over here, 'Magyar from Transylvania. Guerrilla and deserter. Executed by hanging, 1861.' "

Fenimore glanced around for Horatio, but he had disappeared. Ned continued his guided tour of the skulls, and Fenimore obediently followed. Was he going to read every one of those damned placards? His knees felt like jelly and his head ached. Tomorrow's hangover must be getting a head start. Ned droned on. Fenimore surreptitiously stole a look at his watch. Almost eight-thirty. Wasn't this shindig supposed to be over at eight?

"And there, 'Robber. Shot by gendarmes, 1862.' Seems we don't have any priority on violence, eh, Fenimore?"

"Umm," was the best response Fenimore could muster.

240

Whether it was the liquor or the company, he was beginning to feel queasy. The skulls in the case seemed to be aging before his eyes. Once ivory, they were gradually turning saffron yellow. He glanced over his shoulder. The last guest had gone. The bartenders, waiters, and busboys had left. No sign of Horatio. He wondered what he had wanted to talk to him about.

"Take a look at this." Ned had moved farther down the display case.

Fenimore, attempting to follow, staggered.

"Whoa." Ned grinned. "You really did hit that Scotch, didn't you?"

Fenimore leaned against the glass case with care. Each skull wore a bright yellow halo. "Dizzy . . . drink . . ."

Hardwick watched him slide to his knees, his fingernails scraping against the glass. He rested briefly, a surprised look on his face, before toppling sideways to the floor.

Ned waited a minute, gazing down at his inert body. Then he bent and began pawing through his pockets. He found what he was searching for. A ring of keys. Taking them, he headed for the door. Before leaving, he turned and hissed, "Did you really think I'd let my only son marry a squaw, Fenimore?"

CHAPTER 39

LATER THURSDAY EVENING

The entrance hall of PSPS was deserted. A single lamp with a small green shade burned at the reception desk. Hardwick's rubber soles made no sound on the parquet floor. He opened the heavy front door. It swung shut behind him with a soft thud.

Eighteenth Street was empty. He went through the wrought-iron gate, turned right, and walked toward Spruce. A young couple, arms entwined, passed him. He averted his face. Another right and three more blocks to 1555. The front windows were dark. He climbed the three marble steps and with a pocket flashlight tried to determine which key in the bunch would open the front door. Two looked probable. As he rushed to insert the first, he dropped the whole set. They clattered on the marble stoop. He looked around. Fortunately, the day of the foot patrolman was over. He tried again. It didn't fit. The second key opened the door easily. He closed it carefully behind him and stood in the vestibule, listening. A faint glow fell on the hall floor from a lamp in a room at the back of the house. The office? But a light didn't mean it was occupied. People often left lights on—even TVs and radios—to fool burglars into thinking they were at

242

home. He pushed open the vestibule door a little wider. It creaked.

"Is that you, Doctor?" A woman's voice came from the room with the light. "Thought I'd stick around and catch up on these forms."

Hardwick ducked into the hall closet and quietly closed the door. The only sound was his own breathing. Had she decided she was hearing things and gone back to her work? He opened the door a crack.

"*Meowerrrrrr.*"

"Sal? Is that you?"

"*Owerrr!*"

He closed the door.

The sharp screech of chair legs being pushed back. The soft pad of rubber-soled shoes. Nurse's shoes.

"What's the matter, puss?" Her voice, coming nearer.

He could picture the cat crouched in attack position, ears back, tail twitching—facing the closet door. The nurse—staring at the closet door too. He gripped the knob, about to spring out.

He heard a key turn.

He rattled the knob.

Quick, thudding footsteps running away. He shoved his shoulder against the door.

"Nine-one-one? I have an intruder here."

He pounded on the door.

"*Owerrrrrrrr!*"

"One-five-five-five Spruce Street. Please hurry."

He pounded and kicked the door.

Even though Mrs. Doyle knew that Victorian houses were structurally sound, she prayed.

CHAPTER 40

STILL LATER THURSDAY

Horatio peered out from behind the heart-lung machine where he had been hiding. At first all he could see were the rows of illuminated skulls. Hardwick had turned off the other lights when he left, but he had forgotten to switch off the light inside the display case.

"Doc?"

Silence as thick as cloth.

He felt his way around the glass case that housed the giant and dwarf. He bumped into the cabinet full of pins, fish bones, and jacks. His foot touched something. He bent down. "Doc!"

Frantically, he looked around for a phone. He ran out the door, almost letting it close behind him, but stopped in time to remove one sneaker and wedge it between the door and the door jamb. He reached the phone on the reception desk in two bounds.

"Nine-one-one? Emergency. Eighteenth, between Spruce and Walnut. The big brick building with the fancy gates. Guy's had an overdose. No, not that shit. Tell them to bring FAB. No, it ain't a detergent. F-A-B. It's an ant-i-body, for God's sake. And step on it!"

CHAPTER 41

SUNDAY, NOVEMBER 13

When Fenimore opened his eyes, they were all there, standing around the bed—Jennifer, Rafferty, Doyle, and Horatio. The only one missing was Sal. They had planned to smuggle her in, but when they went to look for her, she was nowhere to be found.

"What happened?" He looked from one to the other. His head felt as if someone had cracked it open, removed its contents, scrambled them, and stuffed them back inside.

"You ate one too many tea sandwiches," Rafferty said.

"The sandwich contained a new filling," Jennifer elucidated, "mayonnaise and oleander leaves."

Fenimore moaned.

"I told you you should change your eating habits," Mrs. Doyle put in sternly.

"Next time I'll skip the mayonnaise," he said.

A smile went round the bed. He had cracked a joke, however feeble. He must be feeling better.

He looked toward the window, where a huge floral arrangement blocked his view. They followed his gaze. Mrs. Doyle

245

picked up the card that lay beside it and read: " 'When you're feeling better, give me a call. I'll fill up my mason jar. Myra.' "

His two female visitors looked slightly put out.

"Some private joke, no doubt," said Mrs. Doyle.

"No doubt," Jennifer agreed.

Fenimore cracked a cat-that-ate-the-canary smile and asked, "How long have I been in here?"

"Three days," said Rafferty promptly. "The first day got rid of the arrhythmias, the second, the fibrillations, the third, the syncopes." He couldn't resist showing off the results of his crash course in cardiology.

Fenimore sat up. "Did you get Hardwick?"

Rafferty looked at Mrs. Doyle. "Thanks to her." He related how her quick thinking—locking the closet door—had rendered his capture easy.

Everyone cast a respectful glance at Mrs. Doyle, even Horatio.

"And I thought you weren't interested in this case," Fenimore said.

Mrs. Doyle flushed. "If it hadn't been for Sal . . ." and she related the cat's role in the capture.

"But how did I get here? Who found me? The last thing I remember, I was sinking to the floor with a bunch of skulls grinning at me."

All eyes turned on Horatio.

"If it weren't for him, you'd be six feet under," Rafferty said. "Tell him, kid."

Without lifting his eyes from Fenimore's counterpane, Horatio mumbled a barely audible account of his rescue. As he spoke, Fenimore noticed Mrs. Doyle gazing at him with a peculiarly saccharine expression. Some things had changed since he had lost consciousness.

When Horatio had finished, Fenimore said quietly, "Thanks, Rat." The image of an older Horatio in a white coat, with a stethoscope dangling from his neck, flashed through Fenimore's mind. "What made you think of FAB?"

"Just a hunch." He shrugged. "I saw that fat old doctor hand the waiter a plate, and he said, 'I think my friend over there wanted this.' Guy looked suprised but he took it. I didn't like that."

"You see, Rat, I was on my guard against tough hoods who attack with their fists, not a sneaky poisoner." He closed his eyes.

"Who happened *not* to be a woman, by the way," Jennifer put in.

Fenimore opened his eyes and smiled. The war between the sexes was still going on, How reassuring. It meant he really was still alive. He turned to Rafferty. "Something else I'd like to clear up. What did Hardwick want in my office?"

The policeman grinned. "Sweet Grass's blood serum. It seems your friend Applesauce—"

"Applethorn."

"Whatever . . . discovered that some of her serum was missing."

"How the hell?"

"Part of Applebutter's routine is to do a volume check on his specimens every morning. When he found that there was a discrepancy of a few milliliters in Sweet Grass's tube, he raised such Cain in the hospital that Hardwick heard about it. Naturally, he put two and two together—and came up with you."

"And he had no way of knowing that I'd passed the sample on to you. He thought I might still have it in my fridge." Fenimore was feeling better.

"Now it's my turn," Rafferty said. "How did that poor homeless guy fit in?"

"Ah." Fenimore was in his element as he unveiled the role of the homeless man to his attentive bedside audience. He hired 'Joe Smith' to do the dirty work—dig the grave, rent and drive the van, and bury the body. Hardwick even looked up Lenape burial customs. But after Joe dug the grave, he had to wait until dark to complete the burial. It was during this waiting period that Horatio and I appeared on the scene to perform our own burial. I noticed the van at the time and automatically memorized the tag number, but I didn't give it a second thought until much later. It must have been parked over the grave to conceal it. The driver was nowhere to be seen.

"While I was at my cardiology meeting and Horatio was at home, Joe must have buried Sweet Grass. Hardwick had, no doubt, instructed him in the traditional Lenape way to do it. Then Joe returned the van to Budget Rent-a-Car. He had probably arranged to meet Hardwick somewhere afterward to collect his payment. But he collected more than he'd bargained for—a leaf of oleander discreetly hidden in a burger or hoagie."

"Then who hit you?" Rafferty asked. "If Joe had left before you got back?"

Fenimore was silent, thinking. "I have no proof, but I'll wager it was Hardwick. I'll bet he came back to the burial site to inspect Joe's work. Surgeons tend to be compulsive that way. And, to his horror, who should he find parked a few yards from the grave but yours truly. He must have panicked. Even surgeons lose their cool once in a while. Afraid I would recognize him, he grabbed the nearest weapon at hand—my spade—and clobbered me with it."

His audience maintained a respectful silence, each imagining the dramatic scene.

"I think Hardwick must have left the picnic on some pretext or other and followed Sweet Grass to the hospital," Fenimore continued. "He knew that sooner or later she would collapse. Whether it happened on the road, at the hospital, or later, he couldn't predict. He had to shadow her, remaining as inconspicuous as possible, until the poison took effect. He waited around while she visited her sick friend and when she emerged from the ER, he must have waylaid her. Ned could be very

248

charming and persuasive when he wanted to be. Maybe he offered to drive her home and she accepted. She must have been feeling pretty rotten by then. He drove her around until the poison did its work. Then he delivered her to Joe to finish the job." Fenimore lay back, exhausted.

His friends were quiet, each thinking his or her thoughts.

"Hardwick's plan was a good one up to a point." Fenimore roused himself. "If he had just poisoned Sweet Grass and let it go at that. No matter where she died, in all probability—with her cardiac history—her death would have been attributed to a complication of tetralogy of Fallot. But Hardwick, like most surgeons, was meticulous. He took extraordinary precautions. And his ethnic hatred ran deep. He decided that if her body *were* discovered, why not let the blame for her death fall on another Lenape, her brother, Roaring Wings. Hence the choice of a Lenape grave site and the traditional Lenape style of burial." Fenimore paused, overwhelmed by the evil nature of his former colleague. "The event that he was not prepared for was Sweet Grass showing up in the ER. This caught him off guard and threw a monkey wrench into his plan. He knew that oleander glycosides would show up in the test for digoxin. Once she left, he had to steal her blood serum sample. Somehow he accomplished this. How, we may never know."

"Maybe he just put on a surgical gown, walked in during a frantic moment, and stole it," Rafferty said. "The ER can get pretty wild at times."

"You're probably right," Fenimore said. "The nurse on duty told me it was a zoo that night. But there was no way Hardwick could have known that part of Sweet Grass's serum sample had been sent to Applethorn's lab. That's where the element of chance came in, and it was ultimately his undoing. When he learned that I had the one piece of evidence that could do him in, he had no other course but to do *me* in."

After a pause, Fenimore said, "The thing I don't understand, is why Sweet Grass left the ER in such a hurry. If she'd stayed, and let them administer FAB, she might still be alive today."

"I know why."

All eyes turned on Jennifer.

"It was a simple case of denial. Sweet Grass thought she'd go to the ER for a quick cure. But when they decided to admit her, she panicked. Once admitted, she knew she'd be subjected to a battery of tests. They might keep her for days. That would mean postponing the wedding! She couldn't face that. Not when it was so close. Not after waiting so long."

Fenimore fixed his eyes on a spot on the ceiling.

"So, she decided to take a risk," Jennifer went on, "leave the hospital, and hope her symptoms would subside after a good night's sleep."

"Totally irresponsible," Fenimore grumbled.

"You've never been a bride on the brink of matrimony," Rafferty reminded him. "Sounds plausible to me."

"Me too," added Mrs. Doyle.

Horatio had nothing to add to this topic.

"What about her car?" Fenimore hastily changed the subject. "How did Hardwick dispose of that?"

"That was easy," Rafferty said. "He told me he drove it into the heart of North Philly and abandoned it. It was a nice little Toyota. He said he knew it would be stripped as soon as he turned his back."

Horatio nodded knowingly.

"How did he get back to civilization?" Mrs. Doyle asked.

"He had Joe follow him in the van. Then he waited while Joe returned the van. By that time it was dark. He met up with Joe somewhere in the park, paid him off, delivered the lethal sandwich, picked up his own car in the hospital lot, and drove home."

"One thing still puzzles me," said Mrs. Doyle. "If Hardwick

knew you had discovered the body, why would he want to hire you to investigate the case?"

"He was under a lot of pressure from his wife and son to seek my services. If he'd refused, it would have looked suspicious. And when he found I was already involved, he probably decided this would be a good way to keep an eye on me. I'm pretty sure he had me under surveillance the whole time."

"One more thing," Jennifer said. "Why didn't Hardwick burn that incriminating stalk of oleander? Without that, there'd be no case."

"He tried," said Rafferty, "but it wouldn't burn."

"Of course not," Fenimore sat up in bed, "because he had just cut it from Polly's oleander plant. It was still alive and green, whereas the other sticks had been lying around for weeks and were dead and dry."

"Right," said Rafferty. "And he was such an arrogant S.O.B., he figured it would be perfectly safe to bury it in his own compost pit, on his own property. Who would ever find it?"

"Super sleuth Andrew B. Fenimore, that's who." Jennifer grinned at him from the end of the bed.

Fenimore suddenly felt on the road to recovery.

A nurse popped her head in the door and frowned. "How did you all get in here?" Her tone was brusque.

"They're experts at subterfuge, Nurse," Fenimore said. "I wouldn't trust them out of your sight."

"Two at a time is the rule. I hope they didn't tire you, Doctor." She nudged them toward the door with a look, as effectively as if she were wielding a broom.

"Next time, bring Sal," he called after them. His cat's disappearance was the only cloud on his horizon.

Two days later, when Fenimore arrived home in a patrol car kindly supplied by Inspector Rafferty, he found his friends waiting for him. But they didn't exactly rush out to greet him.

When he came in the door with his little overnight bag, feeling weak and tottery, the house was still.

"Yoo-hoo? Anybody home?"

"*Shhhhhhhhhhhh,*" came a harsh warning from the back of the house.

Frightened into silence, he moved on tiptoe in the direction of the laundry room. There he found Jennifer, Mrs. Doyle, and Horatio kneeling in a circle, staring intently at something.

He cleared his throat.

Jennifer glanced up and smiled. "Look," she said.

He looked.

In the middle of the circle his friends had made was his missing bedroom slipper. Tucked inside the slipper were three newborn kittens, their eyes still closed. Around the periphery of the circle, Sal paced ominously.

CHAPTER 42

A Saturday in Late November

"The Lenape believed in two souls," Fenimore informed Jennifer. "The true soul and the blood soul. Some Lenape medical practitioners claimed to have seen the true soul leave the body in the form of a spark or a miniature person."

She looked at him.

"Seriously."

He was driving her on the smooth, flat road that leads to Camp Lenape, where a Xingwikaon or Big House Ceremony was being held. At the Xingwikaon, the Lenapes celebrate Mother Earth and give thanks to the Creator for a bountiful harvest, he had told her. The celebration lasts twelve days. (They wouldn't be staying the whole course, he had hastened to assure her.) Important events, such as births, deaths, and deeds of valor that occurred during the year are also commemorated. Sweet Grass's death was such an event. The last time this ceremony had been performed was in 1924. Roaring Wings was reviving the tradition. The first part of the ceremony was to be dedicated to Sweet Grass, and Roaring Wings had invited Fenimore and Ted to attend. Fenimore had asked Jennifer to come along. He had also offered Ted a ride, but he had declined, saying he preferred to drive himself. Things had been understandably strained between the two men since Ted's father had been arrested.

"After the true soul leaves the body," Fenimore continued, "it hangs around for about twelve days." He was in one of his instructive moods. "Then it takes off, traveling along the Milky Way until it joins up with Kiselemukonk, the Creator, also known as, 'The One Who Thought Us All Into Being' ".

"I like that," Jennifer said.

"The blood soul, on the other hand, you wouldn't care for. When it leaves the body it forms a black ball and wanders the earth forever, causing trouble. Contact with it can cause paralysis, strokes, or lameness. The Lenapes feared it."

"No wonder!" After a pause, Jennifer mused, "It seems no two cultures have the same idea of the soul. Members of some African cultures refuse to be photographed. When their picture is taken, they believe a piece of their soul has been stolen, a sort of spiritual rape has been committed."

"Actually, some Lenapes believe in a third soul."

"There's safety in numbers."

"The third soul is their reflection. In fact, the word for soul in the Algonquian language is *ciicankok*, or mirror."

Jennifer took a compact from her bag and contemplated her own reflection.

"When I was small," Fenimore said as he maneuvered them around a truck that was poking along at forty, "I imagined my soul looked like a Smith Brothers cough drop—a gold, translucent oval, buried somewhere inside me. And whenever I was bad, I thought a bit of it melted away. If I was bad too often, I was afraid it would melt away completely and I would have no soul to go to heaven when I died."

"What happened when you did your first autopsy?" asked Jennifer dryly. "Did you become an atheist?"

He smiled. "No. By that time my ideas had changed."

They drove in silence for a while, enjoying the fields stretching toward the sky. Traffic was light, and Fenimore was able to take Jennifer's hand. Most of the reds and golds were gone from the fields, but the starkness of winter had not yet come. The landscape was muted, as if someone had dropped a lavender veil over everything, providing a breathing space between seasons.

Jennifer snapped her compact shut and returned it to her bag. "I like your cough drop theology. I can just see you worrying yourself to death over that little gold lozenge tucked in some corner of your chest, wondering if there would be enough left over to get you into a heaven full of chocolate sundaes and baseball games."

"What about you?" Fenimore pressed her hand. "Didn't you ever worry about your soul?"

Jennifer laughed. "The only soles I worried about were on my feet." She had spent long hours standing at the cash register after school and on weekends, helping in the family bookstore. "Speaking of souls, what about Hardwick? Do you think he has one?" She suddenly returned to more earthly matters.

Fenimore was silent.

"How could a man who spent his life saving lives suddenly turn around and start disposing of them?" asked Jennifer.

"The God syndrome." Fenimore spoke sharply. "I've seen it before in a few physicians but never to this extreme. If I'm empowered to save lives, they reason, why can't I also dispose of them?"

"Maybe he kept a tally sheet: so many lives saved weighed against so many lives taken." She shuddered. "How is Ted doing?"

"Back in the family nest. Polly needs him now, and for the present he's trying to atone for his father's sins. I don't hold out much hope for him. Sweet Grass was the force behind his small drive for independence—and happiness."

"Polly had nothing to do with all this?"

255

"Nothing intentional. Unwittingly, she provided the murder weapon. She ordered the oleander plant for her Roman garden." Fenimore shook his head. "I have to hand Ned one thing. He certainly knew his medicine. It's common knowledge that oleander is poisonous, but Ned must have learned that its properties were similar to those of digoxin from the *Textbook of Pharmacology.*"

"And what about Roaring Wings?"

"His bitterness runs very deep. This tragedy simply reinforced his poor opinion of the white man. When he learned what Hardwick had done, he uttered one word, '*Saa!*'"

"Meaning?"

"Shame."

Jennifer sighed. "One step forward, ten steps back. Why do you think he asked you and Ted to this ceremony?"

"I'm still wondering about that."

"Maybe he's grateful to you for bringing his sister's murderer to justice."

"And maybe he's finally convinced that Ted did love his sister."

Jennifer cast him a covert glance, wondering how long it would take to convince him that he too loved . . . someone.

They drove through the open gates of Camp Lenape.

A far bigger crowd was gathered on the grounds than on the day of the funeral. The fields were filling up with cars, campers, and trailers, and three men were kept busy directing traffic. Jennifer and the doctor got out of the car and followed the crowd toward the barn. Some families were sitting outside their campers in lawn chairs, barbecuing and enjoying the parade. Children played tag among the parked cars until their impatient parents called them away. The fragrant aromas of roasting chicken, pork, and beans mingled with the scent of burning leaves (a practice still permitted in rural areas). In the field beyond, the last of the

256

sumac and goldenrod vied for attention. It had turned into a brilliant autumn day. As they stepped into the shadows of the barn, a drum began to beat.

"What an enormous barn," Jennifer exclaimed, looking up at the high roof and soaring rafters.

"Actually," Fenimore corrected her, "the Lenapes call this the 'Big House.' "

When their eyes became accustomed to the dim light, they noticed the costumes of the dancers. The young women wore beaded crowns, the young men beaded headbands. Around their wrists and ankles were bells that tinkled when they walked. They all wore feathers of brilliant hues. Some of the dancers brushed against the visitors as they passed. Fenimore and Jennifer settled down on a bench to wait.

Minutes passed. People wandered in and out of the Big House, some in costume, some not. The drum continued its methodical beat. They could see the drummer now, seated on a dais at the north end of the building. He wore a crest of deer hair, dyed bright red. "He looks like a fighting cock," Jennifer said.

A group of women in beaded costumes gathered behind the drummer and broke into a high-pitched chant. Two fires in large pits at either end of the building were being fanned to life by bands of young boys. Two holes in the roof drew the smoke upward and out. As people began to enter in a more orderly manner, the men took their places on one side; the women on the other. Fenimore discovered that he was on the wrong side. Before he could move across the space, Roaring Wings spotted him and came over. He wore the same elaborate costume he had worn at the funeral.

He shook Fenimore's hand gravely, then turned inquiringly to Jennifer. Fenimore introduced her, explaining that she was a bookseller and writer. "She's thinking of writing a book about the Lenape," he said.

"Welcome," he said graciously. "Not enough is written about

257

the Lenape. Most books are written about the Indians of the west." He turned back to Fenimore. "I'm glad you came. I wanted to clear up something with you."

"Yes?"

"That place where you found my sister?"

"The old burial ground."

"It is not a burial ground. That is a popular belief among the *wasechus*. It is a *camp* ground. Look at the deed again. As soon as you told me that, I knew a white man was to blame. No Lenape would bury anyone there." He paused. "The dance honoring my sister will be the first in the ceremony." He left to attend to his many duties. Fenimore, his mouth hanging open, looked after him.

"Very impressive," Jennifer whispered. "Those eyes . . ."

"Yes," Fenimore nodded, pulling himself together. "They're the first thing you notice."

"What's this about my writing a book?"

He shrugged. "I had to explain your presence somehow."

"Actually, it's not a bad idea." She was thoughtful.

Fenimore left her to join the men on the other side of the Big House.

More activity was taking place in the space between the fires, as some of the more elaborately dressed Lenapes were forming a circle. Fenimore looked around for Ted. It would be a pity if he missed the first dance. The chanting was getting louder. The people in the circle began to shift their weight from one foot to the other in unison, causing the bells on their ankles to jingle more loudly.

Slowly they began to move, counterclockwise, gaining momentum as they completed each circuit.

Where was Ted?

The feathers—bright pink, purple, yellow, green—shifted in the firelight. The chanting was reaching a crescendo. The dancers moved faster, turning from side to side, shaking their rattles. For a moment Fenimore was reminded of the famous Philadelphia mummers welcoming the New Year. Suddenly one leaped in the air, then another, and another. Their feathers whirled in a multicolored blur.

Jennifer was transfixed, but Fenimore's eyes searched the shadows of the Big House, until they finally came to rest on a familiar figure. Near the entrance, turned toward the fire and the dancers, Ted Hardwick's face was alight, almost happy.

DATE DUE			
748 6/98